A CORRUPTION

OF

GILDED

ASHES

JESSICA CAGE

Autograph Page

In the Eyes of the Goddess, we are all one!
Love~

Contents

Welcome to Eldritch

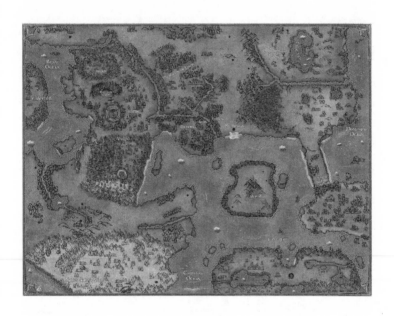

This is Forge

Land of the Griffins, one of the oldest species in Eldritch. During this story, you will explore their home and learn about why the Griffins have fallen from the grace of their goddess.

To those who dare to dream of something unseen.
You shape the world.

JESSICA CAGE

<u>How do I say all of these names?</u>

- Wallai – Wuh-lie

- Eumen – Ooh- men

- Lunai – Loon - eye

- Maluai – Mal-Way

- Kaluai – Kal-Way

- Naluai – Nal-Way

- Valuai – Val – Way

- Masuen – Mah-Su-Wen

- Limua - Lem-wah

- Hasik – Ha-seek

- Fituen – Fit-oo-wen

- Seru- Sey-ru

- Jeraim – Jer-um

- Emixi- Ee- Mix-ee

- Akaien – Ah-kay-en

- Syloki – Sigh-low-key

- Marruk – Mar-rook

- Fralim – Frah-leem

- Cairaix – Ky-Ray

- Genuve – Gen-ooov

- Hende – Hen -day

- Denai – Den-ay

- Dumi – doo – me

- Nizese – nee-sees

- Spirtus / spirtuses

Glossary (In Earthling terms)

- People

  - Earthling = Drichians

  - People/Person = Eumen /Euman

- Common Curse words

  - fuck = Jiiq

  - shit = shezia

  - damn = drakgo

  - bitch = fatu

  - you hoe= ma hezi

  - dumbass= deplu

  - ass (asses)= plu (plu's)

- ○ asshole=pluvuta

- Hello / Goodbye = Hende

- Family = Laenu

CHAPTER 1

S ilence was often the greatest advocate of evil.

The Wallai royal laenu held court in a secret underwater city where the water griffin lived hidden from the rest of the world. Maluai, princess of Wallai and second daughter to the king and queen, floated in the third pillar and begrudgingly performed her duty to her eumen. As taught, she sat shoulders square, chin high, and mouth shut. Her gray eyes scanned the vast room and its members as the council members and the king and queen debated the future of their eumen.

The court, an oval room with limited access, sat at the heart of the royal palace. To Maluai, it was the worst place to be because, though it had painted glass covering the ceilings and sections of the walls between the massive pillars, there were no windows—no access to the outside world. It forced her to pay attention to everything going on within its walls. Even then, she played with the beads on the ends of her silver locks and half-listened to the conversation she'd heard repeated too many times before.

In Wallai, wearing heavy hair accessories was considered the most presentable fashion. Those of high status never let their hair flow freely with the underwater currents. To do so suggested a lack of control and poise. When Maluai was alone, she would remove the beads and dance. The free movement of her unrestricted hair made her heart sing out as it mimicked the freedom she wished for herself.

"We cannot sit idly by while they turn their backs on the lessons of Lunai." Valuai, queen of Wallai, and Maluai's mother, sat on the throne at the head of the room next to her husband. She spoke of the Mother Goddess with reverence. "Their actions affect us all. To the goddess, we are one eumen. She will judge us alongside them."

The opal stone of her crown sat in the middle of her forehead, matching perfectly with the markings that dusted the high cheekbones. A signature trait of their eumen. Her blue and black locs hung past her breast adorned with beads and jewels fitting the queen. As she looked onto the court, her skin, a deep brown, shimmered with the energy of a shift waiting to happen. She would stay poised despite her internal unrest.

"What you say is purely speculation. You cannot claim to know the intentions of the goddess. The griffins have not been called to challenge for hundreds of years. For us to take a stance against our sisters would start a war, Valuai." As Masuen, the king, spoke, his deep voice added a low vibration to the water.

"I love your heart, dear wife, but we have to think about this with a calm spirit."

"My spirit is calm." Valuai turned to her husband, her crown in perfect position. "My patience is not."

"If I may," Limua, a member of the council, interjected and waited for the approval nod from Masuen before continuing. When received, she swam to the center of the room, her white robes flowing from her massive body, to take the speaker's stand. "I know we have maintained a veiled presence in society. However, it is time to rethink that position. Given the changing times, we must consider reframing how we operate."

"Am I hearing you correctly, Limua?" Masuen leaned forward in his seat, his hand clutching the arm of his chair. "You would have us claim independence from our sisters?"

"If it means the survival of our eumen, yes," Limua declared, her aged tone conveying wisdom as she peered around the room. "The agreement our eumen entered long ago was to protect the lives of a version of ourselves who were weaker than we are now. They needed the land griffin's protection. We have advanced far past that need."

"It would mean leaving our home," Hasik, another council member, spoke. Though she was a few years younger than Limua, her voice was just as powerful. "Do you believe they would let us inhabit this place, liberated from the agreement?"

"Again, that would mean a potential war." Masuen regained control of the room. "We have an agreement with Forge. We'll uphold that agreement as long as they do so in good faith."

"Do you honestly believe they've upheld their end of the bargain? We are not to live under their thumb without question. Those are not the constraints of our agreement," Valuai reminded her husband. "We give them our resources, our magic, more and more as each lunar cycle passes, and what do we get? A semblance of protection from a world when there is no evidence of a continuing threat? Should we attempt to separate because of their failures, that is not the call of war you fear. We must lead in a way that is best for our eumen. If that means revealing ourselves to the world and disassociating with the land griffins, that is what we must do."

"Things have not been that bad." Masuen tried to calm his wife. "We can come to an amicable solution. I'm sure of it."

"Not that bad?" The queen laughed. "They take our resources and claim responsibilities for advancements we have made. And what do we get in return for this? We live in their shadows, our water growing more toxic each year because of the runoff from their waste. We have to come up with layers of filtration for our people, and do they help? No! I love you, my husband, but we cannot continue to pretend this isn't an issue."

While they continued their conversation about potential wars, Maluai's eyes drifted across the room to Naluai, her youngest sister. At seventeen, Naluai was granted the liberties Maluai and Kaluai, their older sisters, were never able to experience. She wore frilly clothing, like the common Wallain citizens, rather than the official robes of the royal laenu. And she refused to weigh her hair down like the others.

They adorned the royal robes with gold, bronze, and an assortment of jewels. They were heavy and stood as a symbol of the strength of the royal laenu. The heavier the robes, the stronger the bloodline.

Naluai's reddish-brown afro floated around her face like a cloud of rebellion and a testament to her mother's relaxed stance on protocols. Maluai remembered being forced to sit in those boring meetings when she was younger. It was a part of their inherited responsibility for being a royal. From the age of ten, they had to take part in important conversations for their eumen, despite how horribly uninteresting it all was.

Maluai, who had seen more than her fair share of meetings throughout her twenty-five years, had a keen sense of when her opinions should and should not be shared. This was one time when the king and queen wanted to hear only from the members of the council. They would never expect their daughters to speak up on something that could change the trajectory of their eumen's lives forever. It would also force the girls to choose sides between their parents, which neither of them wanted to do.

Limua, Hasik, and Fituen were the members of the council who remained in their true forms. Covered in the scale-like feathers with wings, two arms that ended in clawed hands, and a tail resembling that of a whale instead of legs. For most Wallains, the decision to present in their true form was an independent choice, and they shifted back and forth between their two forms at will.

5

The council members always maintained their true form. They considered it the pure presence because it meant they were true to themselves and, therefore, true to their eumen.

As Naluai zoned out and Valuai and Masuen continued their debate with the council members, Maluai took her opportunity to flee. She'd taken a position at the back of the court closest to the side exit that opened behind the last pillar. It was an entrance intended for the aides to use as needed, but often became Maluai's escape hatch. They'd been at it for hours, and she had no intention of wasting her day on a topic she knew would come to no resolution. When all else failed, escape.

As her father slipped into another speech, she carefully snuck out the back and floated into the hall. With a sense of triumph, she turned to leave but came face to face with the guardian, Seru. The guardian stood seven over six feet and looked down on Maluai, who barely reached six on her own, still having many years left to grow. She crossed her toned arms over her chest and tapped the tip of her whale bone spear against her shoulder. The sharp point was fused together by magic, making it one of the deadliest weapons in Wallai.

"You cannot keep doing this, Maluai." Seru shook her head and scrunched her wide nose in disappointment. "Your parents will be upset if they find you have once again slipped away from your responsibilities."

"Oh, come on, Ser. You know as well as I do, they do not need me in there." Maluai looked up into the tattooed face of her guardian.

Like most of the guardians, she had scurry ink tattoos. Scurry ink was a special bioluminescent ink extracted from the scurry fish, also known as the ghost fish. It was hard to find, and even harder to catch, but it was a rite of passage for a guardian. They had to catch their own scurry fish and extract its ink without killing it in order to be tattooed. Seru had two vertical strikes on her forehead and four that stretched from the eyeline down each cheek. The vibrant ink against her brown skin made her cool blue eyes stand out even more.

"It is your responsibility to your eumen and to your laenu to take part in the council meetings," Seru pressed. "How else are you going to lead when it is your turn to sit on the throne?"

"My turn to sit on the throne?" Maluai laughed. "Do you really think I'm that naïve? We both know it is not me who will lead our eumen when my parents' time is done."

Seru sucked her teeth and rolled her eyes at the statement. Maluai wasn't next in line to rule, but she would have influence over future decisions. Still, Maluai didn't think it was enough to warrant her wasting away in pointless meetings.

"You know it's true. Kaluai will be the next Queen, and after her, any children she births will follow. My presence in these meeting is nothing more than a formality, and I'd much rather use my time to explore the world than sit through conversations I don't need to be a part of." Maluai looked up at Seru and deftly positioned her head in just the right angle so the light from the orbs, balls of fire magically encased in a thin membrane produced by a plant called the mucilias, hit her eyes.

Maluai used this maneuver on her guardian for years, and it consistently achieved the desired effect. Her father told her there was magic in her eyes because whenever the light hit them just right, it illuminated the gold flecks in her gray iris. He said it was almost hypnotic. It was also why her mother rarely looked her in the eye when Maluai pleaded for something she wanted.

"How many times must I ask you not to look at me that way?" Seru looked away from Maluai.

"As many times as it takes for it to stop working?" Maluai swam in a circle around her guardian. "Tell me, has it stopped working, Ser?"

"Fine." Seru sighed and pulled her spear back to her side. "Be careful. The last thing I need is for you to get hurt and for me to take the blame for it. My job is already on the line because you keep disappearing, and I keep pretending not to know where you are. It makes me look incompetent."

"Your job is safe. Father may pretend like he doesn't understand what happens between you and me, but he does." She moved closer to her ear to whisper. "It's why he assigned you to me. He knew my spirit wouldn't be tamed. And Ser, I appreciate it."

"Yeah, yeah, have fun." Seru waved Maluai off. "Hurry, before I change my mind. Remember, you are supposed to meet with your father today. Whether you will ever sit on that throne, there are things you must learn from him, things that will help you lead a prosperous life."

"You know I've never missed a chance to have a moment alone with my father, and I never will." Maluai patted Seru on the shoulder and left the guardian alone in the hall outside the court.

Maluai swam away from her guardian, who, if questioned, would pretend she hadn't seen her leave. This was their secret vow to each other. Her sister's guardians were much stricter, and she believed her father assigned Seru to her because he understood his daughter's spirit.

Maluai's desire to run free stemmed from the tight restrictions her mother held over her from the time of her birth. That was what happened when a royal child was born differently from every other water griffin in her bloodline. There were the obvious physical differences that worried them. With her grey hair and odd gray eyes with flecks of gold, she looked like no one in her laenu. The members of the royal laenu all had ice-blue eyes and naturally reddish-brown hair they wore in different styles. The differences were far more than the superficial appearances.

When Maluai was born, the doulas feared she was ill. They warned her mother that she may not have much time with the child because Maluai never cried, and she barely ate, but she grew at the same rate as any other child. She laughed, played, and had hopes and dreams.

They waited for her to fall ill, but she never did. In fact, Maluai had never been sick in her entire life. Of all the eumen who lived in Wallai, Maluai was the only one to never get so much as a sniffle. Her father told her it was because she was special. That there was some untapped potential inside of her, and one day, she would show the world just why she was so special.

Her mother, however, thought it was a sign that her daughter was in trouble. She looked at her middle child and worried about her future. She barred Maluai from performing the activities her sisters had no difficulty with. If not for her father, the girl would have never learned to battle or fend for herself. Her mother would have had her put her in a mucilias bubble and locked her away for her own safety, but her father was the one who fought for her to live a life like everyone else.

Valuai's fear only spiked with Maluai's first show of her true form. For most water griffins, they could tap into that other side just weeks after birth. But Maluai couldn't. No matter how hard she tried, nothing happened, and the magic workers could find no reason for it. Despite the troubles of her birth, Maluai was healthy in every other way. They thought it was a sign from the goddess that they'd done something wrong until her eighth year, when she finally connected to her true form. But what should have been a moment to celebrate became one to fear, and her mother begged her not to show her true self again.

She differed from any other water griffin. Where they had scaled tales at their lower half, Maluai had legs like the land griffins with extended fins along the length of each leg. Her brown skin turned dark, and silver webbing covered the length of her body. Instead of a beak on her face, she looked more feline, with a shortened mouth, enormous jaw, and sharp teeth.

Maluai busted into their room as the two moons traded places over Eldritch. She spun in circles, squealing like she'd just found a mountain of her favorite sweet.

"I can do it!" She spread her hands above her head. "Mother, I changed. I did it!"

"Really?" Valuai swam over to her child. "You found your true form? That's wonderful. Will you show me?"

Maluai nodded, then moved away from her mother. She scrunched her nose in focus as she found the connection to her inner being. A moment later, after three strong grunts, her body changed. Ink-black wings with blue tipped feathers stretched and talons marked the end of each wing stretched from her back. Smooth brown skin turned dark with silver webbing as her small body expanded in size.

Her parents' eyes widened as they witnessed her body for the first time. Their mouths fell open with the roar of her lion that created ripples in the surrounding water.

"Stop," Valuai said. "Maluai, please, return to yourself."

A moment later, Maluai's face, as they knew it, returned, and her wide eyes flooded with tears. "I'm sorry."

"What is this?" Valuai asked her husband as she clutched her child to her chest after Maluai returned to her vanity form. "Why does she look like this? What did I do wrong?"

"You've done nothing wrong." He tried to reassure his wife, but Maluai could hear the concern in his voice. *"We've always known she was special. This is just another way that's true."*

"Father?" Maluai looked up at the king. *"Did I do it wrong? I can try again. I can make it better."*

"No, baby." He rubbed her forehead, pushing the grey hairs from her face. *"You did it just fine."*

"No one can ever see her," Valuai blurted out. *"What will they say?"*

"We can't just hide her away, Valuai." Masuen tried to reason with his wife, sitting on the enormous bed next to her.

"Maluai." She looked down at her daughter. *"Tell me now. Promise me you will never show another euman your true form."*

"But I like it." She looked down at her hands and flexed her small fingers. *"It was fun! I felt so strong."*

"I know, but..." her mother searched for the words to say.

"I'm different." Maluai's voice was small as she said the words her mother tried not to. *"Eumen won't like it if I'm too different."*

"They just won't understand." Her mother pulled her closer and held her so tightly she struggled to catch her breath.

Those words lingered with the girl her entire life. She made herself small and refused to show the world her true self for fear of how they would respond to her. But as time went on, the act of shrinking herself inspired something else within the princess. A thirst for adventure, which she told herself was her father's fault.

Of his three daughters, she was the only one to share his love for thrill seeking with him. Whenever she got the chance, she swam away from her city. Never too far away, because though she craved excitement, she didn't want to cause friction between her parents. Valuai always took it out on the king whenever her daughter acted out.

It grew harder for her to restrain herself when she snuck away. Maluai wanted to see more of the world of Eldritch. She loved her home. Wallai was a beautiful place filled with vibrant colors, animals, plant life, and eumen who inherited magic from their ancestors, but it wasn't enough for her. There was only so much adventure she could have in a place she knew like the back of her hand.

Maluai headed for her room first. Once there, she changed her clothing, removing the royal robes and changing into attire more fitting for adventure. She chose a long green dress that flowed around her like the petals of a flower. Once dressed, she slipped out of her bedroom window.

She made it just minutes from the palace when she felt Seru's presence. Though the guardian pretended to let the princess roam free, she never did. This was the game they played together. The predator who never quite caught the prey.

She looked back, expecting to find the shadow of her guardian. Maluai would have rather faced Seru's disapproval than the sound of the kangul shark's menacing growl. The enormous beast was blocking her view of the palace behind her, and the putrid smell of its breath on the current as it opened its mouth to reveal rows of sharp teeth made her heart miss a beat.

CHAPTER 2

M enacing eyes widened as a shriek of pain ripped from the shark's mouth, creating a rush of bubbles that pushed the princess further from the predator. Maluai accepted the moment to flee without question. She thanked Seru, relieved the guardian was close by and able to distract the shark. It was the only explanation she could think of as she quickly swam away from its menacing presence.

After her panic subsided, Maluai's heart smiled as she swam through the underwater city.

Every time she swam through Wallai, the vibrant colors of its coral and exotic sea life mesmerized the princess. The underwater buildings built directly into the ocean floor were a stunning sight, their structures reaching up through the waters in a gesture of reverence to their goddess, Lunai. The buildings were alive with the vibrant colors of coral, enhanced by the gentle sunlight that shone through the water. It added life to the world that couldn't be replicated through artificial means.

Wallai was a curious mix of buildings, some made with eu-man hands and others the result of the ocean's movement. The water griffins carved their homes into the natural formations, while the royal laenu, like most families of importance, lived in the structured buildings. Having control of the layout allowed them more defense, even though their eumen had never known war. It also meant surrendering the vivid colors of nature.

The dwellings of the general populace were usually far more colorful, boasting an array of the most vibrant shades stretching across the rainbow. Maluai often wished she could live in one of those structures because she felt they were more in tune with the world around them.

Though she held her tongue, Maluai thought it hypocritical for her parents and the council to discuss how the land Griffins had lost their way. They complained about how their sisters had forgotten what made them who they were, when they were moving further away from nature. She wondered how long it would be before her eumen, the water Griffins, were making the same mistakes that they judged the land Griffins for.

The singsong sound of a little girl interrupted her thoughts of hypocrisy. Maluai turned to see the bright cloud of red hair floating around the face of a girl who couldn't be over eight years. Her ebony complexion shone as her broad grin stretched across her face. She twirled in a circle, her green tail creating a spiral in the water before she continued her song.

"Fatu! Fatu! Fatu!" She swam along, shouting the curse word and giggling. "Mami! Fatuuuu!"

"Eshi!" Her mother moved furiously behind her to keep up with the girl who had the edge in swimming. "Stop that. It's not right."

"Ah, let her have fun." Her husband, with a belly that shook from his deep laughter, shouted after them. "It's just a word!"

"You think it's okay for our daughter to swim around shouting foul language? I told you to be careful what you say around her!" the mother scolded her husband, then froze as she realized who watched them. "Oh my, Princess." She bowed her head, hiding the look of horror on her face.

Maluai said nothing. She pressed her finger against her up-turned lips, then she swam away as the wife expressed her anger by slapping her husband's arm before she continued to pursue her boisterous child.

Some appeared in their true forms, like the council members, while others preferred to appear like land walkers, two legs, two arms, and hair weighted down with heavy shells and beads. No matter their form, they all stopped and waved at the passing princess, greeting her in the Wallain fashion. Right hand over chest, up to the sky, then wave downward. This motion was symbolic of the heart of their euman, their goddess, and their connection to one another. Maluai returned the greeting to each euman as she passed them.

To reduce the risk of being seen, she veered off onto a hidden route that would lead her to the outskirts of the city, where she hoped to make her break for the surface. After several minutes of skillful maneuvering through the narrow passage, she reached the open water.

"Finally!" She couldn't help but smile as she moved her feet to propel her body closer to the surface. Soon, her face appeared above the water, and she breathed in the fresh, invigorating air for the first time in a month.

Stepping on land never felt normal to her, no matter how many times she did it. Her body felt heavier, and her limbs ached for the first few minutes as she acclimated. Once out of the water, her skin snapped to her body like a dried glove. If she stayed out of the water too long, she would have to pray for rain or deal with the pain. The inner lining of her nostrils changed to allow air to enter without the need for filtration through the water.

On the edge of the water in the small oasis hidden from the world, she stretched her body to limber up as the water dried under the heat of the sun. She felt relaxed and plopped down on the sandy beach, letting the warmth seep into her skin. The thing about being underwater was she could see the sun, but she couldn't feel it. Maluai felt it was a sin to be away from the sun for so long and wished more of the eumen of Wallai could experience what she did in those few moments.

When she grew weary of being still, Maluai began her hike. She climbed to the top of the hill that ended on a cliff overlooking the water she had emerged from. The climb was taxing, but worth it for the view she got when she reached the peak. She could see all of Forge, the home of the land griffins, and glimpses of her underwater home. The beauty of the world was captivating, yet the silence of the air made her aware that there was more to explore just beyond what she could see.

The deep, reverberating tone of a man's voice followed the soft hush of wings cutting through the air. "You're here again?" The satin voice massaged the back of her mind like a familiar friend.

"Oh, you're here?" She looked back at the euman she'd known, in secret, for nearly two years.

"Don't act surprised to see me here. Why else would you keep coming back?" He laughed as he reached the space where she stood.

Jeraim was a land griffin with the same adventurous spirit as Maluai. The euman who stood six inches taller than her was only a year older than Maluai, but acted like he had twenty on her. When they first met, he felt like a friend, someone who she would grow to look at as laenu. But in time, that appreciation for him turned more romantic, though she had yet to admit it.

It wasn't proper for a land griffin and a water griffin to get together. Though they were of the same legacy, there were fundamental differences between the two. Differences that led to the current conversations about the separation of the two cities.

Maluai met Jeraim shortly after she found the secluded cliff. For years, it had been his getaway. He said it was the only place in the Forge where things were quiet. He could sit there for hours in his own silence and meditate. When he found her there, they agreed to share the location, which wasn't a tremendous sacrifice for him, considering Maluai only appeared during the first week of each month. Because it was the busiest time for the king and queen, it was the easiest time for her to sneak away.

"You're the one who comes here exactly when you know I'll be here." Maluai pointed to the sky. "I come here every first of the month. You can come here any other time you like."

"That's true." Jeraim folded his wings back and rolled his shoulders as they retracted behind his shoulder blade. Once they were hidden, he adjusted the collar of the dark blue top that shifted with the motion.

The tall euman lifted his arms to the sky, basking in the sun's warmth on his dark, ebony skin. She watched the muscles that flexed along his bare skin. Maluai averted her eyes before she said something embarrassing.

"So, you agree? You don't have to be here when I am." Mal smirked, as if she caught him in a lie.

"Also, true." Jeraim rubbed his chin beneath the silver markings that stretched across his left eye. "But then, when would I see you, Mal?"

"In your dreams?" she joked and felt the weight of the world melt away as he used the shortened version of her name. "What's new in your world, Jeraim? Anything exciting happening in the land of Forge?"

"Is there ever anything new, really?" He stepped to the edge of the cliff and sat, patting the ground next to him for her to join. "I'm escaping responsibility as always, and I assume you're doing the same, though in all the time we've known each other, you've yet to reveal what those responsibilities are that keep you running from home."

"I am, and I haven't." She joined him.

"And you won't?" He looked at her with those hazel eyes that glowed when the sun hit them.

"Nope." She smiled.

"Ah, well, one of these days I'll get to know more about the mysterious Mal." He picked up a handful of pebbles and rolled them around in his palm.

"Why is it that the elders think that we're supposed to have some grand respect for the ways of old?" Maluai looked at the forming clouds above them. "That is what I'm running from today, as always. Nonsensical rules about how I'm to live my life based on eumen who are long gone."

"They want us to continue the traditions." Jeraim spoke, his voice heavy with his own remorse at the topic. "It's like they think if we don't keep their ways alive, all traces of them will vanish when they are no longer a part of this world."

"If you ask me, most traditions need to die with the generation that created them." Maluai rolled her eyes. "Maybe then we could make real strides forward instead of worrying about the same issues that really have no impact on the current generations."

"If you asked me, I'd say I agree with that." He laughed at her twisted expression. "I love the way your marks on your face glitter in the sun."

"Thanks." She touched her cheek where the discoloration appeared.

It was a genetic marker that all griffins had. For the land griffins, they appeared more uniform, like geometric grains of sand. But for water griffins, they were more free forming. When they were out of the water, the marker looked like gemstones embedded in the skin. Maluai's marks started in the inner corner of each eye, then like waves of the ocean, they flowed down her cheek and up around her eye to end just above the eyebrow. Unlike most water griffins, her marks appeared with symmetrical placement. A mirror image on both sides of her face.

"I'm happy to see you again," Jeraim admitted in a rare display of unrequested honesty.

"You are?" She looked at him. "Is it the marks? I hear they are pretty in the sun."

"You've never seen them?" He smirked. "Are there no mirrors in Wallai?"

"Yes, there are mirrors, but everything is different in Wallai." She touched her face. "I've only heard how beautiful they are above the water. It's that way for everyone, not just me."

"Well, yes, they are beautiful, but it's not the reason I'm happy to see you."

"Care to share the reason?" Maluai felt her heart flutter, and her stomach did somersaults. Was this the moment they would finally stop tiptoeing around each other?

"It's become one of the few things I look forward to. Seeing your face." He paused and then broke the sweet moment with a

22

playful joke. "And watching you struggle to get out of the water, then lay there like a tired fish."

"Oh, hilarious." She playfully punched his shoulder. "Gravity does not impact us the same way underneath the water."

"I wish we could know each other better." There it was again. That unexpected honesty coated in the warmth of his voice.

"What do you mean?" Maluai was almost afraid to ask the question. Jeraim responded with such sincerity that his answer only inspired the need for further clarity.

"Maluai, I like you," he answered.

"I like you too. You know that." She attempted to mask it as another humorous moment, but she could discern by the way he stared at her and the quietness of his voice, Jeraim wasn't joking.

"No, I mean." He intertwined his fingers with hers, and as they contemplated the joined hands, he continued. "I like you as more than a friend I see once a month. You're in my thoughts when you're not here. I even come to this place when I am sure you won't be here, hoping to catch sight of you in the water's depths. I used to come here to get away from everything, but now, my heart soars because I know there is always a chance I'll see you here."

"Jeraim, you know I—"

"Yes, I know. We can't be together, and you already have someone in Wallai." He looked her in the eye. "Still, I cannot be true to myself, or a genuine friend to you, if I leave my thoughts of you unspoken."

"I'm not really sure what to say." Maluai searched for the words, but found nothing that could express how she truly felt at the moment.

She had the same thoughts about Jeraim as he did, even though it was against the rules. Maluai looked forward to seeing him each month and wondered what he did when they were apart. It didn't matter. She knew they couldn't be together, so she never allowed herself to explore the budding feelings.

She also had a secret from the land griffin, and she wasn't sure how he would feel about her if she ever revealed it. Jeraim was unaware of Maluai's standing in Wallai. He didn't know what she ran from was the responsibilities of the royal bloodline and that her moments with him were some of the few times she felt normal.

"Alright, I think I'll leave." Jeraim let her hand go and got up from the ground beside her.

"Why?" She looked up at him. "Why are you leaving?"

"I've embarrassed myself enough, and besides, I know how you like to get lost in your thoughts while you're setting up here." He looked down at her with a soft smile.

"Don't go, Jeraim." She stood. "I didn't mean to make this uncomfortable for you. It's hard to find the right response to what you said."

"You have nothing to apologize for. I swooped in here confessing feelings we've never discussed before." He touched her cheek. "I'm not holding anything against you."

"Jeraim." She sighed as the wind picked up, bringing the scent of the nearby wildflowers.

"I think it's best I go, and I think, if you're honest with yourself, you agree with me. It will give you time to think about what I said. I'll see you again, I promise." Jeraim spread his wings, and the massive span of brown feathers carried him away from the cliff.

Maluai watched Jeraim fly away and, as always, was awed by the power of his wings. A male's wings spoke to their virility. They weren't all the same. They varied in length, coloration, feather type, and strength. A euman with great wings had many potential mates mesmerized by the sight of his wingspan silhouetted against the sky.

The males with the widest wingspans and most dazzling plumes were highly desired. So much that if they wanted, they would have many wives. Of course, they had to care for each equally, but that was never an arrangement that appealed to Maluai. She knew there had to be plenty of females in Forge who sought after Jeraim, and yet, he confessed he wanted her.

When it came time to choose a mate, griffins took part in a simple ritual. The male would present his wings to the female. When the female accepted him, the male soared into the sky, their courtship highlighted by the breathtaking display of his aerial ballet. His dance would end in a series of tight circles above her head.

As she watched Jeraim, something clicked in her mind, and she held her breath. Jeraim didn't just fly away. He moved in tight circles above her, positioning her directly in the center of his movements. Jeraim presented himself to her from above. He sent her a message that was undeniable. He wanted her, and he would break the rules for her if she agreed. She couldn't help it. As she watched his display, she considered risking it all for the man.

Maluai's thoughts shifted to home as soon as Jeraim left her. She considered her mother and father and how they would react if they found out about her monthly trips to Forge. Her mother would already be upset enough to discover that she had left the safety of their home. However, if she were to find out that her daughter wanted to be with a land griffin, it would start a fight Maluai felt she had no chance of winning.

Her father might have been more supportive, but she couldn't be sure. Just because he encouraged adventure didn't mean he would be okay with all her choices. Masuen was one for tradition. Tradition said water griffins were not to mix with land griffins sexually.

Then she considered the euman her parents would prefer she be with. Kenu, the hunter. He was an excellent friend but was the only male unrelated to her allowed in her company for most of her life. The son of the head of the hunters, he often came to the palace when his father did. They would sit together while their father discussed business, and in time, he would come to visit her on his own.

Kenu had expressed his desire to be with her, but Maluai never saw him as anything but a friend. She was debating whether to accept his proposal, but once she got to know Jeraim, she realized if she was to choose Kenu, it would only be because of the simplicity of the choice. He was there. Everyone would almost expect that she be with him. No one would contest it, but she would never know passion or love in the way she witnessed between her parents.

There were reasons the two species weren't supposed to mix. Not only did it ensure the water griffins remained hidden, but there were consequences to their mating. The results of the pairings were offspring born with many mutations. For over a thousand years, no one had explored the unknown because the potential dangers were too great to risk.

The last debates about it questioned if the evolution of the water griffins in the eons had made up for their incompatibility. Though the argument for it was sound, the elders still voted against it. There was more to be protected in Wallai than its eumen. Resources the griffins, both from Forge and Wallai, wanted to keep to themselves.

This left Maluai to wonder how many opportunities had her eumen missed out on. How many chances for love and adventure had they wasted out of fear? All because they wanted to keep their secrets.

Only once had she thought to take a stance about opening their borders and allowing the water griffins new freedom. She'd barely gotten her first point across before Masuen shut her down. He spoke to her like she was a child, stepping out of line. Being nearly thirty meant nothing in a species that lived for an average of a thousand hundred years. They all still looked at her like she was an uninformed adolescent. Another reason she preferred to escape their time at court.

Maluai sat down again to overlook the water. Their hidden location was serene. The still waters perfectly reflected the blue sky above, while the cliffs provided a natural barrier. She relaxed, but only for a moment before she heard eumen shouting. She stood and ran to the other side of the peak, where she could see the source of the yelling. Land griffins shouted at each other, but she couldn't hear what they said. She considered getting closer, but horror stopped her when she saw the dark cloud that erupted from the side of the island and spilled into the sea below.

CHAPTER 3

Two heartbeats later, Maluai ran back to the other side of the cliff and jumped from the edge to the waters below. With a quick dive beneath the surface of the water, she pushed herself to swim faster than she had in years. She moved through her secret passageway that led back to her home. With each push that moved her forward, her heart broke more. She heard the screams of her eumen as the thick cloud of darkness spread across the surface of the water.

She watched it from her vantage point. It was a surreal sight as the fluid hovered above them; the sun hidden behind it, until eventually, the pull of gravity was too strong, and it fell. Like heavy beads, the dark substance dropped to the ocean floor where her eumen lived. The massive black orbs crashed down, exploding on impact, and sending a shower of the foreign threat in all directions.

Her concerns only grew when the screams of fear turned into ones of pain. Those who the substance touched swam away with disfiguring burns. As the chemical was mixed with the water, it created a bright, bubbling reaction. When it touched their skin, it sizzled and produced a rotting smell that spread through their home quickly.

Maluai adjusted her course as the sight brought panic to her own laenu. There was chaos everywhere she went. She passed hundreds of eumen, who fled the unfortunate scene. Just like her, their concern was the safety of themselves and their families. As they swam to their homes, opposite where the spill happened, they hoped to find their loved ones safe.

Maluai hoped their homes would provide enough protection from the poisonous substance that spread across the south side of their city. Where it was unsafe to stay, the guards were quick to act, evacuating eumen from their stations and pushing them to the north side of Wallai.

It was a fortunate occurrence that where the spill happened, there were only a few water griffins. Unfortunately, most of their crops were in the area that suffered the worst of the devastation. It was the laborers, those charged with gathering and tending the food source for much of Wallai, who suffered the greatest injuries.

Wallai's royal palace sat in the direct center of the city, under the heart of the island above them. The elders said the position was a direct link to the strength of their mother goddess. They built the back of the home against the spine of Forge that reached down to the ocean floor. Luckily, the palace was just outside the reaches of the dark substance. But it wasn't so far that she couldn't hear the terror of her eumen.

It wasn't just the water griffins that were impacted by the disastrous spill. Every creature that swam in the magical waters was being displaced. Maluai was careful to avoid the schools of fish. Large bodies of whales and jellies swam by her. She almost cried when an injured Symphoneun, a fish who created beautiful music with the pipelike fins, swam by. She loved listening to them during their mating season and only hoped they would survive the terror. Its injured fins created a despondent sound that echoed the feelings of their eumen.

Despite her conflicting emotions and thoughts, Maluai told herself to focus on finding her laenu. Her father would have gone to the frontline with the others to make sure their eumen were safe. The council members would have gone along with her mother to begin preparations for outreach to the injured. Protocol stipulated the guardians would safeguard her sisters within the palace.

She changed her direction rather than returning home. Her sisters were fine, but her mother and father needed help. She was the only one of them who'd never been sick before. She could go to the front line and help the others. Her mother would be upset about it at first, but if Maluai could do some good, she would get over it. And her father, Masuen, would be proud of her for stepping up for her eumen in a time of need.

"Maluai!" the relieved voice of Seru called out to her through the chaos.

"Drakgo!" Maluai cursed beneath her breath as she stopped swimming. She considered trying to out-swim the guard, but knew Seru was much faster than her. She didn't stand a chance.

"Thank the goddess." Seru reached her. "You're okay. I was about to take to the surface to find you."

"I'm fine, Ser." Maluai brushed off her comment. Seru didn't know what Maluai did when she went to the surface. It was one secret she allowed her to keep after she promised she stayed away from the general population of Forge. "Where are my sisters?"

"They are safe inside." Seru confirmed what Maluai suspected. "Your parents are out trying to help the others."

"I figured they might be." Maluai cast a glance over her shoulder toward the danger.

"And you were going to join them?" Seru knew exactly what she was thinking. "You can't go there, Maluai. You know that. It isn't safe for you, and it's against our protocols."

"Isn't that the right thing to do?" She looked Seru in the eye. "You're always talking about how I need to face my responsibilities. I'm a part of the royal laenu, which means I am responsible for our eumen. I should be out there helping to make sure everyone is safe."

"Now you want to take on the burden of responsibility?" Seru threw her hands up. "I swear, I don't understand you at all. I'm glad you're willing to face your duties. However, this is the one time I'm insisting you put them aside. At least until we know what is happening. We need to keep you and your sisters safe."

"I already know what's happening. It's Forge. They did this." Maluai admitted the truth, knowing it would raise the guardian's suspicions. "Whatever they are doing up there is the reason this is happening here."

"How would you know that?" Seru's jaw tightened as she pulled Maluai out of the way of a scour whale. An enormous creature with seven translucent tentacles that stretched from its belly to sweep the ocean for food.

"Because I saw it with my own eyes." Maluai dropped her eyes from the inquisitive face in front of her. "It was like they cut open this side of the island, and when they did, it bled out into the ocean."

"Okay, we'll discuss how you saw this later, considering you promised to stay away from the land griffins." Seru paused. "What do you mean, the island bled out?"

"It was horrible. There was a loud popping sound, and the ground trembled. A moment later, there was shouting. I ran to see what happened, and the sound of terror filled the air as eumen screamed and ran to escape the danger. A moment later, I saw it pour out the side of the island." Maluai explained what she had witnessed. "We have to contain it. If we don't, it's going to keep spreading through our home, and it's going to hurt everyone it touches. I'm not even sure they stopped it. As soon as I saw what happened, I rushed home. I wanted to get back here so I could help."

"My only concern right now is making sure you get somewhere safe. You need to go inside with your sisters."

"You want me to just sit there and do nothing?" Maluai took one last shot at convincing Seru to give in. "Is that what you would do?"

"You asked what I want. That's exactly what I want. You will go inside and wait until your parents get back." Seru turned and swam toward the palace. "This isn't about what I would do, Maluai."

"They want us to sit back, keep our mouths shut, and do nothing," she replied in a resigned tone. "This is the one time I can't do that. Not when I know we could help our eumen."

"That is not your job. There are other eumen equipped to take care of this. Please, for once, listen to reason. I know you don't like tradition, and I know you want to go against what's expected of you. This is one of those times when it's best for everyone if you stay put. Sit with your sisters. Comfort them in this difficult time and wait for your parents to return."

"Okay, you're right," Maluai conceded, as she thought of her sisters, who were likely worried about her. "I'll go."

They made it back to the palace, and Seru insisted Maluai redress before joining her sisters. There was enough going on without adding more suspicions about her attire. As soon as Maluai was back in her royal robes, they swam to the panic room at the bottom of the palace. It was the safest place for the sisters.

"Maluai." Her youngest sister swam to her and wrapped her arms around her waist the second she stepped inside the room. "I was so worried about you."

"I'm alright." Maluai hugged Naluai back. "It's okay, Nal. Everything is going to be okay."

"Always running off and getting into trouble." Kaluai, her older sister, commented as she swam over, her heavy robes poised perfectly on her shoulders.

"Are you blaming this on me?" Maluai rolled her eyes. "You can't be serious. Just because I skipped out on a meeting?"

"Shouldn't I be?" Kaluai narrowed her eyes. "You left court and went who knows where, and now suddenly—"

"Right, I left the court and cut a hole in the island's side that is spilling acidic fluid into the water. That's my fault," Maluai cut her off. "You hear how ridiculous that claim is, don't you?"

"I'm not about to argue with you about this." Kaluai waved her sister off.

"Because you know how idiotic you sound." Maluai laughed, because yet again, Kaluai's attempt to make her look incompetent had backfired. "Just because I don't want to sit through these pointless meetings does not mean I'm out creating trouble when I'm not here. When I leave, it's a search for peace and for freedom. Something you've known your entire life, but I have not."

"Whatever you have to tell yourself to make you feel okay about stepping out on your responsibilities," Kaluai huffed and turned her back on her sister, her lips pressed together in a thin line.

"Can we not fight right now?" Naluai tightened her hold around Maluai's wrist. "I'm worried about our parents and about the city. How can you be arguing about whether she wants to sit here in meetings? Who cares?"

"She's right. No one cares about this." Maluai put her arm around her little sister's shoulders and ushered her over to the seats. "Our parents will be alright. They're just making sure everyone's alright, and they'll be right back, I promise."

"Is it terrible out there?" Naluai looked up at Maluai. "You're the only one who saw."

"Yeah, it is." Maluai related to her little sister. Though she wanted to protect her, as all older siblings did, she knew it wouldn't help to keep secrets. Especially when the lie would be obvious. Whatever was going on, it was exactly what the court and the royal laenu argued about earlier. Things in their home were about to be changed forever, and it directly resulted from the actions of the eumen of Forge.

The three sisters stood in silence, guarded by their protectors as they waited for word of their parents. Even though they couldn't hear anything outside the reinforced walls that surrounded them, the screams of pain and the sights of their panicked eumen replayed in Maluai's mind. She didn't tell her little sister how bad it was, but all she could do was hope that Naluai would never have to see it for herself.

Shortly after she arrived, Maluai and the others stiffened as they felt the strange shift in the water. The gentle current that typically moved the surrounding waters stopped. It could only mean one thing. The magic wielders lifted a protective border around the palace. If they had, it meant the dark liquid threatened to reach their home.

Maluai considered their guardians. She wondered what they must be thinking. Protocol dictated they stay inside with the guardians, but was that what they really wanted? Wouldn't they prefer to be out helping to save their eumen? They had their own families and friends. They had eumen who were important to them. Instead of being able to go out and make sure they were safe, their duties restricted the guardians and forced them to watch over the princesses.

Lavi, Naluai's guardian, held her position by the door. She kept herself together, but whenever she approached to check on Naluai, her eyes told the truth. Lavi was hurting. The guardian was one of the toughest available, but she also had a child of her own. Maluai wondered if she kept her back to them to prevent them from seeing the tears that flooded her steel green eyes.

Though her laenu lived on the opposite end of where the destruction happened, still Maluai couldn't imagine how much restraint it took for her not to leave and make sure they were okay.

Emixi was Kaluai's guardian. Of the three that watched them, she was the one who looked the least worried. As far as Maluai knew, she had no one else in her life. The guardian was strictly by the book, which matched the daughter she protected. She was also the youngest of the guardians and had the most to prove.

As always, her expression was blank, serious. Tattooed luminescent ink enhanced the natural markings on her face and created a soft glow at the edges. The marks appeared on her forehead and cheeks and complimented the enhanced armor she wore. Emixi always wore her battle gear unless strictly ordered not to. Even in times of peace, she looked battle ready.

Maluai thought the armor, complete with chest plate and shoulder gear built to protect the neck, was a physical representation of the stress of her job. Of the three royal guardians, she probably had the hardest because if she failed, the trajectory of their eumen would shift forever. Kaluai was the next to be queen after their mother. No harm could come to her.

After two long hours, the door to the room finally opened. They expected to see the king joined by the council and his wife, but the only euman who appeared was Valuai, followed shortly by her guardian, Kianna. Her usually strong demeanor softened, her expression taking on a somber note. As soon as the doors shut behind her, she pulled her daughters into her arms and sobbed.

"Mom?" Naluai asked. "How is it?"

"It's bad. I won't lie to you." Valuai touched her daughter's face. "There are tough times ahead for Wallai."

"Are we going to be okay?" Kaluai asked. "Should we be staying here, or should we move somewhere safer?"

"The magic wielders have created a barrier of containment. We don't know how long it will last. They used most of the available mucilias harvest and are trying to figure out how to get rid of it without releasing it back into the rest of the world.

Right now, the safest place for us is right here in our home. We are safe here."

"Where is Dad?" Maluai looked at the door where she expected him to enter. "Why is he not with you now?"

"He is coming soon." Valuai rubbed Maluai's shoulder. "He's helping the others. You know how your father is. He won't rest until he is sure everyone is safe."

Valuai was gentle enough to calm her daughter, but still kept her display of strength. And through it all, her crown remained perfectly placed on her head. Maluai admired that about her mother. From the way she handled the court to the way she was with her eumen, Valuai had perfect poise. She kept their best interest in mind at all times. Despite the ways they clashed, Maluai hoped she would inherit that strength.

Just as they settled in, the palace walls trembled at the sound of a distant explosion.

"What was that?" Kaluai asked.

"I don't know." Valuai looked at Kianna, the head of the Queen's Guard, who listened at the door.

There was silence. A long, horrible silence. And they sat together for another hour before the rapid knocking on the door. Kirua opened it with Seru and Emixi poised to attack should the euman mean to do harm. But when the door opened, there was a young guard standing on the other side.

He swam in, saluting the other guardians, before addressing the Queen.

"Queen Valuai." There was sorrow in his voice that turned Maluai's stomach.

"What is it?" the queen asked.

"It's the King. He was injured in the blast."

CHAPTER 4

"Keep the princesses here until I send word," Kianna, the queen's guard, instructed the other guardians. Her voice was the most powerful of the guardians, and the opal stone in her armored collar hummed with reverberating energy from her words. Valuai was so impressed by Kianna's courageousness during the unlikely shark attack, she chose her to head the guard.

The markings that dusted her honey brown skin like freckles on her face glowed as she issued her orders. She instructed them to lock the doors securely behind her and wait until they received the signal before unlocking it once again.

"Of course." Seru saluted the head of the guardians with a fist over her chest. "We will protect them."

The door closed, leaving Maluai and her sisters in the safe room with their guardians and their ballooning grief.

"What are they going to do?" Naluai asked, tears streaming down her face. "What's going to happen to Dad?"

"They will do whatever they can to help him," Kaluai answered. "He will be fine."

"You don't know that," Maluai muttered.

"This isn't fair." Naluai sobbed into Kaluai's shoulder, her wild hair blocking her sister's face. "This isn't fair."

"Nothing in life ever is." Maluai's thoughts were already turning dark, and she struggled to keep it to herself.

"Maluai," Kaluai snipped at her sister. "Really?"

"What?"

Kaluai nodded to their younger sister. Her eyes bulging at her Maluai's careless statement.

"Oh, I'm sorry, Nal." Maluai moved over to the young girl. "I didn't mean it. I'm just frustrated."

"I understand." Naluai reached out to her sister and took her hand. "This is scary for all of us."

"Yes, it really is, but Kal is right." Maluai addressed her earlier outburst. "We should try to stay positive."

The sisters turned their thoughts to positive moments with their father. Naluai talked about her experiences with art and music. Their father had a beautiful voice, and she inherited that talent from him. Kaluai spoke about their lessons in history. She always had her nose in the archives and would spend hours there, learning from him and sharing their political theories.

Maluai's thoughts were all about the freedoms he allowed her. The moments when he snuck her away from their world and showed her things that would have terrified her mother.

"Once he took me to see the Kivari sharks mating." Maluai spoke of the creatures who had gems down their back and tails. Despite being relatively harmless, they were still intimidating to observe while they mated, adding an edge of risk to the experience. "I didn't know what to expect, but it was beautiful to see. It was like they were dancing, almost hypnotic."

"What?" Kaluai's mouth fell open in disbelief. "There is no way he took you there."

"Yes. He did. It was terrifying and beautiful, and Mom would have killed us both if she knew." Maluai laughed. "He made me promise to tell no one. Even you."

"I can't believe he did that." Kaluai found it difficult to see past the danger. "What if something happened to you?"

"Nothing happened, Kaluai. As you can see, I'm fine now." Maluai laughed at her older sister. "I'm glad he took me there. I didn't understand it, but it was the first time I felt like being different wasn't a life sentence. That it wouldn't hold me back if I didn't allow it to."

"Is that how you felt?" Naluai asked.

"For a long time, yes," Maluai admitted. "Mom treats me like a bomb waiting to go off. Even now, almost thirty years into my life, and she's still afraid of me breathing without her there to supervise. But going there helped me change the way I saw things."

Maluai left her sisters to approach the guardian who stood at the door, giving them space to talk. "Have you heard anything, Ser?"

"He is with the healers now." Seru turned to the princess. "I wish I could say more, but that is all I know."

"Why are we still in here? It has to be safe by now. I mean, if the barrier is up, we should at least be free to move around the palace."

"You're like a fiddle fish trapped in a cage." Seru smirked. "Can't keep still."

"What?"

"They're agitated little things. Hard to keep hold of. You know they swim around fifty miles every day? That's how much they need to move their little bodies. You're just like one of them. Just swimming around in circles trying to burn off untapped energy."

"I'm nothing like that," Maluai vented with a deep, frustrated sigh. "At least they're cute. I used to love watching their colorful little bodies when they would swim by my window each day until their migrating patterns changed."

"I'm sure they will send word soon." Seru nodded.

"I hope so. I'm going to go crazy if I have to stay in here for much longer."

Twenty minutes later, there was a knock on the door. Seru opened it and stepped out. The three sisters watched the door and waited for the guardian to return. When she did, she had a solemn look on her face that she quickly tried to mask before the sisters saw it. Maluai caught the look, and her stomach dropped.

"Your mother is calling for you now," Seru announced. "We will escort you now."

Protected by their guardians, the sisters swam through the long hallways from the bottom of the palace to the top level where they'd moved their father. The moment Masuen was brought back to the palace, they immediately took him to the healers.

"My daughters." Valuai met her daughters as they reached their destination. "Your father wants to see you all. Before you go in, you should know, the healers did all that they could."

"But?" Kaluai asked.

"It is not looking well." Valuai's voice broke as she spoke to her daughters. "His injuries are severe and far beyond anything we've faced before."

"Shouldn't we wait? Let him rest?" Naluai asked. "He's been through so much."

"I think it's best you see him now." Valuai touched her daughter's face, and her voice broke with sadness. "He needs to feel your love and see your beautiful faces. It will do him some good."

"Okay." Naluai's voice was small, frightened, but she agreed to her mother's request.

Valuai grabbed Naluai's hand and led her into the room where their father rested. Their eldest sister followed her mother closely, but Maluai lingered behind. Her stomach felt heavy, and no matter what she did, she couldn't move forward. She stared at the door, the sound of the latch clicking into place still echoing in her ears.

"Maluai." Seru laid her hand on Maluai's shoulder. "What are you waiting for?"

"Ser, I can't go in there." Maluai forced the words out of her mouth. "I don't know that I can take seeing him like that."

"This is one of those times that what you must do isn't for you." Seru's words were gentle, lacking the usual authority in her voice. "It's about someone else and what they need."

"So, I should go in there." Maluai looked at the door.

"Of course you should, but I won't force the issue." She nudged her in the back, pushing her forward. "It's not my place to push you."

"I'm going." Maluai looked over her shoulder at Seru. "Thanks for *not* pushing me."

Inside the room, her mother sat next to an enormous bed where her father rested. The weighted blanket helped to keep her father's body on the bed beneath him and keep him from floating away. Even with the blankets and wraps covering most of his body, she could still see the scars and smell the rot of his flesh in the room.

Maluai took a deep breath and told herself to focus on the man, not his pain, or the smell of decay that filled the room. She was there for the father who raised her, the euman who encouraged her. She moved forward until she met Naluai's side. Her sister quickly grabbed her hand, and Maluai looked at her. The youngest of their laenu struggled to keep it together.

Maluai turned her attention to supporting her sister. That much she could do. She could be the strength for someone else, even when it was hard to do that for herself.

Her father said no words, but he looked at his three daughters. His eyes told her he knew he didn't know how many more times would see their faces. As he always did, he remained strong. He smiled though he was in pain, and he held back terrible coughs as not to worry them.

Masuen's laenu remained at his side until he fell asleep. When his breathing shifted, and his grip on his wife's hand eased, the three girls left the room, allowing Valuai more time alone with her love.

"I just don't understand how this could have happened," Kaluai whispered. "How was he hurt so badly?"

"He sheltered someone with his own body," her guardian reported.

"This is ridiculous," Kaluai snapped. "How could the guards let this happen?"

"Kaluai," Emixi spoke, ready to defend the guard's actions.

"No, she's right," Maluai said. "You all make such a big deal about protecting the royal laenu. He is the head of our laenu, and yet he is in there, hurt worse than I could ever imagine. How could they not protect him?"

"You know your father," Seru spoke. "He wouldn't expect anyone to put their life on the line for him, not really. It doesn't matter the oath they took."

47

"There was a small girl," another guard who'd been with Masuen spoke. "We doubled back to make sure everyone got out of the area. The king insisted. We were on our way out when he heard her. I offered to go to get the girl, but he said it would be better if he went. His presence would comfort her. He pulled her out of her home, but they hadn't made it far enough. The blast was unexpected. We didn't know."

"He saved someone?" Naluai asked.

"Yes, a small girl. No older than ten." The guard nodded. "If not for your father, she would have died in that blast."

"I want to be happy that he saved a life, and that he protected our eumen, but all I can think is that my father is dying in there." Maluai sobbed. "No matter how optimistic I try to be, I know he won't make it out of this alive. What are we going to do without him?"

"You cannot think as if he's already gone." Kaluai approached her sister. "He is still here. Still fighting."

"But for how much longer?" Maluai looked at Kaluai with tears flooding her eyes. "How am I supposed to not consider the reality we're facing right now?"

"Mal." Kaluai paused because she was also struggling to process what was happening.

"I need to get out of here." Maluai shook her head. "I can't just stand here and do nothing."

"You can't leave again." Naluai sobbed. "We need you here."

"I don't want to leave." Maluai tried to comfort her sister. She didn't mean to make her worry. "I just I can't sit here and wait for them to come out of that room and tell me that my father is gone. It doesn't feel right when I could do something meaningful."

"Mal, he wants to see you." Valuai's voice called their attention to the open door to their father's room.

"He does?" She turned to find her mother's bloodshot eyes gazing at her.

"He asked for you, specifically," her mother whispered. "He has something he wants to say to you."

Maluai looked at her sisters. "Why me?"

"I can't answer that." Valuai wiped the tears from her eyes.

"Right, okay." She moved to the door, then glanced at Kaluai. "Maybe you should go first. You're the oldest."

"He asked for you, Mal." She nudged her sister forward. "Go, like you said. We don't know how much time we have left."

"You're still here," Masuen said when she entered the room. He sounded strong, but she knew better.

"I am." Maluai swam forward.

"I admit I am shocked to see you still here." He coughed, and she rushed to his side. "My daughter, the brave spirit, the wandering soul. That's why I asked to see you first."

"I wanted to leave," she admitted. "I thought it would be better if I was out there with our eumen."

"You always run from the hard stuff." He looked at his daughter with kindness in his eyes.

"What?" She shook her head. "I do not."

"Don't misunderstand me. It's not a bad thing. I was the same way." A tired smile stretched across his dark face. "Adventure! That made life worth living. It was also the thing I turned to when I faced something I knew I couldn't change. It was almost easier to go for adventure because the ending is so unpredictable."

"Father."

"Maluai, I am dying." He said the words she hoped he wouldn't. "In this, the ending is quite predictable. I expected I would have so many more years with you and your sisters. I hoped to watch you grow old, find love, and marry. Maybe then we could finally convince your mother that you aren't someone who needs to be locked away."

"That will never happen." Maluai smirked.

"Oh, it will. I believe in time she will see your true spirit." He held his hand out for her to take. "I wish I could see it, but it will happen even if I am not here to applaud when it does."

"This is not fair." Maluai looked at her father and could see the changes. His usual full face looked hollow. In less than a day, he'd changed so much, weakened beyond measure. "The eumen of Forge do something tragic, and we suffer for it."

"That is not my concern right now, nor should it be yours. I know how you are." He squeezed her hand. "When I'm gone, I do not want you to retreat within yourself or to escape to the outer world. Face your grief, daughter. Know that my love is with you always, even if I cannot be."

"I don't want to think about that. Not now when you're still here. We still have time." Maluai tried to summon up all the optimism she could. "There is still time. We can figure this out and save you."

"I can hear it in the way your voice shakes—you believe that no more than I do." Masuen spoke with a quivering voice. "My time is limited, but yours is just beginning."

"I don't want you to go." The tears she fought to hold back flowed freely. "This isn't right."

"It is not my desire to leave you either, but I will be with you always." He placed his hand on her chest. "In your heart. You will find echoes of my love for as long as you live, and even after you're gone from this world to join me in the next."

"I need to go. I need to get out of here." Maluai wiped her face of the tears.

"I know you do. It is your spirit. Maluai, I wanted to tell you that whatever you feel you need to do to process this, do it. No matter what anyone else is telling you is the right way to do so. Know that your father will hold nothing against you. All I ask is you do what is necessary for your survival."

"Even if that means leaving, so I'm not here when—" She couldn't say the words.

"Especially if it means that." He nodded. "Do what you feel is right. Go out there. See our eumen. Help them."

"I love you." She lifted his hand to her lips and kissed the back of his hand before placing a kiss on his forehead. "Forever. You will always be in my heart."

"Such a comforting thought." He sighed. "Thank you."

Maluai left her father alone and did exactly what he told her to do. She listened to her own needs, and they told her to leave, to go somewhere that wouldn't haunt her. When she left her laenu, her mother looked at her with knowing eyes. She understood what her daughter needed, even if she didn't agree with it.

Maluai didn't go far. She couldn't, not with the magical barrier still surrounding the palace. Until the magic wielders dropped it, all she could do was watch. There were fewer terrorized screams, and the dark cloud no longer spread. They had it contained it and were working to clean up the areas already devastated by its touch, but it was a slow process.

It was a slow process because the black cloud was more volatile than they could have prepared for. They found the best way to deal with it was to contain it in smaller batches. Carefully, they sliced it into smaller bubbles and secured them in place with the mucilias harvest. They were at a loss as to how to eradicate it, so this was their only recourse.

She knew what the true concern was. It would be the same for every creature that lived in those waters. What if the toxic matter continued to spread throughout the waters? What would that level of contamination do? Would the harmful effects spread outside of Wallai? How many lives would they lose? It was a never-ending list of questions and not one of them had an answer.

Six hours later, the magic wielders felt it safe enough to lower the barrier around the royal palace. The moment it dropped, she was ready to go. She wanted to be free of the palace and of the emotions. She needed to get away from her sisters and her mother and everything else that reminded her of what she was losing. It made little sense because going out to see the eumen and their home meant facing the thing that her father gave his life for, but it was better than doing nothing. It was better than sitting and waiting for the inevitable.

"Where are you going?" Seru drifted from the shadows where she watched over Maluai.

"To see how our eumen are doing and to be useful," Maluai answered her firmly. "I will not let you convince me not to go, so if you need to report me to my mother, do it, because I'm going."

"I am not here to convince you not to go," Seru said calmly. "I intend to go with you, and I will help you."

"Really?" Seru's statement shocked Maluai. "Isn't that against your rules?"

"It is, but I think what you're doing is brave." The guardian adjusted her spear that was strapped to her back. "It will show our eumen that the royal laenu cares, even during this time when your father's life is at risk. I think it shows good faith that your laenu will do right by the eumen of Wallai."

"That's not why I'm doing this." Maluai shook her head. "This isn't some political stunt."

53

"I know it's not the reason, but that's what the eumen will take from it. I know you just need to get away and that you really care about what's going on out there. Maluai, you're doing what you feel is right, and even that sends a message of strength. Regardless of the reasons behind it, your efforts will be good on many parts."

"Fine. Whatever you have to tell yourself to make it okay for you." Maluai realized that for her guardian, she had to have a valid reason. If questioned, she couldn't tell her superiors that she did it because of emotion. To say that it was a strategic move would grant her leniency for her actions if ever questioned. "Let's go."

Maluai's grief only inflated as she swam away from her home and through the city. She almost turned back, thinking that what she witnessed was worse than what she would face at her father's side, but then she thought of what he said. She always ran from the hard stuff. That couldn't be her truth. It couldn't be how she navigated through life.

Though she knew it would be bad, there was far more devastation and ruin than she thought. She saw the effects of the tragedy in places far away from the point where the murky liquid cascaded into the waters. In areas left untouched, the guard had evacuated the eumen. She couldn't understand why until she looked at the ocean floor. Dark veins spread through the soil. Evidence of disease, and of the long-term damage their home would face.

"Touch nothing," Seru instructed. "We're not sure how this stuff works yet."

"Right." Maluai heeded her guardian's warning.

There was so much damage. More than the land itself. The vegetation, aquatic life, and creatures of all sizes had to find new homes because of what happened. By her estimation, there was a five-mile radius from where the damage hit. Everything within those reaches was pushed aside. With her guardian by her side to make sure she was safe, Maluai swam for nearly two hours and cataloged everything she saw.

She had no plan for the information she recorded, but it had to be done. They would need to keep a record of who needed help and how to provide it. Her healers would need to know what eumen to aid. The hunters would need to understand how their food supplies would shift and calculate what would inevitably become new migration patterns of the creatures displaced.

The harvesters would need to move their work. She counted three patches of vegetation that would no longer serve them. Who knew how long it would take for the soil to recover? If it ever did.

After taking as many notes as she could, she turned away from the devastated lands to join the displaced. She swam to the north side of the city, hoping to help. As she moved with Seru close by, she was relieved to see a school of rotundi fish. They were one of the primary food sources for Wallains because of their high fat content and sweet taste. The school appeared completely unharmed as they stayed on the east side of the city.

Above them were four dumi whales. Their yellow underbellies glowed as always, but she could see dark spots on one of them and knew it meant the animal had suffered injuries, but there was nothing she could do. When it opened its mouth, the normal deep sound was a high pitch that gave voice to its pain. Maluai wished she could help the creature, but to even approach it would be dangerous. The others clustered around it, as if comforting it. She watched closely as the marks spread across its belly. Soon it would perish.

Again, Maluai cried because there was nothing more she could do. But she continued moving forward until she found her eumen. They were also in clusters, grouped around the injured, helping in any way they could, though it appeared nothing helped. She approached Akaien, a healer who exited a home, his shoulders slumped with the weight of his frustration.

"Akaien," Maluai greeted him with their gesture, and he returned it.

"Princess Maluai." He looked genuinely shocked to see her there. "You shouldn't be out here. It is dangerous."

"I want to help," Maluai spoke. "Tell me what I can do."

"I wish there was something you could do." He shook his head, the long grey locks swayed beneath his tired face. "We've tried everything to stop the effects. Even those of us who have magic, nothing has worked."

"How bad is it?" Seru asked.

"Forty have died," he responded, and the wrinkles in his forehead deepened. "Another thirty are ill. They will not make it through the day."

"This is horrible." Maluai looked around. "We have to figure something out."

"All we can do is try to comfort the ill." Akaien sighed, and his grey eyes looked at her like a ghost looking at its past life. "Even our suppressants are not enough to fully ease their pain."

Maluai spent the next hour swimming from home to home and witnessing what her eumen experienced. She comforted when she could, and when best she stood aside and simply observed.

"Maluai, we should head back." Seru spoke as they exited another home. "You've done much more than anyone could have expected of you."

"I don't—" Maluai began her protest, but Seru refused to back down.

"You're tired and hungry. I know you want to help, but you're no good to these eumen if you collapse from exhaustion," Seru spoke reason the princess couldn't refute.

"Maybe you're right." She looked back at the home. "There's just so much pain here."

"You can come back, do more, after you've rested. It's been a long day, and the night is coming."

"Okay," Maluai turned to follow Seru back to the palace, but stopped when she heard the sobs of a small child. "Wait, do you hear that?"

"What?" Seru's ears lifted as she honed her senses.

"There is someone over here." Maluai pointed to the east of them, where a small cliff stood. "I heard someone crying. "

"Let me go look. Stay right here," Seru insisted, but just like her father had, Maluai swam ahead.

She swam around a small cliff and found a girl swimming alone, arms wrapped around herself as she attempted to self-soothe. Her eyes were puffy with tears and her markings, two stripes across each eye, matched her mother's.

"Syloki?" Maluai recognized the child immediately. "Seru, it's Lavi's daughter!"

"Princess Maluai!" The girl swam to her quickly and wrapped her arms around her. "I was so scared."

"It's okay." Maluai comforted her and looked back at Seru, who for the first time in years, she saw struggle with her own emotions. "What are you doing here?"

"I was with my brother, and then we got separated." Syloki looked up at her with wide eyes. "I don't know where he is."

"I'm sure he is okay. You can come with me. Your mother is at the palace. She will help you find your brother." Maluai tried to comfort the young girl and hoped her brother truly was okay.

Maluai carried Syloki back to the palace. The young girl was terrified and could barely keep herself from falling apart. Even in the safe hold of the princess, she cried, and her body trembled. It wasn't until they made it back and Maluai released her into her mother's arms that the child relaxed.

"Thank you." Lavi's eyes watered as she held her child. "Thank you for bringing her to me."

"Of course," Maluai nodded as Lavi, excused by the head guardian, swam off hoping to locate her son.

"Where is everyone?" she asked a guard.

"They are in the court," the guard with deep brown eyes reported.

"Why?" Seru asked.

"The council called another meeting," he reported.

"Are you serious? Now?" Maluai asked before storming off toward the court. "I can't believe this."

"Maluai," Seru called after her when she swam away.

"Is this really the time to do this?" Maluai asked as she entered the court. "What is the purpose of this meeting?"

"Maluai." Naluai approached her. "You're still here."

"Of course I am." She turned her attention to the councilmen. "I'm serious. I want an answer. Why have you called a meeting now? Our father is on his deathbed, and yet you want to have a meeting to talk about something you will not make action on?"

"I think it's pertinent to—" Fituen began, but Maluai cut him off.

"I think it's pertinent for you all to show some respect to the king!" Maluai insisted. "Our laenu should be with him, not here. And you should be out there, with the eumen of Wallai, fixing this mess. What is there to talk about?"

"Mal—" Kaluai was ready to reprimand her sister for her rude behavior but stopped when the queen spoke.

"No, she is right." Queen Valuai entered behind her daughter. "I do not wish to be here talking to the same eumen who refused to take action when we still had a hope of avoiding a catastrophe like this. We knew the eumen of Forge were up to no good and yet we stood aside. Now, I've already approved evacuation plans, and the guards are hard at work securing our eumen. My husband, his life is ending, and yet I'm called here to talk discourse about Forge. Maluai refuses traditions, but this is one time I agree. I've only come here to tell you to end this madness. I will not hear your concerns today."

"I understand you are in pain, Queen Valuai, but—"

"But nothing!" she yelled. "Our laenu is in pain, and you so selfishly wish to brush that aside. We have always strived to do what is best for the eumen of Wallai, but at this moment, I will do what is best for my laenu! End this now. I am going back to Masuen, and I will deal with you later."

The queen looked at the faces of her daughters. The silence hung in the air, and then she abruptly turned and left the room.

"I still think we should discuss this," Fituen spoke after the queen departed. "We can't sit here and do nothing. We should make plans to hold the members of the Forge court accountable for what's happened here."

"You plan to hold this discussion without the queen?" Kaluai asked, her eyes turning dark as she looked at the councilman. "Am I hearing you correctly, Fituen?"

"I—" he began, but she held her hand up to stop his attempt at excusing his disrespect.

"You are stepping outside of your limits, councilman. Remember your place."

Maluai's chest rose with pride as her sister, the one who always played everything by the book, stepped out of place. Technically speaking, the councilman could call for a meeting without the royals, but in an instance where the queen vehemently called for the topic to be held for another day, she wouldn't allow them to disregard her mother's wishes.

"Yes, princess," Fituen yielded.

"We will end this meeting, as the queen requested." Kaluai displayed the same strength as her mother. "Save your thoughts for when we reconvene."

Maluai, proud of her sister for taking a stance, turned to leave the room with Naluai by her side. They stood in the hall and watched the council members leave. Kaluai was the last to exit as if she wanted to be sure they did as requested.

"That was pretty awesome of you," Maluai complimented her sister as she approached them.

"I took a cue from my sister," Kaluai responded. "Sometimes we have to lift our own voices, even if it goes against the rules."

As they hugged each other, the unexpected sound of the alarm startled the three girls.

The bells pealed four times with a solid and powerful sound. A tense silence descended on the room as everyone held their breath.

The fifth sounded, and Naluai burst into tears.
The king was dead.

CHAPTER 5

A ll of Wallai stood still. From the eumen to the creatures, even the subtle movements of the coral. It froze in reverence. Their leader, Masuen, the king of Wallai, had taken his final breath.

The sisters stood together in the hallway outside of the court and clutched each other as if their grip would amend that moment in history. If they held on tight enough, they could erase the sound of the bell and their father would still be with them. Maluai held her breath, but her eyes focused on Kaluai, who had silent tears flowing down her face.

Between their chests, Naluai cried out. Her body trembled with a frenzy of emotions. No matter how long they remained there or how long Maluai denied herself the function of breathing, nothing would ever change that moment. Maluai's eyes burned, and finally, her tears fell just as freely as her sisters'.

There was no more waiting for the inevitable and no opportunity to outrun it. The thing they dreaded the most had happened, and Maluai found herself relieved she was home when it did. There was the consolation of being with her sisters. She could comfort them and feel the same warmth of their emotional support in return.

It felt like an eternity had passed. There were too many moments between the last bell and when they saw their mother again. The guardians ushered them from the hall to the main floor of their laenu quarters. When they entered the room, which was far less official than the court on the floors below, Queen Valuai stood alone. It wasn't often they saw her mother without at least one guard nearby.

When she saw her daughters, she swam to them, arms wide. She wrapped them in all the love she had to give. All the love she could no longer give to their father. And they held on to her, for strength, and for that unseen adhesive that would keep a breaking laenu from falling apart.

"Is it true? Is he really gone?" Naluai looked to her mother for hope, though the young girl knew it was true. But they all needed to hear it from her, the confirmation of their sorrow.

"Yes, my dear." Their mother's voice broke as she spoke the words her heart could hardly take. "Masuen, your father, no longer flows with us in this life cycle."

"What happens now?" Kaluai's logical mind spoke when her emotions got the best of her. She needed structure. Point A to B and on until things made sense again.

"Now we mourn," her mother answered her and attentively stroked Naluai's wild hair. "We care for each other and then for our eumen."

The laenu sat together for hours, alternating between crying and laughing at old memories. They took comfort in the memories. They recalled moments they had together, the laughs they shared, the lessons they learned, even the secrets once hidden. In embracing those moments, they came closer together. They found strength in their shared love. For breaths between moments, pauses as fleeting as the time between blinks, they felt like they would be okay.

Maluai was the first to leave. Though there was comfort together, there were things she wanted to process alone.

"Maluai," her mother called her name as she left the room. "I'll see you tomorrow."

It sounded almost like a question, the slight lift in her voice at the end of her sentence. It was the vulnerable admittance of a mother's fear.

"Yes, of course," Maluai reassured her mother.

As Maluai returned to her room, she couldn't help thinking about her mother's reaction to her leaving. Because even in their time of shared grieving, surrounded by their familial love, there was something in the back of her mind. It was what her father talked about. That thought of escape.

Yes, there was comfort in others, but there was a part of her that wanted to run. Despite the internal urge, she also wanted her father to be wrong about her. Life was going to throw curveballs and difficult moments that she would have to face. How would she make it through if her response was to run?

Despite her aggravation with her own thoughts, it was still what she longed for, and she found it impossible to not contemplate it. Maluai thought of a place, just as her father taught her as a child. He taught her there was power in visualization, though she didn't always use it the way he intended.

She imagined there was a place where the restrictions of reality were malleable. There, she could bend her reality, and their mourning would end. In this fictional space, her father was still alive, and her mother, though firm, was still happy. Her youngest sister's eyes still glowed with optimism, and her older sister, who was often too rigid for her liking, still looked forward to a future where she could continue learning from her father.

If she could find it, that was where she would go. But there was no escape that was far enough away to make her reality different. Masuen, her king, her father, was gone. They would be there without him forever. As she undressed, she told herself that since there was no place that existed that could change her present truth, then she would remain at home.

Maluai got into her bed, pulled the weighted blanket over her body, and attempted to rest. An attempt was all she could manage because her heart felt heavier than the blanket she used to cover herself. Her mind raced with thoughts of escape and fantasy. She told herself stories. Imaginings of waking up the next day and finding that her father hadn't died.

But those stories did nothing but hurt her more. Because in the few moments they brought her comfort, pain followed. Like a fresh cut on a still bleeding wound. There was no amount of imagination, no story she could tell herself that would bring him back.

She tossed and turned, and by the time the light returned to their underwater home, Maluai lay puffy eyed and unrested in her bed.

She thought of remaining there for the day. Avoiding the world and getting lost in her own sorrow. A thought that was quickly chased away by the knocking at her door.

"Mal?" the soft voice of a girl who looked so much like herself called out from the other side. "Are you awake?"

"Yeah. I'm awake. Come in." She wiped the remnants of sleep from her eyes and waited for her sister to appear around the opening door.

"Did you sleep?" Naluai asked as she swam over and climbed into the bed next to her.

"No," Maluai admitted. "Did you?"

"No," she answered. "Every time I closed my eyes, I saw his face, and it just made me sad."

"I know what you mean." Maluai brushed her sister's hair. "I kept trying to imagine it away. Maybe if I dreamed hard enough, when I woke up, it wouldn't be true."

"I wish I could hear him sing one more time." Naluai released a loud, weary sigh, a sound that echoed through the stillness. "We were supposed to have lessons today. He said he would teach me the secrets of that quiver he did with his voice. I guess now I will never know how to do it."

"He tickled the inside of his throat." Maluai laughed as she revealed their father's secret.

"What?" Naluai sat up in the bed beside her.

"Dad had an injury when he was a child. It created a moveable cliff within his throat. No matter how many lessons he gave you, you'd never been able to do it."

"Seriously?" Naluai scoffed. "Why would he tell me he could teach me?"

"He did the same to Kal and me." Maluai sighed. "I think it was his way of extending the time we shared in singing. Our interests were shifting, so he had to keep us hooked. Eventually, he told us the truth."

"I almost choked trying to do that!" Naluai crossed her arms over her chest.

"I did choke!" Maluai's shoulders shook with the memory. "Kaluai was terrified I would die, and she slapped my back so hard I had a bruise for two days."

"Can I come in?" Kaluai poked her head around the open door.

"Of course." Maluai waved her forward.

"It's been a long time since we've done this." Naluai smiled as Kaluai swam over and joined them in the bed.

"What?" Kaluai asked her youngest sister.

"Cuddled up together." Naluai pointed to the bed. "We used to do this all the time."

"I guess it has been a while." Maluai nodded. "As we get older, moments like this come along a lot less. I wish it were for a happier reason."

"They're starting preparations today, aren't they?" Naluai looped her arm through Kaluai's as she lay between her sisters.

"Yes, they are," Kaluai confirmed. "I heard them moving things in the halls when I came over. I think they're moving his body now."

"His body," Maluai repeated the words. "He's just a body now."

"No, he's so much more than that," Kaluai said. "Remember, our physical selves are simply vessels that contain the energy of our true beings. He's moved on, maybe to find a new vessel."

"One that can do the throat quiver?" Naluai asked.

"Oh, the throat quiver, you know when Mal tried it—" Kaluai began the recount of the time Maluai choked.

"I already told her!" Maluai laughed, and her sisters joined in. "My brief life flashed before my eyes."

"I swear, the look on your face was priceless." Kaluai cackled, and her beaded braids clacked against her chest.

"So was the handprint on my back." Maluai reached across their youngest sister and playfully pushed her shoulder.

"Ouch, sorry about that." Her oldest sister struggled to hold her laughter back.

The sisters remained in bed, laughing, talking, and eventually, they fell asleep together. And while they slept, the preparations for their father's recommittal went on.

The process of recommittal, the ritual of death, happened in three phases. First was the preparation of the body. During this time, the herbalist would take the body and coat it in a thin membrane called nizese. This membrane adhered to the body and removed all moisture from within. The process was lengthy, taking twelve hours to complete, but it was important to guard against scavenger fish.

Before this was done, they would cut a lock of hair for each member of the surviving laenu. They would turn the hair into a jewel for them to keep.

After the nizese did its job, they would wrap the body in samos, a thin vegetation that glimmered in the light like a pattern of lace, and adorn it with sweet lilos, whose gentle fragrance was like inhaling a breath of fragrant lavender.

Then, in a private ceremony, they would take the body to the rift. As the officiant chanted the ceremonial rites, the laenu watched solemnly; the sound echoing off the coral as they laid their loved one to rest. Their words were a promise to the goddess, to return every water griffin back to the source. Their souls would be recycled, as they believed, into a new lifeform.

All this would happen two days after the passing. It was another day of mourning before they would complete the ceremony. Maluai spent the day in bed with her sisters. They laughed, talked, cried, and slept wrapped in each other's arms.

When the light left the water, the sisters went in search of their mother. She lay in her bed after a long day of preparations for the services that would take place the next morning.

The girls joined their mother, filling her bed with warmth, and she quickly fell asleep listening to their chatter. Maluai was the last awake. She watched her laenu, her sorrow still lurking in the back of her mind. They would survive the loss. They would band together, heal together, and go on. Because that was what they had to do.

The next day was the hardest.

The next morning, she rose, cleaned herself up, and dressed in her robes. These were different, all white and adorned with gold and jewels on the shoulders and bodice. They did not weigh the bottom down. Instead, they allowed the robes to float around their body as representation of the freedom of the soul rejoining Lunai, their mother goddess.

The laenu, the royal court, and the guardians gathered for the private ceremony when the king's body was returned to the land. As the roots absorbed his body, each member of his laenu placed their new jewel, crafted with his hair, around each of their necks. Each jewel reflected the euman receiving it. The glass case with wire framing held the piece created from her father's hair. Maluai sobbed when she saw it. The pain climbed up her throat and burned in her chest. This was just the beginning of her farewell.

After the private service, all the surviving Wallains gathered on the north side of their home, the only place it was safe, and they sang the songs of mourning. While their voices rang out, they lit their vanishing lanterns and released them. The bubbles floated to the surface where they popped and released a flame that shot into the sky.

If the residents of Forge were unaware of what happened beneath them, they knew then.

"You asked for me?" Maluai peeked around the corner at her mother, who sat alone in her bedroom.

"Yes, I did." Valuai waved her daughter forward.

"Is everything okay?" Maluai nervously looked around the room. "How are you?"

"I'm surviving, which is the best I can offer right now." Valuai patted the bed next to her for Maluai to join her. "I called you here because I am concerned for you."

"Me?" Maluai joined her mother. "Why are you concerned about me?"

"I know your heart, daughter." Valuai smiled, then placed her fingers to her daughter's temple. "And I know that your mind is telling you it's time to go."

"I am not planning on going anywhere," Maluai disputed. "I'm right here."

"You are not planning it. No. You're denying that part of yourself for now." Valuai pulled her hand into hers. "But I've known your heart for quite some time now, and you've always desired to get away from Wallai. I fear that now that your father is gone, that will only grow. I know he supported your desires more than I ever have, and I'm sure that's what he told you to do."

"He..." Maluai thought of what her father told her on his deathbed.

"No, don't tell me what he said to you. Those last words were for you and you alone. I only called you here to ask that you wait. I know your spirit wants you to go, and it might be selfish of me to ask this of you, but please, stay." Valuai choked back her tears. "For me, for your sisters. Just for a while. Stay. Be with us. I know you leave us often. You have your adventures. I'm not a fool, and I've learned to turn a blind eye to it because they never take you too far from home, but I need my daughters by my side. I need to make sure you are safe."

"Mother..." She wanted to reject her mother's claims, but there was a part of her that wanted to escape. No, she hadn't planned to leave. After the time with her sisters, she hoped to stay with her laenu, but for how long?

"Maluai, I know this is a lot to ask, but please."

"I will stay," Maluai agreed.

"Thank you." Valuai kissed her daughter's hand. "There is a lot that is going to happen. There is a shift that needs to take place, one that may put our laenu at risk."

"What's going to happen?" Maluai's brow furrowed as she questioned her mother's declaration.

"Change. I'm not sure that everyone is going to be happy about the way I plan to change things, but we cannot sit by and watch this happen again. This is where it ends."

"I don't know what you mean."

"You will. Now, go get rest." Valuai patted her daughter's shoulder. "We have a council meeting at first light. The council won't wait much longer to address this."

"Are you sure you're going to be okay?" Maluai looked at her mother. "I can stay if you need me to."

"I'll be okay. I'm a survivor, just like you." She smiled. "Where do you think you get your strength from?"

Maluai left her mother alone and headed back to her bedroom. As she swam the hall between their quarters, she thought of her mother's words. Their home had always felt like a limitation to her, much because of her mother's overbearing actions. She never expected her mother to address her obvious desire for freedom. Even when she did, it felt wrong, like she'd pulled the veil back on her shame.

Back in her room, Maluai went to bed. She had a fitful night of rest, the second one in a row where she thought of her father. Their adventures together replayed in the few dreams she had, and every time her eyes opened, her heart ached because she knew there would be no more. There would be no more secret trips they could pretend her mother didn't know about. No more exciting new discoveries they would share.

There would be no more journal entries about how her father did something risky and adventurous and how she hoped to be like him one day. But she made a promise to her mother. She would stay, not forever, but until she could be sure her mother and sisters would be okay without her.

They were all strong, but they needed to be together. They needed to heal and to help their eumen do the same. But once that was done, she would go. She would find her own way. She would explore the world and do all the things she couldn't before, because she realized that life was not promised to her. Her father thought he had centuries to go, and yet, in a flash, that was all taken away. She wouldn't let that be her story.

As she lay there in between fitful naps, she wondered what changes her mother would make. Without her father, the queen had the final say. If she chose, she could eliminate the need for debate with the council and take whatever strides toward a better future she saw fit. The queen was usually a fair euman. Kind and understanding, but Maluai couldn't help but consider that losing her husband may have changed her mother in ways she couldn't comprehend.

An hour after she woke and dressed the next morning, Seru arrived with two other guards. They would escort her to the court.

"Why so many of you today?" Maluai asked as she nodded to the two guards whose names she was unsure of.

"Your mother's orders," Seru explained. "She wants to be sure you and your sisters are protected."

"Protected from what?" Maluai raised a brow. "What does she expect to happen?"

"From anyone who may disagree with the way she does things. She is the queen, and now, without King Masuen, there is no one who can truly contest the choices she makes," Seru reported.

"Do you think anyone will try to stand against her?"

"I think your mother is smart to be prepared for whatever the outcome is."

"Right." Maluai played with the jewel that hung around her neck and hoped her father was still with them to guide them in whatever came next. Then she pushed the thought aside, because despite everything, her mother was a good leader. She always had been. Whatever decision she made, Maluai trusted she did so with the wellbeing of their eumen in mind.

They made it to the courtroom at the same time as Kaluai, who also had her guardian and two additional guards with her. The two sisters looked at each other and embraced.

"This is going to be serious, isn't it?" Kaluai whispered in Maluai's ear.

"Yes, it is," Maluai responded. "You ready for change?"

"Life is ever changing, so yes." Kaluai straightened her shoulders. "I'm always ready."

The sisters entered the court side by side. The council members, their youngest sister, and the head of the guards were already there. At the front of the room, on her throne, Queen Valuai sat with her head held high and shoulders squared. She meant business. In the seat beside her, in reverence to her husband, was his crown.

Kaluai grabbed Maluai's hand, squeezed it, then moved to her usual position to the left of her mother. Instead of hiding in the back as always, Maluai moved to the front and took up to the right of her mother. They needed to show a united front for whatever was to come next.

"This meeting will operate differently than the ones before," the queen began, and the room remained silent as she spoke. "Let me be clear before we begin. I am not here for discussion or debate. I am here for one thing and one thing only, and that is action. We've sat in this room too many times before deliberating what we should do about Forge and its actions.

"There was a time when you could convince me they were no real threat to our survival. That time is long gone. I must now consider the eumen, whose lives I represent in the world, and do what is best for them. The alliance with Forge was there because they kept our secrets. But our secret existence is no longer important if those of us who exist below Forge are at risk because of it.

"The agreement was made to help move the eumen of Wallai forward, as we were still an underdeveloped eumen in the eyes of Eldritch. It is something we don't like to admit, but that is the truth. But in the time since then, we've become something entirely new. We are more than capable of taking care of ourselves and protecting ourselves, and that is what we will do."

The queen stood from her seat, and her voice filled the room with its deep, commanding timbre.

"I look around this room, and I see eumen who want to help, but I also see eumen who are too afraid to take a stand. Before, those eumen might have been able to convince me to go about things differently, but now, that is not the case. We are aware of the changes in Forge. We have monitored them for years, and they are not getting better.

"They go further and further away from the ways of nature. Most of their magic wielders have lost their access to magic, and now they seek to plunder our home for its resources so they can sustain themselves in this new world. I will not continue to be associated with something of that nature. I will not continue to sit here and watch them go further and further away from the true path.

"In the eyes of the goddess, we are one eumen, but I say we need to separate. If you don't think they will see judgment after what they've done, then you all are blind, and I will not have the eumen of Wallai suffer for the actions of those who couldn't give a drakgo about us."

"We haven't spoken to the eumen of Forge. We do not know—" Limua, the council member, started, hoping to calm the queen's fire, but only stoked the flames with her attempted defense of the land griffins.

"How many of their eumen did you see come down here to help?" Valuai snapped. "They watched what happened from above, and they wiped their hands of the mess. It has been three days! Three days since the spill, three days since the devastation, three days and since our eumen lost hundreds of lives. That is the death toll: two hundred and seventy-two lives gone forever.

"Not one euman from the Forge has come down here. They couldn't even be bothered to send a message to offer an apology or to aid in fixing the mess they've made. Why do you think that is? What reason can you give that would explain why they would believe we're just going to sit down here do nothing after they've infected our home? If you are in this room and you believe we should sit aside and allow them to continue their treacherous ways without action, then I suggest you give up your title right now. Because we are going to Forge. And we are severing our ties."

"To do so would mean—" Fituen, the most vocal of the council members, spoke but was cut short.

"To do so would mean we are subject to challenges. That we are standing as an entity of our own. I am well aware of what it means, but I'd rather stand on my own than hide under an umbrella or protection that has holes in it." She paused, taking in the range of emotions on the faces that surrounded her, from worry to excitement.

"Again, let me make myself clear. This is your chance to walk away if you do not agree with my course of action. Your refusal to support my decision will not change what is going to happen from this point forward."

An unbroken silence shrouded the room, yet no one took action. Even though Maluai could see Fituen had an obvious issue with what the queen wanted, he would never take a stand against her.

"Tomorrow, we will go to Forge." She turned to address the head of the guard. "Kianna, prepare our eumen get the guards ready. The entire royal laenu will go above. Please know this is not an act of war. We are simply journeying there to begin this conversation, but be ready should the eumen of Forge challenge our opinion. The time of Wallai living in the shadows has ended."

Chapter 6

From the moment the queen ended the meeting, the eumen of Wallai were in motion. Right away, they sent word of the happenings to keep everyone informed. The guards first went to the capital leaders, notifying them to spread the word among their constituents. The queen would give a formal speech later that day.

"Eumen of Wallai," the queen spoke to the crowd outside the palace. Hundreds of Wallains appeared to hear what she had to say. "I know this is a confusing and sorrowful time in our history. So much has changed in a matter of days, and as you've been told, I plan to make more changes. After what has happened in our home, I cannot stand here as your queen and do nothing.

"It is my intention to break our ties with Forge. We have been under their influence for far too long, and the security their protection once brought us has been shattered, as they are now the ones who pose the greatest threat to our lives. I stand here to say, prepare yourselves for what is coming.

"If you feel it best, leave the city. Though there is no historical evidence that Forge will take any action against us for this decision, history does not always dictate future actions. The guards have sent word to Forge. They are aware of our visit, but not of the intent. Should they decide to act against us, those of you who remain in the area must be prepared to defend yourselves.

"Our guards will stand and protect our home and our eumen, but we are one, and we will thrive together. This choice is not one I take lightly. For years, I, the King, and the council have deliberated it. I say now is the time to stop talking and start acting. I hope the eumen of Wallai will stand by me and trust in me during this historic shift in our history.

"We are one eumen, we are one voice, and they will not sweep us aside to be forgotten under the sea!"

Maluai floated behind her mother, and her chest rose as she felt the energy in the water shift. Her mother's words held power, and that power touched everyone who heard her speak. Moments later, their eumen cheered. They believed in the vision Valuai had for them. This was the time for change, and it seemed more of their eumen agreed. Especially after what happened. Forge had shown no concern for the lives affected, and that was enough to convince everyone it was time to part ways.

"Leaving will not be easy," Maluai said to Kaluai as they swam back into their home. "Even with what happened here, this place is still so beautiful."

"What do you mean?" Kaluai stopped and looked at her sister. "Why would we ever leave?"

"Think about it? When we separate, we will take something away from Forge," Maluai explained. "They will not want us living beneath them anymore."

"What could we possibly be taking from them?" Kaluai asked. "We just want to stand on our own."

"Magic." Naluai jutted her chin out and frowned at her sister. "That's what the debates were all about. Mom even said it outright. They have no magic or very little. It's why they're up there drilling. What other reasons could they have for destroying our home?"

"You're right." Kaluai shook her head. "I'm sorry. It's just been a lot going on. I don't know how you're keeping a clear head right now. Guess I have more learning to do."

"You're fine. I'm just great at compartmentalizing, but the eumen of Forge, they look at us like we're this secret weapon. Something they stored in their back pocket in case they need us. Imagine how epic it would be if there were some major conflicts, and just when the chips are down, we come soaring out of the water."

"That's depressing to think about, but I get it. They had another layer of protection, something they could hold over the rest of the world, and we're taking that from them."

"Yes, we are. I don't think they're going to let us do this with no resistance," Maluai continued. "We've had no problems with them in the past, but we've never threatened their position in the world like we are now."

"I really don't want this to turn into a war."

"In a struggle for independence, when has it ever happened without war?" Maluai looked over her sister at her mother who stood with the guards. "I just hope we're strong enough to survive it."

As her sisters went to do their own preparation, Maluai followed Seru out of the palace. As long as she was with the guardian, she would be okay.

"You really should be home, preparing," Seru insisted. "There is much to be done."

"I'd rather be out here with the eumen." Maluai brushed off her guardian's concern. "Besides, there are plenty of aides at the palace to take care of things in my absence."

"You sound so much like your father." Seru chuckled. "Never one to sit on the sideline while someone else handled the hard work."

"Thanks." Maluai paused, with a small lift to her lips. "Do you think we're going to survive this?"

"Survive? It's just a trip. We'll be back home in no time." Seru winked. "Like your mother said, this isn't a war. It's a conversation."

"You don't have to give me the politically correct response. I really want to know what you think," Maluai insisted. "I'm not talking about the conversation. I'm talking about what happens after it. When the royals of Forge reject our petition for independence. What do you truly believe will happen?"

"I think what we are doing is the right thing. What happened here was horrible, and I will admit I was against the separation before. But..." Seru looked around their home. "This cannot happen again. So, regardless of what happens after those initial talks, I will stand by your side. We will have our independence."

"They did nothing to help us." Maluai took in the same view as Seru, and once again, calculated the insurmountable damage.

"How could they just wipe their hands of it like that? They act as if we are nothing. Shezia, I sat with my laenu and told them that remaining loyal was the way, but this is how they treat us." Seru looked back at Maluai. "I will never understand."

"Such foul language from my guardian?" The princess laughed as Seru's face flushed with embarrassment.

"My apologies." Seru nodded. "I'm just so upset by all this."

"It's fine. I like it. Makes you feel more relatable. You know, you haven't answered my question." Maluai pointed to the spear Seru held. "Do you think we can survive this?"

"Yes, I do. Though I'm not sure it will happen without casualty," Seru admitted. "And after the loss we've already suffered, it will take time for us to recover."

"That's what I was afraid of." Maluai sighed as a school of fish swam by, giving her hope for their own eumen. They would survive. They had to, but there would be so much more loss.

"But it must happen." Seru nodded. "We cannot continue like this."

"You're right." She looked around at them. "How do you think the world will react? I mean, finding out there is a hidden underwater society."

"They're going to freak out," Seru said. "Some may even try to instigate war. They may think of us, an unknown and fully developed species, as a threat to them."

"I didn't think of that." Maluai chewed her lip. "When most species come to be known as a society, they're like babies, but we've been here for thousands of years. We have our own internal structure and understand the ways of the world, if not by a spectator's position, but we have enough knowledge to really be a force in this world. Which means potentially taking someone else's place in the hierarchy."

"It will be okay, Maluai," Seru spoke. "I'm sure your mother has considered these possibilities."

"Can you promise that?" Maluai asked.

"I mean, would a promise from a guardian make this any easier to face?"

"I suppose not, but if you were wrong, I could hold it over your head." Maluai laughed. "At least I'd have that to look forward to."

"In that case, I promise." Seru placed her hand over her chest.

Maluai watched as Seru and the other guardians gathered the members of the guard. She listened carefully as they issued their orders for the next day. They would take one hundred guards with them to the top. The rest would remain in Wallai and prepare, should they need to protect their home. It was enough to show Forge that Wallai could protect itself.

They granted the princess the right to watch the guards until it was time for her and her sisters to prepare. Naluai and Kaluai were in the baths. The communal space where the caretakers toiled over them until they shone like the jewels that graced their robes. Their skin was scrubbed, their hair combed and braided. Even her youngest sister was made to tame her hair. They were each given the same style. Top buns with draping braids that framed their face and formed loops around their ears. It was another form of unity as they went topside.

"How do you feel about this?" Kaluai asked as they brushed her hair.

"What do you mean?" Maluai winced when her hair snagged on the brush. Unlike her sister, she had locks, which meant much more aggressive manipulation to get it in the style they wanted.

"I mean, we are about to make some serious changes which could be very dangerous for us and our eumen. How does it make you feel?" Kaluai expanded her questioning.

"Didn't we have this conversation already?" Maluai raised a brow. "Are you testing me to see if my answer has changed in the hours since we spoke?"

"No, we talked about how it could mean war, but not how we feel about it," Kaluai explained, and it got her another raised brow.

Her eldest sister wasn't really one for heavy discussions about emotions. It made Maluai suspicious. Was there something else going on that her sister hadn't revealed?

"I feel fine," she answered shortly.

"Really?" Kaluai peered at her sister. "Are you being honest with me?"

"Kaluai, I'm not sure what you want me to say. I agree it is time for us to stand on our own. Look what's happening here. If we don't do something, it's only going to get worse. Mom is right. If we don't stand up for ourselves, it only tells them they can continue doing what they just did. It's like they still think we are this underdeveloped group of eumen and that we don't have a say in our futures. If they took us seriously, they would help. They would have acknowledged what they did. Instead, they let us clean up their mess and they go on as if nothing is wrong."

"I know you're right," she said. "How could they have so little concern for us?"

"I don't know." Maluai looked at her sister. "You say you're on board, but you have doubts, don't you? Is that why you're asking me how I feel?"

"Yes. I'm not sure this is the right move for us to make, but I'm trusting in mother. She is a strong euman and a solid leader, and if she thinks this is the right path for us, then I support her, but I would be lying if I said I wasn't afraid of what's coming after this happens."

"Change can be terrifying." Maluai reached over and grabbed her sister's hand.

"I'm always prepared for it, though, right?" Kaluai chuckled. "That's what dad used to say to me. It's like he knew what was coming. Any time I would express my concern for things changing, he would tell me that shifts are inevitable."

"I don't know about you, but I'm never prepared for it, but no matter how terrifying or unexpected change is, we have to embrace it, and we can't let it destroy us." Maluai winced as the hair stylist pulled her hair back tighter than before. "That's what he used to say to me. Never let it destroy who you are."

"You're a lot wiser than I give you credit for." Kaluai winced from the pain of the stylist in her head. "I still think of you as my bratty little sister sometimes."

"Just because I don't want to be at court doesn't mean I don't pay attention to the lessons our parents have taught us." Maluai sighed when the stylist released her grip. "My ears are open just as much as my heart is. But I guess I can understand how you would feel that way. I showed up twenty years after you and had the nerve to appear sickly."

"I always knew you were fine. You were different, but you were okay." Kaluai sighed. "Maybe that's why I was so jealous for a while. The way you got all the attention. Not that it was your fault. No matter how many times eumen told Mom you were healthy, she just kept clinging to you like you were going to disappear if she let you go."

"It still feels like that sometimes. Like if I take one wrong move, she'll have me locked away where nothing can get to me." Maluai glanced at the door as if afraid her mother would walk in. "She doesn't want eumen to know about me. I get it, but it's so hard sometimes. Shrinking myself away to make her happy."

"I imagine it's worse without Dad here to be a buffer between you two." Kaluai followed her line of sight.

"She asked me not to leave." Maluai nodded. "Like she thought I would pack my bags and swim away in the middle of the night."

"What? When?"

"After the ceremony. She called me to her room and asked me to stay. I'm serious, Kal. She looked at me like the moment our father died, I lost all reason to be here."

"What did you say?" her sister asked.

"I said I would stay. For now." Maluai looked in the mirror. "Okay, maybe I left out the, 'for now' part."

"She has to accept that your life is yours." Kaluai touched her sister's shoulder. "I don't always agree with what you want for your life, but I think you should have the right to choose."

"That was kind of manipulative, right?" Naluai, who'd been a silent observer to their conversation, spoke up. "I mean, I love Mom, but to ask you that right now, that seems wrong."

"I didn't think of it that way." Maluai considered her younger sister's words. What her mother did was, in a lot of ways, emotionally manipulative. Was she acting deliberately or because of her emotional state?

"Look at you, showing your wisdom." Kaluai reached over and tapped Naluai.

"Just make sure that whatever you do, you do it for you," Naluai spoke again. Her small voice suddenly aged with wisdom they hadn't considered she'd have. "Don't do it for Mom or anyone else. Because we only have one life. At least in this world, and I would hate to see you wasted trying to save someone else's feelings."

"I want to be here. I know what it looks like. That I would rather be anywhere but home, but I really want to be here with you all." Maluai grabbed her sister's hand, one in each. "We're a laenu, and our eumen is about to go through this monumental shift. As much as I run away from responsibility, I know when it's time to step up and face the hard things.

"When all this is settled, I'll go on my adventures, but I will always come home. Because you're my laenu. And despite my growing need for a thrill, I love you guys. I want to be a part of your lives, and I want you to be a part of mine. Mom thinks my plan is to run away and never come back, but that's never been what I wanted. I just wanted the freedom to explore the world. To go somewhere and not know the destination. But to always know that home is here."

CHAPTER 7

T he sisters shared a bed again that night. Their conversations grew deeper as the two moons swept across the sky, eventually crossing paths in a moment they called the lunar kiss when it looked as if the two moons were touching. Eventually, they slept wrapped in each other's comfort.

When they woke, they put on their official robes. These were special, and it was the first time each of them would wear them because neither of the princesses had ever been on land in their official capacity.

Blue fabric to represent their home in Wallai, with green and gold accents, along with the fabric that represented their connection to nature and their position in the royal laenu. They adorned these robes with jewels, but they were lighter because gravity would do for them what the heavier stones did under water.

Each sister also wore their crown, which they rarely wore. It was a status symbol deemed unnecessary unless they were on official business. They definitely counted a trip to the topside to claim their independence as official business.

"Are my daughters ready?" the queen asked as she entered the room where the sisters were held up as their aides added the final touches to their wardrobes.

"Yes, we are," Kaluai answered.

"You each look so beautiful." Valuai smiled at her daughters. "I only wish your father were here to see how wonderful you all look right now."

"Me too," Naluai said, as her mother touched her face affectionately.

"I know we haven't spoken much about what's about to happen." The queen looked into her daughter's round face as she spoke to them. "I wish I had more time alone with you to further explain my plans, but there was a lot to do. There will be plenty of time to discuss things when we return."

"We understand. And we've talked about it together," Kaluai said.

"And what conclusion did you come to?" their mother asked.

"We support you," Naluai said proudly. "You are a strong euman and an outstanding leader, and we will stand beside you in this."

"That makes me so happy to hear." Valuai kissed her daughter's cheek. Of the three, the youngest received the most affection from their mother. With Kaluai, the next to rule her eumen, she was much more guarded. For Maluai, she was much more reserved and muted in her expression. With her youngest, it was constant kisses and hugs and affirmations of her love.

"We know you only want to do what is best for everyone, and though it may be difficult, this is the best path for Wallai," Maluai said.

"Queen Valuai," the head of the queen's guard came in. "We're ready to go."

"Alright. Let's do this, shall we?" The queen nodded, turned for the door, and her daughters followed her.

They swam by their mother's side, with their guardians flanking each one. The royal laenu exited the palace to an audience of hundreds of Wallains who cheered as they took their places in the formation that would rise to the surface. There were twenty-five guards to each side and fifty were behind them, making sure they protected the royal laenu at all costs. The council members swam behind the royal laenu in front of the guards, who covered their tail. Each would remain in their true form, even above water. When they broke the surface, their tail would split into two legs, and they'd walk on all fours.

As they rose to the surface, the creatures of the sea, those majestic beings that shared their home, swam close by. They created wide circles around their path as if championing them. Maluai believed this was their way of showing they agreed with the choice that the queen was making. The occurrence impacted them too, though they could not speak up for themselves. Wallai's separation would be good for more than just the water griffins. The display was a good omen.

The head of the Queen's guard swam ahead of the others. As soon as she broke the surface, ten from either flank took to the sky. Their duty was to gain an aerial view of what was happening below. Maluai could see above the water that the land griffins had some of their own in the air. While neither side appeared to want things to turn bad, they were both prepared for it.

The royal laenu lingered just underneath the surface until the head of the guard came back to verify they were being welcomed without hostility.

"We're clear to take to land," Kianna spoke to the queen, then signaled for the guards to move forward.

"Are you ready?" Valuai turned to her daughters. "This will be your first time on land, and while we are here, we will sit in important meetings."

"Yes," Kaluai answered for them, and her sisters nodded. "We're ready. You don't have to worry about us."

With their mother leading the way, the three sisters swam to the surface. Maluai's heart raced as she moved. Each one of them shifted as they moved from their vanity form, which the royals typically adorned, to their landform. The water vibrated as they reached the surface, a result of the drums playing above. Her heart found the rhythm and matched it beat for beat.

As her head broke the surface, the fanfare that welcomed them overwhelmed her. The topside was bright as always, but what was new was all the eumen. Land griffins were everywhere, watching their visitors arrive from the world below.

Enthusiastic singing, a melodic chant of welcoming, accompanied the steady beat of the drums. To the sides, just in front of rows of guards, eumen dressed in flowing dresses danced. She watched their fluid movements and held back the urge to dance. They walked forward. Naluai handled herself perfectly. The weight of the gravity was less impactful, thanks to the magic wielders who accompanied them. They made the acclimation much smoother than anything Maluai experienced on her own.

Their presence was a powerful arrival. Their footfalls were in unison, their heads held high, and with the magic wielder who stood behind them, a current of warm air wrapped around each member of the royal laenu to dry their clothing yet left enough moisture on their bodies so they would not need to return to the waters any time soon.

Maluai felt powerful and important as the eumen of Forge looked at them in awe. She looked at her mother and felt pride as the queen held herself in perfect poise. They moved ahead, where across a long aisle of dark carpet with golden lace, the royal laenu of Forge waited for them.

Maluai recognized the laenu that was missing one member. Though she'd never met them before, it was a part of her duty as princess to know them all. She knew their faces as well as she knew the members of her own laenu.

In the center stood Queen Helena, who was as headstrong as her own mother. She had maroon locks twisted into seven knots styled to look like a part of the intricate crown she wore. Her deep brown eyes focused on the euman who led her daughters.

This was a conversation that Maluai could see coming to a stalemate. Both were sure of their stances and took actions they thought were best for their families and their eumen.

Their queen stood proudly at the head of her laenu, but her face was soft and welcoming. There was no sign that the euman, whose red robes with intricate gold webbing that dusted the ground, had any ill intentions. The soft smile lifted the corner of her full lips as she laid her eyes on the approaching princesses.

To either side of the queen were her children. To the left were two sons and to the right, two daughters. Maluai took their faces in and recounted the information she knew about them.

Prince Marruk was the oldest son. He had dark skin, a low-cut afro, and wore a crown that looked like they made it from the beaks of fallen birds. His suit was the same shade of red as his mother and adorned with gold feathers at the shoulders. He was arrogant and apparently a playboy. Her father often told them of his antics and how the king of Forge complained about being worried Marruk wouldn't be ready to rule when his time came. Maluai often joked that Kaluai could tame the man. She poked at her and laughed about how they would end up together, even though Kaluai showed no interest in the opposite sex.

To the left of him was the youngest prince. Fralim was a lot like Naluai. As the youngest of four siblings, they gave him a lot more freedom. He had brown skin, short hair, and dark eyes that locked on her youngest sister. Maybe theirs was a connection waiting to happen. He also wore their signature red, adorned with gold embellishments.

The Princesses were as beautiful as their mother. Her eldest daughter, and next in line to rule, Princess Cairaix, stood at her side with straight shoulders, a lifted chin, and a serious look on her face. She wore a crown with feathers on either side that blended with the locks that fell past her shoulders. She wore a golden collar fitted with red gems that matched the color of the dress she wore.

Tera was dressed similarly to her older sister; except she had large gold hoops hanging from her ears and her crown looked more like armor than a royal ornament. It matched the gold breastplate. From what Maluai knew of the princess, she always thought they would have been friends if they had been allowed to know each other. Her father often told her of Tera's adventures and how she'd taken up combat skills most in her position would have avoided.

When they were ten feet away from the other royal laenu, Maluai and her sisters stopped walking, but the queen continued ahead. Her guards, of course, kept in step with her. And on the other side, Queen Helena stepped away from her laenu, her own guards shadowing her. Despite the lack of any threatening signs, the atmosphere was still charged with anxiety.

"Queen Valuai," Helena greeted her. "It's so good to see you. It's been too long since you've come topside."

"Yes, well, the occasion seemed fitting." She smiled. "It's good to see you too, Queen Helena."

"I'm so sorry to hear of your loss. Masuen was a great man." Helena took her hands into hers, a show of her remorse.

"Yes, he was. And thank you for your condolences." There was a slight edge to Valuai's voice as she spoke of her husband, but she easily recovered. "You look well."

"I'm glad you've come here." Queen Helena smiled. "We have so much to discuss."

"I agree." Valuai glanced back at her daughters. "There is a lot to cover."

"Let's go inside. I know how much you preferred to be outside of the sun. Don't want you all to dry up out here under the sun," Helena joked, and Valuai's lips curled into a stiff, plastic smile.

"No, we don't want that." The queen chuckled, and Maluai recognized it as the fake laugh she used when she was trying to keep up appearances. They would keep everything cordial until they were in a private setting. To do anything else would be unfitting for the queens. "I notice your husband is missing. Where is Lequad?"

"Unfortunately, our king is away on business. Had we known about your visit sooner, he would have made sure he was here to greet you."

"I'm sorry to hear that." Valuai nodded in understanding. "I hope to see him soon."

Just behind the platform where Queen Helena stood with her children were massive golden vessels. The royal transports. Maluai dreamed of being able to get inside one since she was a child. The vessels were made to resemble the body of a griffin, from the feathered wings to the clawed feet that held them up.

This was how they would travel from the water's edge to the palace.

As they walked, surrounded by the guards, Maluai looked around the crowd, hoping to see a familiar face. Jeraim was not there. And the crowd of moving colors made it more difficult to find the euman who never dressed in typical attire. In Forge, most of the population identified themselves by the colors they wore. Unlike the underwater city, they separated themselves into classes, and the colors they wore showed where they belonged in their society.

It was a curious thing to observe because it made it appear as if the eumen of Forge weren't unified. They were a collection of individuals hoping to do all they could to reach the next level and change one color for the next.

She recalled her lessons. Lower class only wore green. It was easiest to achieve the color and often the shades were less uniform. Orange meant they were of the middle class. They had no actual power, but were considered productive members of society. They designated dark blue for the upper class. These were eumen who held power and could affect a change in their communities. Ash gray was the color of members of the guard. They blended in with shadows and made their jobs easier to do. And of course, the royals wore red and gold.

As they climbed into the foreign ship, Maluai looked back at the eumen who greeted them and hoped the eumen of Wallai would never be like that. She wanted them to remain as one.

One thing Maluai had yet to experience was flying above land. Though she, like the other water griffins, had her wings, she never used them for more than extra power in her swim when racing her sisters around the palace grounds. And even though she still wasn't using her wings, she was still technically flying above the city of Forge, and that made her heart swell.

The large metal contraption provided silent transportation over the vibrant city. Forge was so different from their home. Though almost identical in the layout, things were much shinier, everything had touches of gold. Only the areas outside of the clear view looked dull. She assumed that was where the lower-class citizens lived. Out of sight of the royal laenu.

There were eumen everywhere, looking at the sky to watch the aircraft. They appeared in varying forms. Just like the water griffins, the land griffins had different forms they could present in. First was their true form, which was their full out griffin complete with massive wings, four powerful legs, a beaked face, and a tail ending in long wispy hairs. In their phase form, they had the lower half of the griffin but the top half of their euman-like appearance. Their vanity form presented their majestic wings but bipedal body. They typically saw this when men were ready to mate. And then there was the recluse form, beaked face and wings, but euman body, and they usually kept their wings positioned to close out others.

Maluai looked out the window, because inside the ship, though beautiful and comfortable, it was awkward. When they boarded, each laenu and their guardians took to a different side.

The queen wanted them to feel like they were welcome there, but it felt anything but. They stared at each other across the aisle that felt like it expanded the longer they sat there.

Outside the windows, on either side of the vessels, were their guards. A mix of land and water griffins protected the important cargo on board.

The landing was smooth but still jarring as they heard the crunch of the ground beneath the clawed feet. They remained seated until the engines powered down and the doors opened. Soon, they climbed out of the vessel, which left them standing at the foot of the palace.

Maluai looked up at the palace and gasped. It was at least twice the size of their home and was almost too bright to look at. Her grandfather always referred to the Forge as the gilded city. Now, seeing it in front of her, she understood why.

The framing of the structure shot up in the sky like a pair of wings and flowed down to the center in layered pillars that glistened as if imbedded with jewels. Outside the massive structure, the royal guard stood at attention. Again, this was different in Wallai. The guards' job was to protect the palace at all costs. Maluai wondered if it would be like this in their future home. Once the rest of the world found out about them. Clearly, they feared some external threat. Why else would they be on guard like that?

"You made changes since our last visit," Queen Valuai commented as they climbed the steps to enter the palace. "Everything's much larger, I see."

"Yes, touching up things." Helena nodded. "You know how it is."

"And making them shinier." Valuai pointed to the golden post that lined the foyer.

"Well, we must show a strong front," Helena explained their excessive display away with a generic political statement.

"I thought they allowed no outsiders in their home. Who are they showing a strong front for?" Maluai muttered in her sister's ear.

Kaluai shrugged, then straightened when Queen Helena looked over at them. Had she heard Maluai's comment?

"We will meet in the court. Please follow the guards. I have something I need to check on first, then I will join you." The queen waved them forward, throwing another side glance at Maluai before she turned to head off in the opposite direction.

They followed the guards and the rest of the royal laenu through the halls of the palace, and their gaudy display of wealth didn't stop at the front door. Throughout the building, there were gigantic statues and ornaments of gold. The further she went, the more she heard her grandfather's words replaying in her mind. A gilded city.

Maluai was surprised to find herself yearning for the familiarity of her home, despite being in such a strange place. The simple finishes and the cool colors that would have contrasted the gold and bright colors of cream and marbles. They fortified their home for their protection, but they never flashed their status like the royals of Forge.

As she looked around, she glanced over at Marruk, the eldest prince, and he had an odd grin on his face. It looked like pride, but what could he feel so prideful over?

"You like it here, don't you?" he asked her.

"I mean, it's okay, a little bright, to be honest," Maluai answered in a way that wasn't exactly fitting for a princess.

"Hum." He turned his nose from her and walked ahead.

"I think I made your boyfriend mad," Maluai whispered to Kaluai, who nudged her in the side with her elbow. "Ow."

"Girls?" Valuai glanced at them, and the two straightened.

In the court, Maluai and her sisters stayed as close to their mother as possible. Their guardians formed an invisible line between them and the other laenu in the room. The Wallain council members sat with them as well. You'd think they'd share small talk, but the entire laenu looked both smug and guilty. They knew the true reason behind the visit from the Wallai royals.

They sat in the courtroom, which actually looked a lot like the one in Wallai, for nearly an hour, until the queen rejoined them, followed by her own council members. Not a word was uttered the entire time. Just awkward glances across the aisle. When Helena entered the courtroom, Maluai presented herself like her sisters. Shoulder straight and at the front of the room. She wouldn't fall back for this meeting.

"I apologize for the delay," Helena commented as she entered.

"It is nothing to apologize for." Valuai paused, tilting her head just so. "Besides, your heart is heavy now. I know how difficult a time this must be for you."

"Well, thank you." Helena took a deep breath. "But I don't know what you mean."

"I know that look in your eyes. I had it myself just a few days ago," Valuai continued.

"What look is that?"

"The look of grief and of worry for the love you may lose. Lequad." Valuai brilliantly deduced the reasoning for Helena's absence. "I take it he isn't doing well?"

"We are trying to be discreet." Helena lowered her voice. "This is a sensitive topic."

"You think I would use your husband's circumstance against you?" Valuai placed her hand over her chest. "I can assure you I would never do something so heartless."

"No, I—" Helena stumbled. "I didn't mean to insult you. I'm just worried about him."

"I hope he heals soon." Valuai nodded. "I don't wish the loss of a cherished love on anyone."

"He is improving," Helena revealed. "It's a slow progress, but we're happy to see he is on the mend."

"That is good."

"I'm sorry. I didn't mean the secrecy, but as you said, you understand. My concern was for my husband and our laenu."

"Oh, yes. I understand. My husband is dead, and so are hundreds of our eumen." Valuai laid out the facts, and the tone of the conversation shifted. "How many lives did you lose to this?"

"Fortunately, we didn't have any casualties. A few injuries," Helena confirmed what they all suspected.

"I'm glad to hear that, but I must ask, after you realized your eumen were okay, what did you think of those in Wallai?" Valuai asked calmly, but there were undertones of fire in her voice. "Were our lives so invaluable that you couldn't even send someone to check on us?"

"As I said, my concern—"

"Your concern was your king and yourselves. I heard you." She sighed and looked around the room. "We cleaned up your mess, not that it seems you were concerned with that, either. The world will never have to know what you did here. Is that right?"

"Valuai—"

"I am here for one thing, and I'm sure you know what it is, so let's get to it so you can return to your husband's side." Valuai lifted her voice to make sure everyone in the room heard her announcement. "Wallai intends to discontinue the union with Forge."

"You can't possibly mean that. Why would you do this now?" Helena asked. "With all that has happened, now is not the time to part ways."

"Are you deaf or blind?" Valuai asked. "I mean no disrespect, but all that has happened is exactly why we are doing this. This doesn't have to be a big issue. We can do this peacefully. A mutual termination of an archaic contract. I understand your shock, but the Wallains will no longer live like this."

"We've protected you, and this is how you repay us?" Helena stepped back from Valuai, her guards responding to the movement by tightening up their formation.

"Protected? You poisoned our home but couldn't be bothered to do anything about it. My husband died because of the spill! And don't pretend to deny your part in what happened because we have witnesses." Valuai lifted her voice. "Don't get me started on the centuries of issues we've had. Things you all continue to sweep under the ocean as if it's no concern. Our voices go unheard because they fall on deaf ears. I know what your priorities are. Wallai is far from the top of that list."

"Listen, I get your emotions are intense after losing your husband. I can't imagine what you're going through," Helena tried to reason. "Maybe we should take a break. You all can rest, and we can reconvene with clearer heads."

"There's no need for that." Valuai refused the offer. "I've rested plenty. Wallai rested while waiting for Forge to do right by us. The time for rest and waiting is over."

"Valuai—"

"We will handle this now," Valuai spoke sternly.

"There is a lot to consider. For one thing, if we end the alliance, where will you go?" Helena asked.

"Excuse me?"

"Well, you live in waters under our protection. I hope you don't believe we would still lend that to you." The queen dropped her act of soft concern.

"Lend it?" Valuai stepped to the Queen of Forge, and all the guards in the room tensed. "Don't pretend we do not know how much you need us. We are not a city of simpletons. The land griffins, the eumen of forge, have changed. And it's not just the glint of greed in their eyes that I'm talking about. Do you really want to go down this road?"

"I—"

Before Helena could finish her words, the door burst open, and a land griffin, a short boy, ran in waving a roll of paper in his hand. He handed it over to the guard and backed away slowly.

"What is it?" Helena demanded to know why they were interrupted.

"The Iris. It's active." She handed over the paper. "The goddess has challenged us."

CHAPTER 8

The unexpected announcement instantly changed the energy in the room. Where moments before, it looked like the two queens might soon come to blows, there was a blanket of concern and even fear. Valuai's jaw tightened as her eyes met those of her counterpart, and Helena's entire demeanor changed.

It was like the Queen of Wallai had slapped her across the face with a loud *I told you so*. This was what the Wallains wanted to avoid, judgement from the goddess, but it was far too late for that. The years of disregard for their world and the blatant negligence of the spill were more than enough to warrant a test from the goddess.

Eldritch was a world created by a goddess who believed that when one created something as beautiful as a world capable of producing and supporting new life, they should stick around and make sure they took care of it. Mother Goddess was her common name, but the griffins called her Lunai. She was a gentle goddess until the creatures she gave life to showed they held little value for all she provided.

Following the edict of their goddess, whenever a species grew to the point of independence, able to make decisions that affected the world around them, they were deemed a civilization and given the goddess' challenges. The Eldritch Trials, as they were called, were a set of puzzling psychological tests that a single member of each civilization had to complete, each task crafted to assess a variety of values chosen by the goddess. Even though they did not know when they would be tested, a sense of security was there if they did their best to make good choices and paid respect to the land. Throughout the years, the griffins had been known as a distinct society. The goddess only tested them once.

The Griffins were one of the oldest groups of civilized eumen of their world. And so, they held somewhat of a superiority complex. It was what led to the changes in Forge. They were so concerned with keeping themselves at the top of the food chain that they made unfortunate shortcuts and detrimental decisions.

"Is this true?" Helena looked past the guard to the small boy who delivered the message.

He simply nodded, no words. Maluai's stomach dropped before they all ran out of the courthouse.

The aircraft was already waiting for them when they stepped out of the palace. The two queens, followed along with their children and the council members, flew directly to the center of Forge where the Iris stood. The Iris, said to be the direct connection to Lunai, was a fountain older than the griffins themselves. It was the way the goddess used to communicate with the species. The relic sat in the center of the island and it remained inactive until she issued a challenge.

Once it became active, new challengers would volunteer by placing a drop of their blood in the fountain. After forty-eight hours, a challenger would be chosen. Their face would appear in the water above the fountain, and the water would change to a color showing how difficult the challenges would be for them. If the water continued running blue, then the challenge would be simple; the closer the color got from that cool tone to a deep red, the more difficult the challenge and the more likely the euman was to fail.

There were great stakes at hand because should they fail, the griffins, like any other species who failed, would suffer a one-hundred-year curse.

"Beltan, is it true?" Helena repeated her question as soon as her feet touched the ground. She addressed the temple guardian as he stepped out to greet them.

Beltan was a mature land griffin who appeared in his vanity form. Grey hair touched his temples and went up like strikes of lightning on either side of his head. His heavy robes covered him from neck to toe and had hints of red at the seams, which showed they considered him of the royal class in Forge. His massive size made him a spectacle to look at, and Maluai could only imagine what he would look like in his true form.

"Queen Helena," he greeted her before the others. "Yes. The iris is active."

"How long?" She glanced at the others.

"I sent word as soon as it started. It hasn't been long. Less than an hour," he reported.

"Why is this happening?" Helena peered around the euman toward the center of the island where the fountain stood.

"You can't be serious." Valuai laughed. "After everything you've done and how far the eumen of Forge have swayed from the ways of old. How can you stand here and question why this is happening now?"

"Are you blaming us?" Helena turned on her.

"Who else is there to blame?" Valuai spoke, and the wind kicked up as if encouraged by her anger.

"I don't remember seeing you or anyone else from your underwater world coming up here to say anything about how we were running things before." Helena narrowed her gaze at the queen of Wallai. "If you had such a big problem with it, why not take a stand sooner?"

"Oh, believe me, it was not my decision to sit by in silence. It was my husband who hoped you could keep yourselves out of trouble. He wanted to give you the benefit of the doubt." Valuai paused, her jaw tightening with her own grief. "Look what that got him. It's exactly why I've come here to declare the end of our union as one eumen."

"Excuse me if this is out of place, but should we really be talking about that right now?" Cairaix, who stood among the other children watching their mother's point fingers, spoke up. "We have to face this. Someone has to enter the challenge."

"The princess is right. I suppose you have someone in mind." Valuai looked at the Forge Queen. "I'm sure you know who the strongest and most willing eumen would be."

"I'll do it." Marruk, the eldest prince, stepped forward. "It's only right."

"There, and I'm sure there will be others who are just as fitting," the queen said and looked at her son like she didn't want him to do it.

Maluai exchanged looks with Kaluai. They both caught the look the queen gave her son. Maybe she didn't believe in his abilities as much as he did.

"And what about your eumen?" Helena asked Valuai.

"My eumen?" Their mother frowned. "What about my eumen?"

"Surely you have someone who would step up to the challenge." Helena issued her own challenge for the underwater queen.

"I'm sure we do, but why should we? It is not our fault the goddess has issued this challenge."

"We are one eumen in the eyes of the goddess, and if we should not act as one now, do you think that will play in our favor in the trials?" Helena leaned into her question. "Or do you think that bias will be used against us?"

"It's astonishing that you now seek to present a unified front, yet when your actions poisoned our waters, we were not even a consideration for you."

"I told you—" Helena began, but Valuai interrupted her.

"Yes, you were too busy caring for *your* eumen, *your* laenu, and *your* king. You were so busy; you couldn't even send one guard to check on what you'd done. So busy that apparently you never even put any protocols into place should something like this happen before you started drilling holes in the side of our island."

"Our island?" Helena scoffed. "Since when is it our island when you live below it?"

"Yes, our island. You see how you seek separation when it doesn't favor you? Or did you forget this is one connected being from the root to the top, and where do you think the root of this island is? It's in the center of our home!" Valuai looked around at their children who watched them. It looked as if she might soften until she met her daughters' faces. Each one gave her a new fire for her fight. "So, I'll ask my question again since it seemed to confuse you the first time. Before you even considered cutting into *our* island, did you stop to think what would happen if you messed up? Or did you think it wouldn't matter since the spill didn't directly impact you?"

"I think we need to focus on the challenge," Helena snipped. "This debate is better for another day."

"We will focus on the challenge, and when this is done, Wallai and Forge are no longer one." Valuai looked at her daughters and their guardians. "For now, we will return to our home and tend to our eumen. Good luck with the challenge."

The Wallain royalty and their guards headed back to Wallai while Helena put the call out for challengers to submit to the fountain.

Maluai hesitated for a moment before she left the temple. It felt like someone glued her limbs in place. She could see straight through the temple doors and the windows on the other side of the structure. Just beyond the massive frame was the view of the Iris, the activated fountain. The waters rushed up to the sky, peaked, and fell again.

Her heart and mind followed the flow, and with each pulse of the water, she felt something deep within her grow. A desire, a feeling stronger than anything she'd experienced before. A duty. Something inside her told her she had to volunteer. Lunai meant this challenge for her. Before she could process the weight of the thoughts that rushed through her mind, Seru tapped her shoulder, encouraging her to join the others. She turned from the temple, heart climbing into her throat, and boarded the aircraft that would take them back to the water's edge.

As they swam back from the surface to their home, Maluai held her tongue. This was not an easy thing to do, considering how many thoughts she had, but she knew it was not the right time to question her mother, especially when there were so many members of the guards surrounding them. They had to appear to be unified in the decision. But the moment the guards left the laenu to themselves, she voiced her opinion.

"Mother, I mean no disrespect in what I am about to admit," Maluai began, "and typically, I would never question your judgment."

"Which means you are about to question me?" the queen addressed her daughter, who stood with her sisters by her side.

"I think someone from Wallai should enter the challenge," Maluai admitted.

"Excuse me?" Valuai straightened her shoulders, which meant she was prepared to debate whatever points her daughter presented.

"Before you get mad or whip out your superior argumentative skills, just hear me out." Maluai held her hands out, a symbol of the peaceful discussion she wanted to have. "We're in this situation because of what we allowed the land griffins to do. I know you feel the same way I do because it's something you've expressed before. We sat by for far too long and allowed them to make decisions that were against what we knew Lunai would have wanted. And I've seen you fight and debate the legitimacy of the union between the water griffins and the land griffins. You wanted to take that away from them, the responsibility for our eumen. Why are you giving it to them now?"

"I am not giving them anything." Her mother refuted her claim.

"Your anger and your grief blind you. You've moved in strength like I can't imagine, despite the loss you've suffered, and I am so proud of you for that, but I think now your hurt is louder than your logic." Maluai moved closer to her mother to express that she wasn't there to fight, but she recognized her mother's pain. "I say this out of love, but if you allow them to take this challenge without even the consideration of someone from Wallai, then you are giving them the responsibility to save us from this. We've already seen they are not capable of doing what is best for all of us. Is there anyone in Forge who has been immune to the same moral decay that has consumed the Royals?"

"She's right." Kaluai moved forward. "I mean, look at them. They're all so concerned with superficial things, and they have this weird class system. Am I the only one who thinks it's strange they wear colors according to their status in the system? Is that the type of eumen we want to represent us in something so important?"

"You agree with your sister?" Valuai addressed her eldest child.

"Yes. I do. I mean, if they fail, and I think anyone they send in would fail, that means we fail. That means on top of having our home destroyed, losing hundreds of eumen and our king, we then get cursed for one-hundred years. How was that fair?"

"You both feel really strongly about this." She looked at her youngest daughter, who remained in place behind her sisters. "What do you think?"

"Me?" Naluai pointed to her own chest. "You want my opinion?"

"You are as much a part of this laenu as anyone. I want to hear your thoughts."

"I think my sisters are right." She paused, chewing on her lip. "It won't be smart to sit aside and not give ourselves a chance. Volunteering will prove to Lunai we can stand on our own. Which is what we want, right?"

"All right. There you have it. Perhaps my daughters are correct." Valuai touched Naluai's cheek before she moved to sit at the table. "I did not expect to be so angry. But as soon as I witnessed the lavish lifestyle they live, free of any consideration of the lives they've impacted, I have to admit, my emotions got the best of me. And here I am supposed to be teaching you how to be prominent leaders, but it looks like you've taught me a thing or two."

"So, we will enter the challenge?" Maluai asked enthusiastically.

"Yes. I must admit, setting emotions aside, I agree with your logic here. It would be a mistake to let Forge represent us if we can help it. We will establish our independence, beginning with the challenge. We will call for eumen of Wallai to volunteer. I will force no one to do this. Not after what we've been through."

"I want to do it," Maluai spoke up. "Like I said, we've been through a lot, and our eumen need a leader. I think it would be good if I volunteered."

"Absolutely not." Her mother quickly rejected the thought.

"What?" Maluai stared, wide-eyed, at her mother. "Why not?"

"I agree we should be a part of this, but not that my own child should be the one to put her life on the line."

"You just said we were right." Maluai looked at her sisters, who both looked away. They would not be backing her up on this point.

"You were right. About allowing Wallains to take part in this. Not about this." Valuai shook her head in disbelief. "You are the princess. You are not to risk your life like this."

"Do you think I will fail?" Maluai asked. "Or am I not good enough to be chosen?"

"That's not what this is about."

"Mother—" Maluai wanted to explain the feeling she got when she looked at the Iris. She thought if she could just express how it felt to her, like it was her duty, her mother would allow it. But she couldn't get another word out before the queen shut her down.

"Maluai, enough." She turned to Kaluai. "Let Emixi know my decision, please. Put the word out. And if they can find someone worthy, let them."

"I can't believe this," Maluai huffed after her mother turned and left her with her sisters.

"Let it go." Kaluai grabbed her sister's hand, but Maluai pulled away from her.

"Right, just let it go. My own mother has so little faith in me, but I'm just supposed to drop it." Maluai turned from her laenu. "I'll be in my room, since that is all I'm allowed."

Maluai was supposed to go back to her room. She was supposed to clean herself up and go about her day as if what her mother said to her hadn't hurt her, but she couldn't do that. She couldn't pretend she wasn't deeply affected by her mother's lack of belief in her. Instead, she snuck away from her home. With her guardian doing the queen's bidding to find a challenger, she had ample opportunity to get away unnoticed.

She snuck through the city's pathways and found herself back on land in the same rendezvous point where she met the land griffin. Even though her body ached, she found it easier to push through the climb, and when she reached the top of the cliff, she felt an immense sense of accomplishment. With each visit, her body adjusted more comfortably to the surface climate.

It surprised her to see him, but the sound of his wings beating the air and the feel of the wind on her skin brought her relief when he touched down safely beside her.

"You didn't tell me you were a princess," Jeraim spoke as soon as his feet touched the ground.

"I didn't think it was important." She turned to face him, the wind causing the fabric to shift around her body.

"Interesting. If I was a prince, I'd tell everyone." He laughed. "You'd never get me to shut up about it."

"The difference between a male and a female, I suppose." She shrugged. "I didn't see you out there today. Were you hiding from me?"

"I wasn't sure it would be good if you saw me. Didn't seem like anyone knew you were coming to visit each month. Could you have hidden your recognition if you saw me out there in the crowd?" He raised a brow, the smirk on his lips meaning he already knew the answer to his question.

"Probably not," she admitted with a soft sigh.

"That's what I figured. It would have blown your cover, and I might never see you again."

"Well, it worked, because here I am." She smiled. "Why are you here? I didn't think you visited this place that often."

"I had a feeling you would be here." He pointed to the sunset behind her, and she turned to watch it with him. "Does the sunset look different above water than below?"

"It does." She nodded. "The colors are much more vibrant here, but lack the rainbow effect we get beneath the water."

"Hmm, I would love to see that." They stood silently, watching the sky. "What's troubling your mind?"

"I convinced my mother to allow a water griffin to volunteer for the challenge."

"And now you feel guilty?" He looked at her. "Worried they might fail?"

"No, now I feel pissed because she won't let me volunteer."

"Of course." He smirked. "That sounds a lot more like you."

"I mean, what's the big deal? So, I go, and they take part in the challenge. Even if I put my name in, there's nothing saying I will be the euman chosen."

"If that's the case, why do you care so much?" he asked. "Odds are you won't be the chosen one, anyway. Why get so upset that you can't put your name in?"

"It's the principle of the thing. I mean, I want to do something meaningful. She's so afraid of me leaving home that she'll do anything to keep me there. My eldest sister is next to be the queen, so she has all the responsibility for our eumen on her shoulders. All my life they've told me how I run from responsibility. And this time I'm stepping forward, and it's like they don't care. They want me to turn my back on something that feels like my duty."

"Why let them?" he asked.

"What do you mean?" She frowned at his question.

"I mean, if this is something that really feels like you're supposed to do, like it's your responsibility, then why would you let anyone talk you out of it? If I felt as strongly as you did, nothing could stop me. Think about how many times you've visited here against their wishes. You sneak away and you come here and hang out with me." He held her gaze, and it felt like he could see right through her to the truths she hid from him and the rest of the world. "Are you telling me your mother would agree with you being here now?"

"No, she wouldn't."

"All right. Sounds to me like I was right about you. You're the rebellious type." He nudged her shoulder. "So, Maluai, Princess of Wallai, rebel."

They sat together until sunset, and Jeraim once again left Maluai to her thoughts. All she could think about was what he said. Rebel.

Forty hours later, Maluai returned to the surface with her laenu, the guardians, and the council members. They went straight to the Iris where the Forge royal laenu, and those who'd entered their name as challengers, stood at the temple beyond the fountain.

"I thank you all for being here. For the royal families and the brave souls who've volunteered to step forward as our new challenger," Queen Helena addressed the crowd who gathered. "Over the last forty-eight hours, those of you who wish to stand for our eumen have flown over the iris and dropped your blood into the still waters. Soon, we will learn which of you the goddess has chosen."

Maluai looked around, and this time, Jeraim was there, standing next to an older euman who shared the strong features of his face. She wondered if Jeraim entered the challenge. He'd never specifically said he wasn't going to. Maybe that was how he saw her there on the cliff that night.

Moments later, the water in the fountain, which was calm when they arrived, shot up into the air. It landed in the surrounding water, which rushed around the base violently. They watched as faces appeared in the flow. Maluai recognized two of the men from her home, but the others moved too quickly for her to tell who they were.

When the rush ended, the water shot back into the air, landed in the fountain, and settled.

The hushed crowd waited patiently until the water lifted again, this time a gentle event that formed a face above the fountain. And then the gasps spread across the crowd.

The Queen of Wallai nearly fainted with recognition.

Maluai.

Everyone turned to her, but before a word could be said, Beltan called their attention back to the fountain.

"Now we learn how difficult the task will be," he spoke as the water spun in a tight spiral.

From the cool water, the Hasking stone appeared. The tool they would use to monitor her progress in the trials. As it floated above the fountain, the cool water shifted in hue until it settled in a bright, bloody red.

CHAPTER 9

"How could you do this?" Valuai questioned her daughter the moment they were alone.

As long as they were in front of the crowd, she tried to remain calm. While shocked, she appeared to support her daughter. She quickly recovered from any show of disbelief and held her poise until they were back underwater. The moment they entered the palace, she expressed her true feelings.

"I had to," Maluai said as the guardians left the room. "I know you didn't want me to, but I had to do it."

"What do you mean, you *had* to?" The queen shook her hands around her face frantically, creating bubbles in the water with the motions. "I'm having a hard time understanding your reasoning."

"This felt like something I had to do. Like it was a calling. I know you don't want to hear it, but that's how I feel," Maluai explained. "When I looked at the fountain, it felt like Lunai herself was telling me to come. How could I deny that feeling?"

"You put your life in danger! Do you not get that?" Her mother spoke as if she hadn't heard her daughter's statement. "Maluai, the waters turned red. You know what that means!"

"It means this will be a tough challenge for me." She nodded. "It means it won't be easy. I'm up for it. I know you don't think it's true, but I am."

"It doesn't just mean it will be difficult! Maluai, my daughter, it means you can lose your life. This isn't just a game you run off and play and come back from unscathed. You could die in there. Do you understand what I'm saying to you? You could go in there and never come out again."

"I can do this," Maluai insisted, this time being the one to ignore her mother's statement. She didn't want to think negatively about her chances. "I will not die."

"You don't know that." Valuai's voice trembled with her building fear. Her eyes turned red from the strain of tears she held back.

"Why are you so certain I will?" Maluai asked. "Do you have that little faith in me?"

"I'm not saying that," Valuai said. "This isn't about faith. This isn't about me believing you're good enough or not."

"Then explain to me what you are saying, because I don't get why you're so against me doing what I feel is right to me," Maluai said. "I'm not a child. I haven't been for years, and yet you treat me as if I am. I'm old enough to make this decision. Old enough for Lunai to have accepted it."

"I just lost your father." Her voice broke. "Do you think I want to lose you, too?"

"You were the one who told me we can't live our lives in fear of what's coming. Am I supposed to ignore that lesson?" she pointed out. "When our grandmother transitioned, you said death is inevitable. It's not something we chase or run from. Why is that different now?"

"Because right now I'm facing it twice in a matter of days." Valuai's rage brought an edge to her voice. "I'm looking death in the face, and it's taking away the eumen I love most in this world."

"You're looking at me like I'm already gone," Maluai said. "I know my father is gone. I wish I could do something about it, but I can't. You can't treat me as if I'm not standing here in front of you, alive and well. I'm not gone."

"I know you're not." She grabbed her by the shoulders. "I see you, I hear your voice, and feel you in my hold now, but my heart, how it aches right now. It feels like you're fading away, and there is nothing I can do to stop it."

"Mother, I'm sorry. I never wanted to make you feel that way."

"But this is something you feel you have to do." Valuai nodded. "I want to understand it. I really do, but I need time."

The queen kissed her daughter's cheek and then turned and left her standing alone in the room. The soft light of the lanterns danced on the walls around her as Maluai watched her disappear around the corner. Maluai stood alone after her mother left her.

Her thoughts swam through her mind like a school of wild fish. She didn't want to hurt or disappoint anyone, but she couldn't turn her back on what felt right for herself.

"You're still here?" Kaluai came in after her mother left.

"Let me guess, you're upset with me too?" Maluai turned to her sister.

"This is a selfish thing you're doing." She swam over to her. "I can't believe you actually went and did this after mother specifically said she didn't want you to."

"Selfish?" Maluai scoffed. "How could my entering the challenge to save our eumen ever be considered selfish?"

"Depends." Kaluai peered at her sister. "Are you doing it for the right reasons or are you just telling yourself you are?"

"Why are you so certain I'm not?" Maluai looked at her. "And tell me, what reasons do you think are valid enough to be considered the right ones? Give me a list now so I can give them to our mother. Because the ones I've chosen clearly aren't good enough."

"Maybe there are no reasons good enough. Think about what's going on outside of yourself. Our laenu has been through so much." Kaluai's voice broke, but she quickly regained her composure before she continued. "We're trying to claim our independence. I mean, I get it. We all know how much you want to get away from Wallai, but is this really the way to do it?"

"You all claim to know me so well. You act as if you know my deepest desires, and yet you still think the one thing I want most in this world is to get away from home and the eumen I love. I hate to say this to you, big sister, but you don't know me nearly as well as you think you do. Neither does our mother." Maluai turned to leave her sister, but Kaluai wasn't done with the conversation.

"I don't know you? Really?" Kaluai followed her sister. "I've watched you your entire life, itching to break free. This is what you've always wanted! Maybe you're the one who doesn't know yourself."

"I'm not doing this for myself!" Maluai screamed as if shouting the words would get them through her sister's head better. "I'm not doing this for adventure or as some ridiculous excuse to get away from my home. There are so many things I could say hoping to convince you, but I just realized something else. I'm not doing this to prove anything to anyone. Something inside me tells me it is the thing I am supposed to do. If none of you want to believe it, that's your business, and it is not my duty to change the way you feel about me."

"You don't even know what you're walking into," Kaluai pointed out. "Aren't you at all worried about that?"

"How many days do you wake up knowing exactly what you're walking into?" Maluai challenged her sister's point. "Did you wake up a few days ago and know our world was going to be changed forever? Did you foresee the spill into the ocean, the poisoning of our lands, or all the lives lost?"

"Of course not, but that is not the same thing." Kaluai backed away as if physically hurt by her sister's words.

"Is it not? Life is changing constantly. It challenges us, and that can be a difficult thing to face. I know we're all grieving the loss of our father, but something I learned from that euman is that when life gets hard, when the decisions get difficult to make, and when the challenges present themselves, you don't hide from it." She thought of his last words and his impression of her. Maluai ran when things got tough. She wouldn't do it this time.

"You don't turn and run away. You face it head on. And you don't take the easy way out. Tell me right now, look me in the eye, and say to me that if there was something inside of you so strong that it made your heart ache to think about walking away, you would. If something was calling to you right now to go out there and throw yourself into the mix of madness, would you let anyone tell you not to?"

Kaluai looked away from her sister, chewing on the question, then her shoulder slumped with a heavy sigh of agreement. "No. I wouldn't."

"Exactly. And you know why? Because that's the way our parents raised us. So, tell me, why is it you and everyone else around here think I should allow any of you to sway me from doing what feels right to me?" Maluai had her, and she knew it. There was no way she could say, without sounding like a hypocrite, that she was right.

"We just don't want to see you get hurt," Kaluai admitted.

"One of these days, you're all going to have to stop looking at me like I'm some piece of glass that's going to shatter in front of your faces. I would have preferred that day had come before this. I know that even if I make it through this, it doesn't guarantee the way you, my mother, and everyone else look at me will ever change. But I am tired of waiting for you to see me the way I'm fighting to see myself."

"You really mean it, don't you? You feel you have to do this." Kaluai's expression and voice softened as she looked at her sister. "I believe in you. I swear, I just, it's all so much to take in such a short time."

"I've never felt so strongly about anything in my life as the moment I saw the fountain and felt the energy. I knew what I had to do. It feels like shezia that it's been so readily dismissed by those I love most in this world. I will not walk away from what I believe is meant for me. If it wasn't, why would my name have been chosen?"

"I don't know. Maybe some cruel joke from the goddess." Kaluai forced a tight chuckle to cut the tension.

"Of everything they have taught us of Lunai, when have we ever believed she was a jokester?" Maluai nudged her sister's arm and narrowed her gaze.

"You have a theory?" Kianna asked. "I know that look in your eyes."

"I believe this test is more for us than Forge. Here we are claiming we want to be independent. We've announced to the world that we want to stand on our own. Maybe this is the goddess telling us to prove we're ready. Isn't that how it works when new species are ready to stand on their own? The goddess tests them. Why should we be any different?"

"I didn't think about that," Kaluai said. "And the fountain woke after Mother made her decision."

"I love you, and I love Mother. You both need to understand I will do everything I can to come back home." She paused. "This is my challenge, Kal. My challenge. I'm not backing down."

"I know." Her sister sighed. "I know you will do your best to return to us."

"Good." Maluai smirked. "Now, maybe you can help convince our mother of that."

"There are a lot of things I would do for you, sister."

"But not this?" Maluai asked.

"I'll support your cause... from afar." Kaluai's laughter was natural and unforced.

"Maluai?" the songlike voice floated over to her as she lay on her bed.

"Genuve!" Maluai jumped from her bed and swam over to her window, where she would find a friend she hadn't seen in nearly a year. "Hende!"

Genuve was a mermaid. She had short locs and green eyes with blue and green speckles scaling on her face and chest. She wore a necklace of large marbles wrapped with wire that matched the color of her eyes and stood as a vibrant comparison to her dark skin.

"You know I had to come see you." Her friend shimmied outside her window before settling her wide hips on the ledge. "Word travels fast under the sea."

"You know about the challenge." Maluai leaned against the window frame.

"Yes, and I can't believe you actually volunteered to be the champion. Very brave and possibly foolish of you to do." She tapped her chin. "I haven't decided which one it is yet."

"I had to do it." Maluai sighed. "Everyone is telling me I was wrong to do it, but it's hard to explain. I just know I had to do it."

"Really?" She swam in tight circles and held her hand over her eyes, squinting to look off in the distance. "Tell me, where is the euman who put the blade to your neck and forced you to do this?"

"Hilarious." Maluai pushed open the glass frame that partially closed her room off. "You remember when we were kids, and you told me about how you faced all these impossible challenges? There were things you just couldn't turn away from, no matter what. That's what this feels like."

"Your calling." She nodded. "Been there, done that. Going back again tomorrow."

"Yes." Maluai sighed. "I swear I've felt nothing like this before. You know I've always wanted adventure. I wanted to get out and see what the world was like. There had to be challenges for me to face, but this isn't about that. I know the risks that come with this. Yes, I want adventure, but I never dreamed of doing something that would actually be a threat to my life."

"Admit it, the possibility of adventure is also enticing." Genuve leaned in. "I mean, this is an adventure provided by the goddess herself! That's exciting, even if you may not make it back from it."

"Genuve, that's not why I did this." Maluai was starting to really hate repeating herself.

"I know it's not, but it is a nice little side perk to it, right?" She waved her hands in front of her face as if painting a picture on the current. "You finally get to get away from your home. See all the corners of the world and create memories and stories and adventures of your own. You know, instead of waiting for me to show up and tell you about all the exciting things I've been up to."

"Fine, I'll admit I am looking forward to just seeing what's outside of our world. And another secret? I am worried that maybe I'm not exactly ready for this." Maluai looked over her shoulder. "It would be nice if I could talk to anyone else about this, but I'm too busy defending my decision to reveal my insecurity. I can't turn around and then tell them I'm worried I'm not fit for this."

"Well, you can tell me anything. It's an enormous weight on your shoulder." Genuve swam through the window into her room and moved over to the bed. "I say think about the positive. Like how after the world finds out about water griffins, you won't have to hide anymore. That means you can travel the world with me. I'll be your Eldritch tour guide!"

"That would be amazing." Maluai joined her. "You know how many times I've thought about running away and joining you out there."

"I'm glad you didn't. The last thing I need are those scary plu guards of your chasing after me! I'm just happy they let me float on in here to visit you without tackling me." Genuve laughed. "Can you imagine us on the run?"

"No, I really can't." Maluai laughed. "I'd be too busy trying to explore."

"You know, this is also a relief for me! Hell, it's so hard knowing about you all but not being able to talk about it." She laid back over the bed dramatically. "So many times I wanted to talk about my amazing best friend, and I've had to zip my lip!"

"I'm your best friend?" Maluai joked.

"Play with my heart like that, and I will bring sand from above and rub it into your hair. Let those caretakers of yours pick at you for three days trying to get it all out."

"That's so mean." Maluai laughed. "You know I'm just joking. I love you, girl."

"Sure, sure." Genuve waved her off. "You're lucky to have me."

"I really am. If it weren't for you, I'd probably go crazy here." Maluai relaxed. "I guess it's a good thing our eumen shared this corner of the waters for so long. Made it difficult to stay hidden from you."

"I'm sorry to hear about your father." Genuve touched her hand. "I should have said that sooner, but you know how I get about death. What happened here? I can't imagine how you all got through it."

"Thanks. And yes, I know." Maluai moved back to the window to look out over her home. "We're still getting through it."

"How are you holding up?" Genuve joined her. "I know your father was the only member of your laenu who really supported your wild side."

"I won't lie. It's been difficult, but it means I have to stand up for myself for once, which has not been the easiest." Maluai looked at her friend, who met her with soft eyes and allowed herself to be vulnerable. "I feel like my mother needs me most right now. She's suffering such a tremendous loss, and here I am, trying to take a stand for my independence at the same time. But how long am I supposed to let her run my life or make the most important decisions for me?"

"She didn't want you to enter the challenge." Genuve got what she meant.

"What do you think?" Maluai laughed. "Our mother freaks out whenever I step outside of a hundred-foot radius of our home. After I told her I wanted to volunteer, she said no. She said the guards would find a worthy champion, and if the goddess thought they were fit, she would choose one of them."

"So, you defied her and went and volunteered, anyway?" Genuve looked like she needed a snack while she listened to the story. "What did she say when you found out?"

"She pretended to support me until we got back here. Then, as soon as we were alone, she snapped."

"Good for you." She swam in circles. "I mean, it's not good that your mother is mad at you, but she'll get over it. You're not a child anymore. Your mother needs to understand that. I know for a lifespan that on average reaches almost a thousand years, you're a baby, but you're old enough to know what's right for yourself."

"I appreciate you for seeing it my way."

"Okay, enough with the rebellion. Tell me, have you seen the hunk from up above? I've been gone for a while. You gotta catch me up on everything." Genuve nudged her with her tail.

"I have, a few times in the last days, actually." She smiled. "The last time was weird."

"Weird in what way?" the mermaid leaned in, eyes wide. "Did he do something? I swear I have friends. They'll kick his ass."

"That's unnecessary. But I don't know. The energy was just different. He was actually the one that convinced me I should enter the challenge and not let my mother and others sway me." She thought about seeing him at the Iris. "We didn't get to talk, but he was there when my face appeared above the fountain. I don't think he was happy about it, not that I had time to check with the way they swept me out of there."

"He convinced you to do it, but he didn't want it for you." Her friend looked understanding. "I'd say that's a good sign."

"How could that be a good sign?"

"Because he supports your choices, even if he doesn't completely agree with them. That's the kind of partner you want in your corner. He's not pushing you to do bad things. He's supporting your effort to stay true to yourself, which, to me, sounds like you've done."

"So, you support my decision?" Maluai asked. "You think I'm doing the right thing?"

"You're doing what's right for you. Do I support it? Yes, absolutely. Do I like it? Hell no. But I believe in you. I, like everyone else, just want you to be safe. The difference between me and everyone else is that I know your spirit and your heart. I have a feeling you're the best euman to represent Wallai and the water griffins, and that's why the goddess picked you."

"I've missed you so much." Maluai swam over and hugged her friend. "I'm so glad you came to see me. I needed this."

"You too, girl. So, when do you leave?" Genuve spoke into her shoulder.

"At first light, I return topside, and they'll introduce me to my mentor."

"You better rest up then." She kissed her cheek. "I'll let you rest. I should get going before your guardian realizes I'm here and yells at me for forgetting to check in."

CHAPTER 10

W hen the light touched her room the next morning, Maluai was ready to go. Sleep proved an impossible thing to capture. She dressed and headed out of her door, where her guardian waited.

"Let me guess, you're just as disappointed in me as everyone else is," Maluai blurted out as if she read the negative thoughts on Seru's mind.

"I am not." Seru greeted her before they swam down the corridor.

"You're not?" She looked up at her guardian. "Why not?"

"I think what you're doing is brave. Possibly foolish, but fitting." She looked over at Maluai and winked. "I only wish you the best on your journey. And I hope it proves to be something amazing for you and for our eumen."

"That's shocking. You usually scold me for going against my mother's wishes." Maluai pointed out their typical conversation pattern whenever she rebelled.

"You are no longer a child. I understand you do not wish to be looked at as one, so I am attempting to see the validity in the claim you hold on to your own future. I, like your mother, have realized this is a difficult thing to do." Seru paused. "Besides, I can't really scold you. You're the princess. I'm the guardian. My job is to protect you, not make your decisions for you."

"So, you're saying I shouldn't be upset with my mother because she's only acting out of love?"

"I'm saying I'm proud of you, and I want you to stay safe." She swam ahead. "Whatever other meaning you take from my words is completely up to you."

Seru left her to her thoughts as they swam to meet the queen, the other guards, and the councilmen, who would go on land with them. Maluai felt her heart swell with a new sense of affirmation. Her guardian was proud of her. It had to mean she was on the right path, not that she needed the external validation, but it helped.

As they reached the others, it surprised her to see her sisters waiting to greet her. She was sure they would hide away and avoid facing her before she left, but they were there. Her youngest sister swam forward, approaching her when no one else would, and wrapped her arms around her waist.

"Please be safe." Naluai looked up at her with wide eyes. "I believe in you, but I'm worried."

"I will. I promise I will do nothing reckless." Maluai hugged her sister back.

"Good." She moved aside, and Kaluai approached Maluai. "Because I want another sleepover."

"You got it." Maluai kissed her forehead, then looked over at their older sister. "Kal."

"Are you ready for this?" Kaluai touched her shoulder.

"Honestly, I'm not sure, but I have time to prepare." Maluai nodded. "I'm not jumping right into the fire. My mentor will help me get ready."

"I wish we could be there with you, but they instructed us to remain here." She glanced over her shoulder at her mother, who stood with the others, face a mask of worry.

"I understand," Maluai said. "It's probably for the best. Less distraction for me, and fewer eumen for the guards to watch over up there."

"I'll miss you," Kaluai said, her voice cracking. "I really will."

"I'll miss you, too." Maluai hugged her sister, and when their embrace ended, she joined Seru with the others.

"Maluai," her mother said her name with an unfamiliar edge to her tone.

"Mother." Maluai dropped her eyes.

"We are ready to go," Valuai called out, and the guard fell into formation, forming a protective circle around the queen and princess.

They headed for Forge. While Maluai would have preferred her sisters by her side, they remained home. No one questioned the decision made by the queen. Of course, she was more protective of them. She'd lost her husband and was battling with fears of losing one daughter. Valuai would risk losing no one else.

As they broke the surface of the water, the Queen of Forge and her guards were there to greet them, their armor glinting in the sunlight. There was no fanfare this time, no music or dancing men and women. The two queens greeted one another before turning to Maluai.

"I want to thank you for your sacrifice," Queen Helena said in a tone that revealed she didn't have faith in their chosen champion.

Maluai simply nodded before the group boarded the royal plane that would take them from the edge of the island to its center, where the Iris fountain was still active.

"Maluai, it's good to see you." Beltan approached as they stepped out of the plane. He used the Wallain greeting gesture to welcome her.

"Thank you." She returned the gesture.

"There is much to do, but none more important than this. Before you begin your journey, you will need a guide." He waved his hand to the open door, where two figures appeared. One she recognized. "This is Kerulo, the last champion. He will be your mentor for the trials."

Maluai's heart fell into her stomach as she found the euman he pointed to. His frail form slumped beneath the weight of the cloaks that draped over his shoulders. His skin was dry but glossy in some areas, as if they had dipped him in preserving oils to prevent him from expiring. This was the euman meant to train her and guide her through the toughest moment of her life.

Before she could fully process the wave of disbelief, her eyes flashed to the euman who stood at his side. The familiar face of a friend she shouldn't have any claim to. Jeraim. She didn't acknowledge him. Instead, she looked back to the man, who lifted a shaky hand to his chest. They saluted in the way of Forge.

"Valuai," Helena spoke. "I believe this introduction can continue without us. There are things we need to discuss."

"Will you be okay?" Valuai looked at her daughter.

"I'm fine, Mother," she responded shortly, then watched as her mother followed Helena onto the plane, followed by their council members and their guards.

"Let me introduce you to my nephew." His shaky voice paused as his eyes caught the way they looked at each other. "Though it appears an introduction may not be necessary."

"Jeraim," Jeraim unnecessarily introduced himself and lowered his head to her in respect.

"Princess Maluai," she said back.

"Short." Kerulo looked between them and then to Beltan, who turned and left them alone. "Interesting. Well, there is much to be done and little time to do it in. I've spent years training the wrong eumen. So, I hope you're ready for a crash course."

"Training?" Maluai asked as Kerulo turned to walk into the temple, leaving them to follow him. For a euman who looked like he was ready to keel over, he didn't seem to be in any shape to train anyone. "You trained others for this?"

"Yes, despite it being so long since we were last challenged, it is our rule to stay prepared for this to happen. Everyone who entered their name, apart from you and the other Wallains, had been training and were ready to take the challenge. But of course, it chose someone who couldn't be any further from ready." Kerulo's voice caught as he coughed. His shoulders jerked with the force of the mucus attempting to expel itself from his throat. The fit lasted until Beltan appeared with a cup, giving the sickly euman something to ease his throat.

"Are you okay?" Maluai asked.

"He was caught in the spill," Jeraim answered for his uncle.

"What?" The horror hit her. There were eumen in Forge who the disaster impacted.

"My usual walk led right into the path of the affected area. I tried to get out of there, but my reflexes just aren't what they used to be." He looked at his nephew. "Jeraim, please give us a moment."

"Yes, uncle." Jeraim saluted him and left the two alone in the temple. Beltan followed shortly after him when he was sure Kerulo would be okay without his watchful eye.

"Impressive man. I'm proud of who he's become." Kerulo sat down on the bench in front of the large window that opened to a view of the fountain. "Taught him everything I know. There's no one better apart from myself to have by your side."

"Um, okay." She ignored the cryptic message and joined him on the bench. "So, how does this work? Do you hand me a cheat sheet so I can go in there and pass the test?"

"If only it was that simple." His laugh was a hollow sound that echoed in the temple. "I don't know what you will be tested on specifically. Each test is unique to the challenger. All I can do now is prepare you for what would be an exhaustive mental challenge. What I experienced inside that place was nothing I could have ever expected, and it was nothing like what my mentor went through."

"So, this is going to be difficult, is what you're saying?"

"Did you expect it not to be?" He looked at her. "The eumen I've trained spent years dedicating themselves to a deeper understanding of their inner being. That is what will be at stake."

"I wish I had that kind of time." Maluai dropped her shoulders. "I didn't have any expectations of what this would be. Maybe if I'd thought about it more, I wouldn't have volunteered for the job."

"So, why did you enter your name?" He asked her the meaningful question.

"I felt like I was supposed to," she answered honestly. "There was this nagging feeling inside me I couldn't ignore. It felt like if I turned my back on it, I would regret it. Not just because I didn't do it, but because I'd never know if I could truly succeed."

"I'll tell you a secret." Ge adjusted in his seat. "That's exactly the same reason I did it. I understand the feeling when you're called to do something, even when it terrifies you. The last thing

I wanted to do was enter my name into a challenge that could nearly kill me, but I did it, because despite the threat and the danger, jumping into this made sense. It felt almost like it was my purpose. No matter how much I tried to explain that to the eumen in my life, they just did not get it. Something tells me you have experienced the same thing."

"My laenu thinks I'm doing this just for the chance to run away from home," she admitted. "My mother is not happy about any of this."

"Now, if you wanted to do that, wouldn't you choose somewhere less deadly and more tropical?" He laughed.

"That's what I said!" She looked at the man, and her heart ached because this was someone who understood her, and yet she could sense he wouldn't be around for much longer.

"Well, we have a lot to do, young princess. We've made accommodations for our training close to the water, but you will need to stay on land for the duration so I can monitor you progression."

"Sounds good." She swallowed the lump in her throat, suddenly feeling pangs of homesickness.

"This is your last night of freedom. I suggest you use it wisely." He smiled. "Jeraim will return to show you where you'll be staying. I'd like for you to use the time to meditate. Clear your mind and set your intentions for the challenge. It isn't enough to wish to make it through this. You must have a purpose, a goal."

As if scripted, Beltan returned and helped her mentor to his feet and ushered him from the room. They left her alone in the temple with her thoughts and the swelling fear that she'd made the wrong choice. There were eumen far more prepared than her. Still, it felt like this was what she was meant to do. After a few minutes of unsettled thoughts, she stood from the bench and moved to the center of the room.

Maluai dropped her head back and looked up through the eye shaped hole in the ceiling. She imagined what it would be like to stand there during the rain. When her thoughts grew heavy again, she busied her mind with cataloging the details in the space. The large pillars, the stone carvings, and the earthen floor that flourished after recent rains.

It was fitting that the temple felt so in tune with nature. It was one of the first official structures built on the island. A symbol of their thanks to Mother Goddess. The eye looked up to the heavens, and they said it was a direct connection to the goddess. If one stood in the center, the goddess could hear their heart louder than all others. She sat on the floor in the center of the eye and looked up. She thought about what her mentor told her. It wasn't enough to want to succeed. She needed to have a purpose. What was her purpose?

Of course, she wanted to protect her eumen from being cursed. And there was the point of proving to Lunai that the Wallains should be judged separately from their sisters in Forge. Still, she couldn't properly define what that meant. What impact would their separation truly have on their eumen or the rest of the world? If they separated, would it really make things easier for them or would it get worse?

Outside of the desire to make things better for her eumen, there was an underlying motivation that was more selfish. Maluai was honest with herself. To lie in the goddess's presence wouldn't be a great way to start off such an important journey.

The princess of Wallai wanted more than to save her eumen. She wanted to prove to herself and her laenu that she would be okay. Now that she didn't have her father there waiting for her, cheering her on, pushing her forward, she had to do it for herself, but she wasn't sure if she could. She wanted to explore the world and have adventures of her own. Overcoming thirty years of being told you're incapable of doing something wasn't an easy feat, but it was the only way she was ever going to live a life she defined.

"Are you ready?" his warm voice called from behind her. "I hate to interrupt you. You look so peaceful there, but Kerulo asked that I show you to the campsite."

"Oh." She looked back over her shoulder at Jeraim before standing up from her spot on the floor. "Yes. I'm ready. Thank you."

"This way." He gestured toward the doorway opposite where she entered.

"My mentor is your uncle," Maluai spoke as she followed Jeraim out of the temple and down a set of winding stone stairs.

"Yes." He nodded, not looking back at her.

"You knew he would be my mentor and that it would mean we would spend more time together if I were chosen."

"Yes." Again, he nodded, not looking back.

"Did you enter your name?" she asked. "Kerulo said he taught you everything he knows. Means you were prepared to face this challenge."

"I did not." He stopped as they reached the bottom of the steps and met the sandy grounds that would lead to the ocean-side campsite.

"Why not?" she asked. "Did you not think you could survive it, even with all your training?"

"I didn't feel compelled to," he answered honestly as the wind picked up. "This isn't my fight."

"Is that why you told me to enter?" Maluai looked up at him. "Because of the way I felt?"

"Yes. I've listened to my uncle talk about this for years, and he's always said how he felt like he had to be there. Like the goddess was calling him. I didn't feel that, so I thought it meant I wasn't supposed to enter. You felt it. That's why you she chose you." His answer made it all sound so simple, despite the pit of worry in her stomach.

"You could have told me the mentor was your uncle." Maluai smirked. "Why wait for the grand reveal?"

"That may have swayed your decisioning, and this isn't about me." His lips lifted into a crooked half-smile. "Though I will admit it's nice to spend time with you without having to hide what I'm doing."

"Yes. Your uncle seemed to realize we knew each other." She sighed. "How likely is it he'll be the only one who recognizes it?"

"He's really perceptive like that." Jeraim chuckled as they continued walking. "Maybe with all the chaos, the others won't notice what's happening."

"Well, I'm glad you didn't enter your name." She brushed her locks over her shoulder as the wind picked up.

"Why is that?" he asked.

"If you had entered, and she chose me over you, you might be upset." She smirked.

"Only a child would be upset over something like that." He chuckled. "Besides, being upset would be equivalent to being angry with the goddess and questioning her judgment. Only a fool would do that."

Jeraim came to an abrupt stop, eyes wide as he watched the winged body come plummeting down to the ground before him. When the wings retracted, they revealed the red suited body of the prince of Forge.

"Jeraim." The oldest son of Helena stepped forward.

"Prince Marruk." Jeraim greeted him as they did in Forge, fist over heart.

"I see you've found your way back here." He looked at Malu-ai.

"It wasn't a difficult thing to do," she responded coolly, scanning the skies for his guardian, who was nowhere to be seen.

"I hope you're prepared for this." He looked her in the eye with a bitter expression. "I've trained for years. Built the fortitude to stand in challenge. I'm more prepared than anyone else here."

"It must be difficult to feel so prepared and yet not be chosen to prove yourself," she responded and could see the smirk on Jeraim's face.

"Difficult? No." Marruk's jaw tightened. "Unsettling? Yes. But this is your challenge. I wish you the best. For all our sake."

The prince's exit was as dramatic as his entrance. He whipped out his wings and took to the sky with such force that he kicked up the sand around his feet.

"Only a child?" Maluai waved away the dust in front of her face and looked up at the retreating prince.

"I have nothing to say about that." Jeraim smirked and continued to lead her to the campground.

They approached an area that had four large tents structured along the shoreline. And as the tents, fire pits, and training stations all came into view, Maluai felt the true gravity of the moment. In her head, she had visualized an area for them to just sit down and talk about what was impending. This wasn't just a location for hanging out and talking over snacks. They designed the campsite for intense training.

At the far end of the area, she recognized the stations used for training the Forge guards. They were tests of endurance, strength, and ingenuity. This wouldn't just be a test of her mind, but also of her physical capabilities. Those stations built muscle and mental fortitude.

"And this is where you'll stay." Jeraim pointed to the second largest tent built in the area. He'd been giving her an overview of the area, but she was too busy considering the physical nature of what she'd have to do.

"All of this is just for me?" She pointed to the massive blue tent with silver rope holding the two panels of the entrance open.

"Maluai, you are a princess. Despite what you're going through, they would treat you like nothing less. It should have everything you need. If not, let me know, and I'll make sure you get it. It's also the closest to the ocean, so whenever you feel you need to take a dive, you have easy access."

"What about my guardian?" She stepped toward the tent.

"What do you mean?" he asked.

"Seru, my guardian. She goes everywhere with me." Maluai placed her hands on her hips. "Come to think of it, I'm surprised she's not here now."

"You realize you will have to do this without your guardian, right? It's not like she can go into the challenge with you."

"I guess you're right. I hadn't thought about it like that." Maluai chewed her lip. She didn't think Seru would be with her, but she thought they'd part ways when it was time for her to enter the challenge, not so far before it.

"You will be on your own from this moment forward. Outside of your mentors' help, of course," he amended. "I mean, you can still talk to them if you want, it's not like you're forbidden to talk to anyone else, but I can tell you, my uncle is going to prefer you do this with as few distractions as possible."

"You'll be here, won't you?" she asked. It wasn't like there were many eumen she wanted to see or talk to. Most of the eumen closest to her had little faith in her. That wouldn't be helpful to her.

"Yes, I will be here. At least until you go to Elderton where the trials happen. Once you're there, the only euman that you'll be able to contact is your mentor, and even that's limited."

"Right. I remember reading about that part. The challenger can only communicate with their mentor four times throughout the trials," she repeated the fact she'd committed to memory. "Careful not to use them too quickly, or you will have to go without aid."

"That's right." He looked impressed. "I've heard stories of challengers from other areas who burned through their chances quickly, and, well, it didn't end well."

"That has to be the worst."

"That won't be your story," he reassured her.

"Jeraim." A land griffin with a short wingspan dropped to the ground behind Jeraim, out of breath. He pushed the long red braids away from his face as he called out to his friend. "You need to come quick."

"What is it?" Jeraim turned to him. "Peliak, what's wrong?"

"It's Kerulo." The man's expression turned sorrowful. "They've taken him to the healers. It doesn't look good."

CHAPTER 11

Jeraim took Maluai into his arms and carried her over the city to the healers' tower, where they held his uncle for care. She'd never flown above land and was unsure of her ability. As soon as they entered the building, they pulled Jeraim into the room where Kerulo lay. Maluai could only glimpse the foot of the bed before the door shut in her face, leaving her standing in the hall alone.

She heard the latch click shut, and she knew they had barred her from entering. This was too delicate a time, and all she could do was hope things turned out for the best. Maluai paced the floor, trying to keep her thoughts focused on the two men inside and not worry about what it would mean for her if Kerulo didn't survive. This wasn't about her. She refused to be that selfish.

As time ticked on, she sat in the seat across from the door and kept her eyes on the wood barrier between her and the others. She was so engrossed in her task that she didn't notice the sound of footfalls getting closer until a frantic female voice shouted Jeraim's name, prompting her to look away from the door.

The blue feathered robes billowed out behind her as she ran. Short, dainty legs carried her compact frame down the hall. Maluai watched the long, dark afro bounce around her face as she ran. She came to a sliding stop just outside the door but looked around the hallway as if the euman she called to would appear at her side.

"He's inside," Maluai offered the information. "They've been in there for a while now."

"Oh." She looked at her, then frowned. "I'm Wintia. Who are you?" she asked with a snipping tone, as if she were ready to curse the princess out for being there.

"I'm a friend." She stood from her seat and looked down at the euman, who was nearly a foot shorter than her. "My name is Maluai."

"The princess." Wintia gasped, realizing the mistake she'd made in snapping at someone from the royal class. Though her blue robes showed she was of an upper ranking class in Forge, it still gave her no right to speak out of turn to a royal.

"Yes," Maluai said with a soft smile. She wouldn't lord her status over the euman, who was clearly frantic.

"Where's Jeraim?" she asked as if she hadn't just been told.

"He's inside," Maluai repeated the information. "They took him in as soon as we got here. He hasn't come out since. How do you know Jeraim? Is he laenu? A friend?"

"No, he isn't laenu. It's deeper than that. He's—" she stopped speaking.

"What is it?" Maluai insisted she continue her explanation.

"Jeraim is my mate," Wintia spoke, and the weight of her words slammed into Maluai's chest. She placed her hand on her chest, where a large jewel hung like an echo of her own heart. "I love him. That is why I came."

"I can see why you're so upset," Maluai responded coolly. If being a princess did nothing else, it taught her how to keep her composure in moments when it felt like her stomach was about to drop out of her body. "I'm sure everything is fine."

"Yes," Wintia sobbed. "I really hope so. I don't know what will happen if he loses his uncle. Kerulo is the reason Jeraim and I are together."

"Oh." Maluai looked at the door, her thoughts muddled by unwarranted emotions. Kerulo wanted Jeraim to be with Wintia. Did that mean Jeraim agreed with his uncle's wishes? Why hadn't he mentioned it to her before? She swallowed the lump in her throat and comforted the upset euman by her side. "Let's hope for the best. I'm sure the healers will keep him well."

The door opened, and Jeraim stood there, shoulder slumped, face puffy, swollen and wet from his tears. Though she could already see his devastation, she held her breath, hoping his words would provide relief.

"I..." He took a deep breath, straightened his shoulders, and continued. "He's gone."

"Oh, Jeraim. I'm so sorry," Maluai said, her heart heavy.

"I can't believe this. Just a week ago, he was racing the young boys around the island, and now he's just gone."

"Jeraim, can I do anything?" Wintia asked, her voice soft and loving.

"No thank you," he answered without looking at her.

"Oh." she stepped back awkwardly but didn't leave.

"What do you need?" Maluai asked.

Jeraim took a deep breath, looked out the window, and rolled his shoulders. "I need to fly."

"Let's go then." Maluai's body shivered as her blue and grey wings unfolded from her back. She pushed aside her nerves of using her wings above land for the first time and pointed to the window. "Lead the way."

Jeraim unfolded his wings and flew through the open window. Maluai looked back at the envious face of the euman who claimed to be her mate before she followed his path through the sky.

Maluai paid close attention to the euman who flew ahead of her. The powerful push of his wings, the way he dipped slightly with every fourth push. There was a rhythm to his flight, that when mimicked, she coasted the currents instead of forcing the wind to carry her. Flying wasn't something she ever did. Though the water griffins all had wings, few used them to go above the surface of the water. Gravity made her wings feel heavier above water, but using his method took the effort out of the flight and allowed her to enjoy the experience.

They reached the peak of their rendezvous point, and though he continued to fly, she landed and watched him from below. Her heart ached for him, but she knew what he felt. Losing someone so close to him. She'd just experienced it and had a long way to go until she healed from it, but she told herself as she watched him fly circles above her head that she would support him. This wasn't about her loss. It was about him.

"Are you okay?" she asked when he landed beside her. "Actually, don't answer that. I know it's such a frustrating question. As if you could be okay right now. Just know I'm here for you."

"Thank you," he said as his wings folded back into his shoulders and disappeared beneath the smooth surface of his dark skin.

"Talk to me," she breathed. "It doesn't matter the words."

"Kerulo was the last laenu I had," he spoke and looked up at the willow birds that flew from the nearby treetops. "He was my anchor in this world."

"Oh, Jeraim. I'm sorry," she said. She'd known he lost his parents to a fire when he was young, but not that he had no other living laenu.

"This is so unfair. He should still have so many years left." He swallowed back tears, his pride making it impossible for him to cry in front of her.

"Death is an uncaring thing. It doesn't worry about how many years someone believes they are owed." She said the words that rang true to her, and the soft breeze pushed through her locs as if agreeing with her statement.

"I shouldn't cry," he huffed. "Death is inevitable."

"That's a foolish thing to say." She shook her head. "Not to call you foolish while you're mourning, but death is heavy. It's difficult to deal with. You should let yourself feel it and process however you need to. If that's crying, then cry. If it's flying, take flight, and I'll follow you, but don't hold back because you think somehow it means you're not as strong as you want to be."

"I just want him to be here, to lead me, and to train you." He pointed to her. "He's supposed to be here for you, too."

"How can you possibly be worried about me now?" She shook her head. "There are other eumen who can train me. Maybe they aren't as good as him, but I can get a new mentor. You can't replace what you've lost."

"Because it's easier to consider your needs than it is to process the weight of my own emotions," he answered honestly.

"I guess I understand that." She nodded. "When my father died, I wanted to run out and help the city instead of sitting at home thinking about how he wasn't with us anymore."

"You need a mentor," he said. "They're going to make you choose one or choose it for you."

"That's a concern for tomorrow, Jeraim." She placed her hand on his cheek, and her chest swelled as his deep eyes met hers. "Today, just feel what you need to. I'll stay with you."

"You have much more pressing things to worry about," he insisted. "I will be fine. I can handle this."

"Name one?" she challenged him. "I dare you. If you can name one thing that I find more important than being with you right now, I'll go."

He looked at her, then sighed. "You're not going, are you?"

"No." She squatted on the ground near the edge of the cliff and patted the ground beside her. "Join me."

As they'd done so many times before, they sat on the cliff and talked, but this time, she didn't leave after a few hours. She didn't rush back home and pretend like it didn't happen. Maluai stayed by his side until the sun drifted from the sky and gave way for the two moons to perform their dance across the night sky.

When Maluai's stomach growled, Jeraim, despite his emotional state, flew off to get them something to eat. While he was away, Maluai noticed a small griffin with a blue cloak flying nearby. She thought she was paranoid, but the bird flew just close enough for her to recognize the jewel hanging around her neck. Wintia was spying on them.

She didn't approach. She simply flew close enough to see the princess sitting on the cliff and then took off in another direction. If she expected Maluai to follow her, she was mistaken. Whatever issue she had with Jeraim, she'd leave her to take it up with him. When he returned, she mentioned nothing about their visitor, and they shared the meal of fish and fruit.

When the night took over the sky above them, they should have left the cliff, but they didn't. Instead, they remained there and lay together in the grass watching the stars until Maluai drifted to sleep with her head on his shoulder.

The soft song of the willows woke them to the rising sun. Maluai opened her eyes to Jeraim. His eyes told a story she didn't understand and chose not to question. One that made her stomach tighten and her breath quicken. She was afraid of what he would say if she asked for clarity.

"Good rising," she said in a dry voice.

"Good rising." He smiled in return.

"How are you feeling?" she asked.

"Sore." He laughed. "It's been a long time since I slept on the ground."

"I've never slept on the ground." She groaned as a painful knot formed in her back. "I'm not a fan."

"We should really get back." He looked over her head back to the city of Forge. "I'm sure they are looking for both of us."

"Oh, you're right. My mother is probably losing her mind now."

"Princess missing her first night out of the water." He sat up. "This may cause trouble."

"No more trouble than me deciding to volunteer for the trials." She stretched her hands above her head and groaned. "I think I'm really going to regret sleeping on the ground."

"You know, you may have to do that during the challenge." He stood and held his hand out to her.

"Oh, great." She took his hand and pulled herself to her feet. "Thank you."

"Ready to face this?" He turned in the palace's direction.

"Do I have a choice?"

"No, Princess. You do not." Jeraim chuckled as he unfolded his wings from his back.

Maluai followed suit, and when his wings lifted him from the ground, she joined him in the sky.

CHAPTER 12

"Where have you been?" her mother's tight voice called out to her as soon as she entered the palace. "The guards searched everywhere for you."

"I was with a friend," she answered, leaving out how the guards couldn't have searched everywhere if they hadn't seen her clearly lying on the top of a cliff. "I was safe."

"A friend?" She looked over her shoulder at the euman in a disapproving glare. "This euman is your friend?"

"Yes, Jeraim is a friend." She looked back. "He lost his uncle yesterday, and I was consoling him."

"How has he become a friend in such a short time?" Valuai asked with no concern for Jeraim's loss.

"Does that matter?" Maluai answered, offended by her mother's remark.

"No, it doesn't, at least not now." Helena stepped forward, interrupting the conversation between the two women. "What matters is figuring out who will mentor you now that Kerulo is gone."

"Excuse me?" Valuai looked at the queen.

"There is a decision to be made here. We cannot have an inexperienced challenger enter the trials without a mentor. The council members have already gathered. I suggest we join them in the deliberations." She waved her hand toward the corridor that led to the court.

Entering the court, Maluai felt her stomach knot up. What would happen when she got a new mentor? Would they be as knowledgeable as Kerulo was? Would they understand what was on the line for the eumen of Wallai? Would Jeraim still be able to be there with her? She found comfort in knowing he would be along for the journey and didn't want to lose that.

The court buzzed with the frantic energy of the clashing council members. They debated the merits of their chosen mentors, and clearly, the Wallain council was not on the same side as the members of the Forge council.

"Maluai is of our world. Clearly, we should be the ones to decide who is best to guide her," Fituen spoke.

"And she is representing all of us, all of our values. Not just yours." Shunti, the head of the Forge council rejected his sentiment.

"If it weren't for your values, we wouldn't be in this mess, and Kerulo would still be alive," Fituen bit back. "Or should we overlook that part of the issue?"

"This is getting us nowhere," Hasik voiced her concern.

"I agree," Helena spoke, and the council members shut up as they finally noticed the members of the royal laenu who stood at the entrance watching their debate.

"How would you like to proceed?" Shunti asked.

"Present your selected mentors to us. We will decide," The Forge Queen announced as she climbed to her seat at the head of the court. They had put a temporary seat in place beside her, intended for Valuai.

"No." Maluai shook her head. "This is ridiculous."

"Maluai," her mother snipped at her. "Mind your position in this court."

"I get to choose who my mentor will be." She stepped forward. "Whoever we choose is someone I'm going to have to work with, not any of you. I have to be comfortable with the euman chosen. Why should I stand here and let you all make this choice for me when, excuse me if this appears disrespectful, but your leadership has left us lacking any kind of unity in this court?"

"And who would you choose?" Valuai asked her daughter.

"I choose Jeraim." Maluai pointed to the euman who stood by the open doorway.

"What?" He looked at her and then the other suspicious faces that turned to him, ending with the Wallain Queen. "Me?"

"Yes, you," Maluai confirmed her choice.

"A mentor who has never been in the trials. That is insanity," Queen Helena spoke up.

"He is the best choice. Kerulo told me himself." Maluai looked at the Queen. "I think he knew he wouldn't be here to guide me, and that's why he said Jeraim would be the best euman to be by my side."

"You can't be serious. He's never even been to the challenge." Limua, the Wallain council member, repeated the queen's thought.

"But he's worked closely with Kerulo, learned everything from him," Maluai defended her choice again. "He is the best choice. He is the mentor I choose, and I will work with no one else. So, if you don't want to lose this on a technicality, I suggest you drop the issue and let me do this my way."

"Are you sure about this?" Jeraim asked.

"Yes." She turned to him.

"Maluai," her mother spoke. "We should discuss this before you make this choice."

"Mother, I love you, but this is my choice to make, and I've made it. One of these days, you're going to have to accept that I'm capable of deciding what's best for me. I'm not here to debate my reasoning with you or anyone else."

"I guess that's final." Helena stood from her seat and stepped forward. "If this is who you're more comfortable with, then it makes sense that he is the one you work with. Standing here and debating it will change nothing. You two should begin training."

"Then I guess I should get to it then." Maluai dropped her head in respect before she turned from the court and headed for the door where Jeraim stood.

"Are you sure this is the right choice?" Jeraim asked as they left the court.

"Yes, unless you're not up to it. I'm sorry. I didn't stop to consider that this may be too difficult for you right now." She stopped walking and looked at him. "If you want me to go back in there and listen to what they want, I will."

"No, I mean, I'm up to it. I just... I'm not sure I'm the right one for the job," he explained.

"Who has your uncle taught more about the challenge than you?" she asked.

"No one." He nodded. "I spent my entire life learning about what he went through. Sometimes it felt like I was there with him."

"Then it's settled. There is no one else I want to help me with this." She smiled. "I know this isn't exactly how things typically go, but that's the whole reason we're in this now. For so long Wallains set aside and let those of Forge do whatever they wanted to, even though they didn't think it was right. And because of that, we lost so many lives, including our king, my father. So, excuse me, but I don't think that going with the norm is the way to approach this.

"You told me your uncle believed those of us meant to be a part of the trials have an internal force that urges us to volunteer. That internal push, that understanding of what my path was, is the same thing telling me you're the one who's supposed to be by my side. I think I should listen to it. So again, I'm going to ask you if you want to do this, and I want you to be honest with me because there's no going back. Will you be my mentor?"

"How could I say no after a speech like that?" He chuckled, and they continued to walk. "You know, you sounded a lot like my uncle when you spoke."

"Let's hope that's a sign that I'll be just as successful as he was." She winked at him.

"You will be," he reassured her. "I have to go take care of things for my uncle. If I'm going to be training you, I need to make sure everything is in place before we begin. Do you think you can make it back to the campsite on your own?"

"Yes, I can manage." She nodded. "Give me a chance to break out my wings again. You know, that was the first time I flew above water."

"Really? Well, you did great." He nodded. "I'll meet you there in a few hours. This hopefully won't take too long."

An hour later, Maluai was back at the campsite, settling into the tent that was designated as her own. The tent was simple. A bed, a desk with pen and paper, and an area she assumed they meant for meditation. She stood at the chest full of simple brown clothing, going through the items they selected for her.

For a moment, she considered what it would be like to dress in the nondescript clothing and run away. No one would know who she was. She could explore the world anonymously, with no one knowing her true identity. Though it sounded like a sweet deal, she knew it would only cause more issues than it solved.

"Princess," the low but firm voice spoke from behind her, and she turned to find the short figure in blue robes synched at the collar with a griffin head pendant.

"Wintia, right?" she asked, though she knew exactly who she was.

"Yes." She nodded. "I wasn't sure you would remember me."

"You're not someone who's easily forgettable." Maluai closed the chest. "Jeraim isn't here. He went to see about the arrangements for his uncle."

"I know." Wintia took a deep breath as she looked around the simple tent. "I saw him headed for the towers."

"I guess that means you're here to see me then. How can I help you?" Maluai asked her.

"Respectfully, Princess, I'm here because there's something I have to tell you." Wintia straightened. "You need to stay away from Jeraim. The two of you being together is not a good idea."

"Prefacing your words with the word respectfully doesn't eliminate the contempt from your message," Maluai corrected the euman, who had the nerve to come and tell her what she should and should not do.

"I just mean to say I don't think the two of you being together is a good thing," Wintia spoke, her voice rising with emotions. "It can't be. Besides, Jeraim is going through a lot right now, and he needs someone who understands him. Someone who is like him."

"You mean someone whose recently lost a father figure and is now trying to find their place in a changing landscape?" Maluai reminded Wintia of why her laenu was in Forge to begin with. "You're absolutely right. He should be around someone who understands what he is going through."

"I don't mean to dismiss what you've been through."

"And yet, you have." Maluai narrowed her gaze. "Look, it seems to me that you're making some assumptions about my relationship with Jeraim. Has he said something to you about what we are to each other that has you so concerned about my intentions?"

"No, but like everyone else here, I have eyes, and I've seen the way you two are around each other. I saw the way he looked at you and how you looked at him." She stepped forward. "Whatever is going on between you and him needs to stop. Like I told you before, I am his mate."

"And yet, in the time I've known him, he's never mentioned you," Maluai said coolly. "You would think that would come up any of the times we've met before. And you'd think you would have known he was meeting me, since you seem to have no issue with tracking down his whereabouts. And yet, before yesterday, I did not know you existed. If you ask me, whatever issue you have is one you need to take up with your mate. Perhaps you should go find him and speak to him about it."

Her jaw tightened. Wintia looked like she had more she wanted to say, but Maluai didn't care about what her opinions were about her situation. No one was going to tell her how to live her life, least of all someone who had what was clearly a one-sided crush on a euman who barely knew she existed.

"I hate to have to say this to you because I'm sure you are truly nice when you're not feeling threatened." Maluai stepped forward and postured herself, lifting her chin and pushing her shoulders back. "But I have far more important things to think about right now than some issue of unrequited love you have going on with Jeraim. Whatever your issue, it is with him, not me."

"Unrequited?" Wintia looked insulted. "Jeraim loves me! What do you mean unrequited?"

"You're standing here defending a love I've never heard him speak of. I've known Jeraim for some time now, and we've shared a lot about ourselves, but never once did he speak of a romantic interest, and no one he intended to be his mate."

"You," she sniffled. "You two can't be together. You know that. It's not right for our eumen to mix. You are Princess of Wallai! A water griffin. What example would you be setting if you were to be with him? He is a land griffin. You know what you get when you mix water and earth? Mud."

"I understand your feelings are bruised right now, but I'm not here for a man, Wintia. I am here for the future of my eumen. That is my focus. So again, whatever concern you have, take it up with him. I have been more than patient with you with this because I know right now it is a tough time for all of us, but I'm done. This is the last time I'm going to address this with you." Maluai stepped around her and opened the draped curtain that covered the entrance to the tent. "I don't want to be the euman who holds her status over anyone else, but I'll remind you of who you're talking to right now and of what would happen to you should my guardian or worse, my mother, find out about your actions."

"My apologies." Wintia gave a tight nod, then walked out of the door with no other word. She knew her place and wouldn't risk the punishment that came with the continued disrespect of a royal.

Three hours later, Jeraim arrived. He stood outside her door, calling to her. Maluai sat up from the bed where she lay and walked outside to meet him.

"Everything okay?" he asked.

"Yes, just resting. Sleeping on the ground was far from comfortable." She laughed before stretching out her back.

"Tell me about it." He stretched his arms over his head. "My lower back doesn't like me at all right now."

"Did everything go okay with the arrangements?"

"Yes, to be honest, there isn't much to do. We don't have an enormous laenu, and the royal laenu will handle most of the arrangements, considering who my uncle was. He's a hero, and they will give him the home going of one."

"I'm glad. And how are you?"

"I'm managing." He smiled.

"Your friend came by," she said when he made no mention of the angry little land griffin who came to see her.

"Friend?" He raised a brow. "Peliak? What did he want?"

"No. Not him. Wintia," she corrected his assumption.

"Hmm." He frowned. "Why was she here?"

"She says she is your intended mate," Maluai informed him. "She wants me to stay away from you."

"What?" He stepped closer to her, jaw tight with obvious annoyance. "What exactly did she say to you?"

"She feels threatened. She believes you're supposed to be with her and thinks I'm here to interrupt that."

"Did she threaten you?" he asked sternly. "If she did, we need to report her now."

"That's unnecessary. I don't think she is foolish enough to threaten a princess. I simply reminded her of who I am and told her it would be best if she took up whatever issues she has with you."

"Good." He looked up at the sky. "She didn't come see me."

"How do you feel about her?" Maluai asked. "I mean, you've never mentioned her to me before. Is there something there?"

"I didn't mention her because she wasn't worth mentioning. I barely know her and definitely don't have feelings for her. She is one of a list of potential mates who have approached me in recent years about matching with them."

"Ah, a sexual magnet?" She nudged his arm. "Look at you, turning heads."

"I wouldn't go that far, but I'm not foolish. The standards of beauty in our community make me a desirable match. I'm strong and appealing in the ways a suitable mate should be." He rolled his neck with a deep sigh. "Not one of them knows anything more about me outside of that. With me, they will make strong babies. That's all they see."

"And you've chosen no one from this long list?" she asked, trying to keep the air of hope from her voice.

"I've chosen someone." He looked her in the eye. "She just wasn't on that list and isn't aware of my choice yet."

"I suggest when this is over, you make her aware and let Wintia know about it." Maluai winked. "It will make life better for everyone involved."

"I'll do that." He chewed on the thought. "What do you say we leave Forge?"

"What?" Her eyes bulged. "Leave Forge? Are you serious?"

"Yes. There are too many distractions here." He pointed to the top of the palace in the distance. "Too many opinions and petty feuds. You need to focus, and you won't be able to do that here."

"Are you referring to your long list of potential mates?" She laughed.

"Funny, but there's more to it. There are feuding royals, political mayhem, and, well, the emotions. We've been through a lot, and this place will not let you forget about any of it."

"Where would we go?" She looked out at the ocean. "I wouldn't have a clue. I've been nowhere besides Wallai and Forge."

"I know a place, if you trust me." He stepped in front of her and unfolded his wings.

She called her wings to appear. "Lead the way."

CHAPTER 13

S he hoped their path would take them near other territories where she could see more of the eumen of Eldritch and get a glimpse of their cultures. Instead of flying over the land, they soared above the expanse of water, the only movement from a distant boat, its rider asleep.

As they flew, Maluai had to dip into the water time and time again to keep herself from drying out. That was the burden of the water griffin—they couldn't get too dry, and flying eliminated the moisture in their skin. As she flew, she considered how they could develop a mechanism that might fix the issue. As it was, there was no need for it, with most water griffins never going above the surface. If they were to become free, their eumen would want to explore the world. How much exploring could they really do if they couldn't get too far away from the coastline?

After a few hours, they touched down on an island north of Forge. It was the perfect location for them. The area was entirely cut off from the outside world and had bizarre rock formations that made it feel even more eerie.

"This it?" She looked down on the island from the cliff where they landed.

"Yes." He looked around. "These are protected grounds. We will be in total isolation here."

"Protected grounds?" She pushed her locs over her shoulder. "Who protects them?"

"We do. The land griffins keep this land safe and uninhibited by outside forces," he explained. "It's a part of the original accords."

"Why?" she asked. "Why are the lands so special? There looks to be nothing here. No civilization."

"In Eldritch, all new life begins here. It's like the heart of Mother Goddess. Few eumen know it, but on this island, in the center of the world, there are new species that appear. Hundreds of them each year. Most never make it off the island." He pointed to the ground below where an odd creature with short legs, a fat rolling body, and ten tentacles crawled along. "Few evolve past their infancy. Those that make it potentially evolve into the future civilizations of our world. We must protect them until they make it off the island. Once they do, it's up to them to ensure their survival."

"I remember my father talking about this place before. I thought it was something he made up. Is it okay for us to be here?" She looked at the ground, checking to make sure she wasn't stepping on potential new life. "I mean, what happens if I accidentally squash the future of our world?"

"It's fine. We won't disturb anything while we're here. There are safe areas we can camp, but I figured this was the best place because no one comes here this time of year."

"Oh, good." She looked out at the water and rubbed her drying flesh. "I think I will take a swim. The quick dips were helpful, but not nearly enough. I need to soak for a while."

"Have at it." He pointed to the campsite up ahead that had a simple cabin structure. "I'll get us set up here while you do that."

Each time Maluai dove beneath the surface, she noted how much the underwater world changed. The further they got from Wallai, the more awe-inspiring the view became. Over one hundred miles from home, when she dropped beneath the surface, she was in a new world entirely. A kaleidoscope of fish, animals, and plants created a bustling ecosystem. She took it all in, and her heart swelled with hope. This was just the beginning for her. All the familiar sights and sounds of her home were replaced with an unfamiliar expanse of ocean.

The salty water swirled around her as she explored the depths of the ocean, and she swam for longer than she needed to simply to rehydrate. She kept a safe distance from the life she found, understanding the importance of leaving the ecosystem undisrupted, but she couldn't help but observe as much of the scene as she could. Stomach growling and fully restored, she returned to the island and carefully approached the campsite, still weary of harming the delicate life that claimed it as their home.

With the sun setting, the cycle of the two moons began in the sky as she approached the cabin. A soft candlelight lit the frame of the window and Maluai found herself nervous. She realized this would be the first time being so far from her underwater home, and more than that, she would share this cabin with a man. A euman who made her stomach knot whenever she thought of him being with anyone else.

Maluai took a deep breath, reminded herself of her reason for being there, and entered the cabin to find him sitting on a small bench and reading text from a leather-bound book. He looked up at her with a weak smile on his lips.

"Enjoy your swim?" Jeraim closed the book and sat it next to him on the seat. "You look refreshed."

"Yes, sorry to have taken so long. I didn't expect even the ocean to be so different away from home," she explained. "It felt like my first time in the water, even though it's where I've been my entire life. I never thought it would be so different, even though the guards told me it was."

"You don't need to apologize. I'm here to help you, remember?" He stood from his seat. "This is your journey. Do what you need to do."

"Thank you." She nodded, then took a deep breath, inhaling a tasty scent that reminded her of her empty stomach. "What's next? Something smells good in here."

"I thought you might be hungry. I caught fish and cooked it, but I wasn't sure if you ate it that way, so there is also a raw option." Jeraim pointed to the pots that held the prepared food. "I remember you saying you eat some kinds of fish, but I'm sure cooked isn't typical."

"It's not typical, though we have methods of cooking beneath the water. It's not done often." She looked toward the stove where the food waited. "It really smells delicious."

"Good, I'll prepare our plates." Jeraim stood and went to work, putting together a plate for both of them. He plated them on the small wooden table that had three stools.

They ate in a silence that turned more awkward with each bite they cleared from their plates. As her fish disappeared in front of her, thoughts of the conversation they weren't having rattled around in her mind. She avoided talking to him about what Wintia told her. How everyone thought they were trying to be together and how it would be bad if they tried. She refused to bring up conversations about his uncle because she was afraid she'd make it more about her than him. So instead, when she reached the last mouthful of food, she pushed it around her plate and waited for him to speak first.

"Tomorrow, we begin the hard stuff." Jeraim broke the silence with a neutral topic. "Need to get you fit and ready for whatever the challenge throws at you."

"Sounds good." She nodded. "I can't say I'm completely ready, but I think with sleep, I will be good to go."

"There is a bed in the back." He pointed to the door opposite the one that led outside. "It's yours. Please rest."

"Where will you sleep?" She looked around the cabin, not seeing any place that looked comfortable enough to call a bed.

"I'm going to take a flight. I need to clear my head and check out the island. When I'm done, I'll find somewhere to rest my head." He grabbed her empty plate from her and placed it in the sink.

"Okay." She nodded as he worked and stood from her seat at the table. "I guess I'll go to bed now."

"Sleep well," Jeraim said as he finished his task and headed for the door, leaving her alone inside the cabin.

She found it hard to sleep, and it wasn't just because of the never-ending sounds of unknown creatures outside her window. Those thoughts she refused to give words to at the dinner table kept circling in her mind. A whirlpool that repeatedly sucked her in and spit her back out.

After hours of struggling to sleep, she considered going outside and exploring the island on her own. Her instincts told her the smartest thing to do was to stay in the cabin. The last thing they needed was for her to get injured, or worse, eaten by some beast that hadn't yet earned a name. Eventually, despite the odd noises and unsettling feeling of being in bed without the weighted blanket, she drifted to sleep.

By the time she got out of bed the next morning, Jeraim had returned and had breakfast waiting for her. They quickly ate and then headed outside, where they sat on two logs facing each other. Jeraim ran through the basic rules of the trials. Some she already knew and others that threw her for a loop.

"I'm sure you understand the general rules. You go to the island, walk through the gates alone, and then enter the house that signifies the griffin to start the trial."

"Yes, I got that, though I'm not sure how I will know which house is ours."

"It will have the symbol of the griffin on the house. I'm not sure where, but it will be easily recognizable."

"Good."

"Once you enter the gate, you have forty-eight hours to enter the house," he continued. "If you do not, you fail."

"Okay, time crunch. Good to know." She nodded.

"Inside the house is where the challenge begins. Once you are there, it will be as if you never entered at all. This is a test of mental skill and emotional intelligence. The trials mess with you on a level that most find difficult to contend with."

"Once I go inside, I won't know I'm in the house?" she asked.

"Exactly. It'll feel as if you're just waking up in the morning or like you were in a weird moment and just spaced out. You'll blink and forget all about everything that happened before you stepped through the door. As far back as it takes to make you forget, you're there for a reason. It's going to be up to you to remember why you're there and what your goal is, and the trials will do everything to make you forget. At least that is the way Kerulo explained it to me."

"But you will be there to remind me, right? Isn't that the whole point of having a mentor?" she asked. "You can remind me why I'm there."

"Our communication with each other will be limited. You can reach out to me three times. I can only reach out to you once. I will use the Hasking Stone to monitor your progress, and I will only reach out to you if I truly feel you need my help, but I have to be careful about when I use it. If I reach out too soon, it will leave you to face the rest of the challenge alone."

"So limited communication, got it. I guess I also shouldn't overuse that." She paused. "If I can remember it and you are a thing."

"You'll be fine. I'm sure of it."

"How will I know I'm succeeding?" Maluai asked. "There has to be some way for me to know, right?"

"You will see the gateway." He nodded.

"Gateway?"

"Yes. Apparently, it looks different for each euman, but at the end of each challenge, should you succeed, a gateway will form. When you walk through it, you will enter the next challenge. We will see this happening with the Hasking stone. It will kind of light up to let us know your progress."

"There's so much to learn," Maluai huffed. "I thought I knew so much about this, but I don't. The text we have in Wallai, they barely scratch the surface."

"We have time. Just take it all in. You still have a few weeks before you have to go to Elderton. While we are on the island, we will focus on your mental resilience. The physical stuff doesn't matter nearly as much as that, but we will still make sure your body is strong. It helps when you're going through the trials."

"Really?"

"Kerulo told me about how much his body hurt when he left the trials. It took him weeks to recover," he said. "And even then, he said he never really felt like himself. He was an active man, but he had many ailments. I think that's why he succumbed to the poisons of the spill. His health had been deteriorating for years, and I could hear the despair in his voice when he spoke about the trials."

"Good to know. I can look forward to years of failing health." Maluai's shoulders slumped.

"There are plenty of champions who have gone through the trials and have reported none of the health concerns that my uncle had. I shouldn't have even mentioned it."

She looked down at her arms. "I'm not the strongest, but I'm not weak, either."

"We'll make you stronger," Jeraim said with confidence.

"Okay, how?"

"Meditation is up first." He stood from his log.

"What?" She frowned. "How is meditation going to strengthen me?"

"Meditation is the key to centering yourself and becoming whole. Without doing that, your body, though we can make it physically strong, will never truly connect to your greater self. That is what you need to do for this to work." He pointed to

189

the log where she sat. "That is where you will sit and meditate until you find your center."

Maluai sat on the log and closed her eyes, but realized she felt nothing. Her mind raced with wild thoughts, and then she became distracted by the sounds of the animals nearby. After less than three minutes, she opened her eyes to find Jeraim staring at her, frowning.

"You're not meditating." He pointed at her. "You're fidgeting too much."

"Possibly because I don't know how to do that," she admitted.

"You've never meditated before?" He sat back down on his own log.

"If I had, we wouldn't be having this conversation, would we?" she snipped, then caught herself. "Sorry, just a little frustrated."

"I guess I better teach you the basics. We can't move forward until you learn to quiet your mind. It will help you connect with me when you're there. With your thoughts as wild as they are now, you'll forget all about the outside world and me as soon as you cross into the trials, and you will lose."

"You're the mentor. Whatever you say, I'll do."

"First off, you need to control your breathing. It's all sporadic and uneven. I'd think you were sick if I didn't know any better."

"I've never spent this long out of the water. I'm still adjusting," she explained her condition.

"You're right." His eyes widened with a new idea, and he clapped his hands, creating a sharp echo around them. "We should take this to the water. Best you learn in your own environment before you try it on land."

He spread his wings, and she stood and did the same. The two flew from the top of the cliff to the sandy shore below.

"Okay, we'll start simple. Once you're in the water, you need to take account of your body. Push everything away and think of how you feel inside of your physical body. As you do that, you will sense your mind clearing. Allow it to do that. It may wander, but that's okay."

She walked into the water and did as he instructed. As soon as her head dipped beneath the surface, she tried to clear every errant thought from her mind. She didn't think about the strange new creatures that lived in that part of the ocean, or the way it made her feel like she was in a different world so far from home.

Maluai focused all thoughts solely on the feel of her physical being. How the water felt like a gentle caress against her skin as she entered it but slowly became as unnoticeable as the air above it. She thought about the relief her drying flesh received from the water, and how her body, which ached when she woke, found relief in the ocean.

As she floated, allowing the current to push and pull her freely, she continued to focus herself. One by one, she pushed away the thoughts that lingered. The absence of her father. The concern of her mother. The discontent of her sisters. And the euman who would guide her. Most of all, she pushed away all thoughts of the apparent consequences of their friendship.

Her efforts worked until they didn't.

All the thoughts she had managed to push away rushed back to her, and she found herself floating and calculating all the ways she could avoid the problems that seemed to have no solution.

The next four days were the same. She'd wake, and head to the ocean, dip beneath the surface, and fail. On the fifth day, it worked. She held on to it. By the ninth day, it was easy.

She cleared her mind and everything else felt like it fell away, leaving her feeling safe, free, and whole.

On the tenth day, she moved her meditation above the surface, and to both of their surprise, was successful. The translation of the process was the same from water to land. Despite the additional noises from the animals nearby, she could clear her mind and stay in deep meditation for hours at a time.

Meditation wasn't her only focus. He wanted to make sure she was strong in all areas. As soon as she mastered meditation, Jeraim was ready with custom-built training courses that mimicked the ones they left behind in Forge. Each worked to build her endurance for activities on land. The more she worked out, the more she needed to eat, and Jeraim made keeping herself fed a part of her training. Though he cooked most of the meals, Maluai foraged for fruits and caught any fish they ate. If she didn't do the work, they didn't eat.

"I told you. I'm ready!" Maluai tossed a large stone across the field. "Physically I'm strong. I can meditate for hours. What more do you need me to do to prove that I'm ready now?"

"You are doing well, but you aren't ready." Jeraim shook his head, refusing her protest of doing more work.

"Why not?" she huffed, wiping sweat from her brow. "I'm going to need another swim soon."

"You need to tap into the reason you're really doing this and try to understand why Lunai chose you for this challenge. It's about a lot more than your physical and mental strength, though they are important. Why are you here right now, Maluai? Why did you volunteer?"

"To help my eumen," she answered simply.

"That's a surface answer. Dig deeper." He sat down on the ground and watched her. "There is something deeper driving you to act. What is it?"

"I don't know what you mean." She looked offended. "I want to help the eumen of Wallai."

"On this surface, what you said is the truth. I don't doubt that you would want to help your eumen. No one wants to have to suffer a curse for one hundred years, or worse, to be the reason their eumen have to. But there's something different about what you want, something deeper. You need to connect to that reasoning before you go into the challenge."

"I mean, of course there are more things I want." She paced the ground as she thought about what he said.

"Good, what are they?" he urged her to dig deeper.

"Anything I say right now is just going to sound extremely selfish."

"Who cares? Be selfish. Why do you think anything is wrong with that?" Jeraim stood across from her, sipping a cup of water. "I'm gonna tell you right now there's not one euman who would have signed up for this who didn't have a selfish reason for doing it. Do you think the prince really wanted to risk his life? No. What he wanted was to go in there and prove himself a worthy leader.

"If he would have gone in there and won, he would be next in line for the throne of Forge. It wasn't some honorary thing he was doing. He didn't care about saving these eumen. It was a ploy to take something from his sister. The problem is, he would never have been honest with himself or anyone else about that, even though the rest of the world could clearly see it. You need to be honest with yourself about what it is you really want from this and know that any other motives do not negate the one you just said."

"You're right. I mean, I did this because I felt like I was supposed to. It was weird, but from the moment it happened, there was this urge inside of me to step up. But since it happened, and since I was chosen, I've thought about the possibilities. With everyone doubting my abilities, it was hard not to think about what it would be like to go out into the world and live my life.

"Everyone kept acting like that's the only reason I could possibly want to do anything like this. As if it's my fault my mother basically held me captive for my entire life. No, I wasn't a prisoner, but there were certain freedoms that were never given to me, even in my own home. Everyone else in Wallai is so careful and most never leave the territory for fear of the rest of the world finding out about us. But what she did to me, what my mother decided was best for my life, was so much more than that.

"I was the daughter who was different and had to be hidden away. She didn't allow me to live at all. So yeah, part of me is excited about the opportunity to live and for the ability to prove I am capable of so much more than what my mother believes. I'm not someone who needs to be hidden away, because if the world sees who I really am, they will be afraid of me."

"Is that the way you feel?" he answered in a calm voice. "Do you fear the world would be afraid of you? Do you worry that your mother was right?"

"It's what they made me believe, and I'm still struggling to reset the functions of my own brain. For the first few years of my life, I was coddled and kept away from anything that could have possibly hurt me. When I attempted to branch out on my own, my father stepped in a little more and tried to advocate for my independence, but it was too late. My mother had it in her mind that it was too dangerous for me. As much as I try, it's hard to go against something that is firmly implanted in your mind.

"It's taken me decades to feel like I could go on my own adventures, and then when I reach that point, she refused me the opportunity. For water griffins, when they are ready, are allowed to leave. They can explore designated areas of the oceans as long as they remain hidden. That is the rule. Even though most never take the opportunity, they give everyone else a chance to prove themselves. When I came of age, my mother looked me right in the eye and told me that no matter what, it would never be safe for me to leave my home."

"How did that make you feel?" he asked, encouraging her to explore her true feelings.

"It crushed me. I spent my whole life dreaming about what it would be like when the day came. I guessed they would make me take my guardian, but I'd still be able to swim free. My mother would realize I could take care of myself, and I was stronger than she gave me credit for. When the day came, and she still refused to see it, there was nothing I could do to stop myself from caving in. I stayed in my room for almost a month, contemplating running away for good. It was my father who kept me sane, and now he's gone. If my mother has her way, any glimmer of freedom, any hope I had to live my own life, will die right along with him."

"I know that must be hard for you to admit."

"You mean admitting I'm here not just for my eumen but for myself? Yeah, it's hard." She stopped pacing and sat on the ground across from him. "I feel terrible about it."

"You shouldn't, but you have to know that when you go in there, your own desires, your true motivations, are going to be a huge part of the challenge. It's going to reveal your true intentions, and it's best if you're honest with yourself about what those are before you go in."

"They think I want to run away." She sighed. "My laenu. My sisters and mother. They think all I want to do is get away from them."

"Are they right? Is that what you want?" he asked, as if they hadn't talked about what she wanted during their many meetings.

"Sometimes, yeah. Sometimes I think my life would be better if I could be on my own. I wouldn't have to worry about pointless meetings and rules. It wouldn't matter what my mother's ideas of what I'm supposed to be are, and I could stop worrying about how I'll never be good enough to do what I want. Who wouldn't think of running away?"

"And now you can do just that."

"This isn't an opportunity to run away. If anything, I'm running straight for disaster if you listen to the way they talk about it. I'm doing this because my mother wants Wallai to stand on her own. If I, the supposed weakest of the royals, can go in there and face this and come out successful, then it will prove to the goddess that we are ready for our own consideration of independence."

"You're right about that. I'm not sure there has ever been a separation of species, but I'm sure, like everyone else, you would need to be tested first."

"There's something I keep thinking about." Maluai rubbed her shoulder of the ache that formed there.

"What's that?" He watched her closely.

"What if the challenge really isn't for Forge? What if it was never about your eumen but about mine?" Maluai asked, then watched as Jeraim considered her questions.

"If that's the case then, there is far more at stake," he finally responded, his words echoed by the chirps of nearby birds.

"Why do you say that?"

"Because it means your eumen would be free. But think of the ramifications if Wallai is cursed and Forge isn't. Do you think the relationship between our eumen would get any better during the hundred years that yours are in suffering?"

"I guess not."

"Something for you to think about." He stood. "Time for dinner."

"Yeah." She followed him into the cabin where they shared yet another meal.

As always, they rarely spoke while they ate, and as soon as the meal was done and the dishes were clean, he took flight. Maluai remained in the cabin, her thoughts racing as she tried to find solutions to her unanswered questions. Unable to settle her mind, she considered her mentor. The euman who was her friend long before she chose him to guide her through the challenge.

She needed to figure out what was going on with him. He was her mentor and as much a part of the journey as she was. If he wasn't in a good state of mind, how could he help her when or if she needed him?

"What are you doing?" She landed on the ground behind the euman, who sat perched on a cliff on the opposite side of the island. The soft breath caught in her chest as he turned to her with tears streaking down his face and wiped them from his skin.

"Nothing." He wiped his face and looked away from her.

"You are crying, Jeraim. That's not nothing." She cautiously approached him. "You need to talk about this."

He paused, looking up at the two moons that hung in the sky. "You're right. I am crying."

"Okay, you admit it. That's a good first step." Maluai sat next to him on the cliff. "Is that what you've been doing every night when you go on your flight?"

"Yes." He nodded. "I fly up here and sit here watching whatever creatures I see until I fall asleep."

"Why hide it?" she asked. "Why would you feel the need to hide your tears from me? Is it something I did?"

"I'm your mentor. I'm supposed to be helping you, not making you worry about me."

"Do you think just because I don't see your tears, I don't understand you are hurting? You just lost the most important euman in your life. If anything, I would be more concerned if you weren't sad or crying. I mean, I've been concerned. I just didn't want to bring it up."

"This will not help you focus on what you need to." Jeraim looked at her, eyes still glossy from his tears. "You have way too much to be thinking about. So much on your shoulders. My sorrow, it can wait."

"Don't ever say that. What kind of friend would that make me if I told you to put your mourning on hold for me? This is what I need to be focused on. You're my mentor, which means you're a part of this. You're part of the mental connection to the physical world. I chose you, which means the goddess is going to be looking at that choice. So, I need you to be honest with me, and I need you to tell me everything. Even when you're not okay. I need to know that."

"I'm not okay, Maluai," he admitted.

"I know." She put her arm around his shoulder. "And it's okay that you aren't. Just don't hide it from me. Please."

"All I keep thinking about is when I go back home, there's nothing there. Yes, there's a city and there are eumen and there's work and all these mundane tasks, but there really isn't anything there for me. I don't have any laenu. I'm an only child. My mother was from a line of only children. My father and his brother were the first in his laenu to have a sibling, and my uncle had no kids. Two very narrow laenu trees come down to me, and I'm all alone looking out at the world, feeling like I no longer know my place in it."

"You're not alone. You're here with me." She laid her head on his shoulder. "Don't you feel me here next to you?"

"Yes, I do. And it's nice, for now, but we both know that after the challenge is done, no matter the outcome, you will return to a life that doesn't include me."

"Yes, it does. I don't care how, but we'll make it happen. You're my mentor, and right now, you're the most important euman in my life. That doesn't change just because the challenge ends, whatever the result is."

"How are you here with such mental fortitude after losing your father?" he asked her. "I'm falling apart every night, and yet you are here strong and with a clear mind."

"Honestly? I shut part of myself off to it. What I'm allowing myself to feel is not nearly as intense as it should be. I'm sad. I feel the loss, but it's like static at the back of my mind, not completely in tune. My brain knows there's this important thing I need to do, and I feel it lingering, waiting in the back of my mind and weighing down my heart. When this is over, I will just about crumble. And it's going to hurt like hell when it happens. You know, I think that's part of the reason I wanted to take this challenge. Maybe there's a little honesty I missed earlier. Doing this, facing this insurmountable thing, feels so much more doable than facing the fact that my father is gone, and I will never see him again."

"I'm sorry," Jeraim said, his voice rumbling in her ear.

"So am I, but we're going to get through this together. We'll get through the challenge, and we'll get through the mourning of our fathers. And after that, together, we'll get through whatever comes next. I don't think you and I came into each other's lives accidentally. This friendship we've formed, the bond between us, is important. I'm not giving that up."

"I think you're right." His sigh was one of relief. "It feels good to know that."

"Now, can you please come back to the cabin? You can cry there in peace and not have to worry about random creatures coming for you. I won't bother you. I just hate sleeping there alone. There's some weird stuff out there, and they make the strangest noises that night."

"Yes, I will come back." He chuckled. "To be honest, I wasn't getting the best sleep out here, anyway."

He spent the night in the cabin, and when it was time to sleep; he climbed into the bed next to her. Just as she had the night on the cliff, Maluai laid her head on his shoulder and drifted to sleep. That was the first night the noises of the creatures outside didn't keep her up. She slept peacefully.

CHAPTER 14

The next day, fully rested, Maluai started her day the same as she had since they arrived. Energized by her night of rest, she swam further away from the island than she had ever before, and her heart soared as she saw more of the ocean life. Some were familiar, and others were not.

After a race with some felusian pups, she waved the orange babies away. While they were cute to play with, they would grow into whale-like beings that could be up to twenty times her size. They swam back to their mother, who watched them from a distance. Though she couldn't speak to the other creatures in the ocean, she recognized them. Their mother once swam in Wallai when she was half the size. Maluai recognized the star-shaped scar just above her eye.

After she watched them swim away, Maluai propelled herself forward, increasing the distance between her and the island. She thought of going further but knew it would only worry Jeraim if she hadn't returned soon. Just as she shifted her course to go back to their private training grounds, Maluai saw something move above the ocean. She looked up, patiently waiting to see it again, and gasped as she recognized the shadow cast from above. It was an euman.

She couldn't help herself. The curiosity around the mysterious being drove her to swim toward the shore. Whoever it was, it would be the first euman she ever met who wasn't a griffin or mermaid. Though she was nervous about it, her excitement far outweighed the butterflies that fluttered in her stomach.

Minutes later, Maluai emerged from the water to see an euman with bright red hair walking away from the water. She quickly shifted to her vanity form, afraid any variation of her true form would scare the euman.

"Hello?" she called out nervously.

The euman stopped and scanned the area before turning to Maluai, who stood there waving like a child at a festival. Her excitement was palpable.

Maluai looked at the euman who surveyed her. Scars stretched the length of her body, which was covered in stripes. Some wounds still bled. Maluai followed the length of them to her face, which had strange spots that blended in with her flesh. Her red hair stood wild around her face, a frenzied reach to the sky.

This euman was someone who'd been through something intense. What it was she did not know, and she wasn't about to ask. She considered turning back to the water and escaping, but this was the first euman she'd ever met. If talking to just one euman freaked her out, how could she face a full challenge?

"Hende," she called out again as the euman watched her, calculating what she would do next.

"Hen... de," the euman said, curious and suspicious of her.

"I'm not here to hurt you. I just saw you from beneath the water."

"From beneath the water?" The euman looked out at the vast ocean behind her. "You were in there?"

"Yes." She looked back over her shoulder at the water, and for the first time, considered how far this conversation would go.

"You know there are Kivari sharks and Dumi whales that swim out there, right?" She lifted her thin finger and pointed to the water, a look of concern on her face.

"Yes, I know." Maluai nodded. "I saw some whales."

"And you were just swimming alongside them?" she asked, disbelief now coloring her tone.

"They're really not that dangerous if you're careful around them," Maluai explained. "You respect them, and they respect you."

"Right." The red-haired euman took a step back from her.

"Did I say something wrong? I'm sorry. You're the first euman I've met outside my home," Maluai rushed to speak. She didn't want their encounter to end so abruptly.

"Excuse me?" She paused. "Where exactly is your home?"

"I'm not really supposed to tell anyone that." Maluai frowned as she realized how difficult the conversation would be with the limited information she could share.

"If you can't tell me where you're from, then this conversation is over." She turned to walk away.

"Wait." Maluai ran forward. "Please, don't go."

"And I should stand here talking to this mysterious water euman who can't tell me anything about herself. Why?" Red hair jutted her chin out at Maluai.

"I just wanted to say hello. Are you okay? You look hurt." She pointed to the wounds on the arms and legs. "I'm not like the thing that did that to you, I promise. What happened?"

"Just got mixed up in the wrong crowd. I'm fine. I'll heal." She shrugged, an invisible wall of defense lifting around her.

"My name's Maluai." Maluai recognized the apprehension in red hair's eyes and wanted to do anything to ease the tension. "I know that's not telling you where I'm from, but maybe it's enough to make you trust me?"

"Maluai? Interesting name." She raised a brow.

"What's your name?" Maluai asked, hopeful she would share it.

Red hair looked away from Maluai as if she would run from her, but she turned back, took a deep breath, and said, "Denai. My name is Denai."

"It's nice to meet you, Denai." Maluai smiled, her heart full of joy about the new friend. "You looked troubled."

"Yeah, well…" She shrugged. "That will happen when someone puts the weight of the world on your shoulders."

"You too?" The dry laugh slipped through Maluai's lips.

"What do you mean?" Denai again raised her brow, and Maluai noted the expression.

"The Goddess challenged my species to the trials, and guess who volunteered and was chosen?" Maluai raised her hand.

"Seriously?"

"Yep, so you see, whatever you're going through, it can't be as bad as that. Right?" Maluai sighed and felt the tension in her shoulders melt away as the cool breeze blew past her.

"Wrong." The euman laughed dryly. "I can't believe I'm actually meeting someone else who has to do this stupid challenge."

"Wait. You too?" Maluai gawked at the euman. "No way."

"Yes. I was chosen too, but my eumen, they don't want it to be me," Denai said, her voice breaking with unexpressed emotion.

"My mother was against it, too," Maluai tried to relate. "She doesn't think I'm fit for this."

"No, I mean, I'm different from the rest of my laenu," Denai explained. "The eumen in my home. They are lynas."

"Lynas? You don't look like any lyna I've ever seen." Maluai scratched her chin. "Of course, I've only seen pictures drawn in underwater books, so my knowledge could be skewed."

"That's because I'm not one. I'm a chimera." Denai dropped her shoulders and looked up at the sky, her wild hair blowing around her face in the wind. "And that's exactly why they don't want it to be me. They don't think I'm good enough to represent them. Here I am, putting my life on the line for a bunch of eumen who would rather I not even be a part of them. How messed up is that?"

"Damn. Come to think of it, I think you have it worse."

"Ha, well, thanks for the validation, I suppose." Denai chuckled. "I just never thought it would be like this."

"Why do you want to do it?" Maluai asked the question, even though she found it difficult to answer.

"Honestly, I'm still battling with that question."

"I'll tell you something my mentor shared with me," Maluai sighed. "Whatever it is, even if it's a selfish reason, you need to come to terms with it before you go in there. I thought my reasonings were bad because they weren't totally without selfish motivations, but it turns out, that's a part of the reason she chose us. The goddess knows you better than you know yourself. You better start being honest with yourself before you head in there, or you're going to have a hard time coming out."

"You look like you're a lot more ready for this than I am." Denai gave a weak smile. "I'm sure you'll be successful."

"Thanks for the vote of confidence, but looks can be deceiving." Maluai shrugged. "I'm going in there, and I will do my best. That's all I can do, right?"

"What are you?" Denai blurted out the question.

"What?" Maluai acted confused, but she knew it was coming.

"I've met mermaids before. They aren't like you. And I don't see a boat out there. So, whatever you are, you can swim great distances alongside sharks without being hurt."

"Promise not to tell anyone?" Maluai asked. She wanted to tell someone, anyone, but she had to be safe about it.

"I'm a chimera outcast with no one to call a friend. Who the hell am I going to tell?"

"I guess that's true. Well..." Maluai chewed her lip. "I'm a water griffin."

"A water what?" Denai's eyes widened.

"Well, you know the griffins, right?"

"Big egotistical things that fly around thinking they own the world?" Denai shrugged. "Yeah, I think I've heard of them."

"You can think of us as their underwater cousins. Only less egotistical. They developed before us, and we've basically been living in a hidden world underneath Forge."

"Get the hell out of here!" Denai shouted.

"I'm sorry?" Maluai took a half step back.

"No, I mean." She laughed. "That's just too unbelievable."

"Well, it's true. And as far as I know, you're the first euman, outside of land griffins and mermaids, to know about us." She turned to look at the sea. "And if I win the challenge, you won't be the last."

"Well damn. I feel strangely satisfied. I wish I could rub it in the lyna's faces, but I won't. Your secret is safe with me."

"Want to know something else?" Maluai glanced back at Denai.

"Now you're just free with the information?"

"Honestly, it's kind of thrilling to tell someone." Maluai smiled. "You don't know how hard it is to keep your entire identity hidden."

"Okay, lay it on me." Denai took a deep breath, as if it would ease the blow of whatever Maluai said next.

"I'm a princess," she announced in a whisper.

"I'm sorry, you're a what?" Denai's eyes widened. "Did you just say princess?"

"Yep. Princess Maluai of Wallai." She did the water salute, right hand over chest up to the sky and wave downward.

"What was that?" Denai frowned. "Did you just put a curse on me or something?"

"No, nothing like that." Maluai laughed. "It's our salute. It represents the heart of their eumen, their goddess, and the connection to one."

Denai gave an uncertain grin as she performed the gesture in return.

"Perfect." Maluai looked back at the water. "I really should get back. I've been away a lot longer than I usually am, and I don't want my mentor to worry."

"Oh, right. Okay. Well, it was nice to meet you, Maluai."

"You as well." Maluai turned to the water, then paused. "Denai?"

"Yeah?"

"You know when this is all over. If you want, you can call me a friend."

"Friends with a princess?" Denai bit her lower lip as she furrowed her brow in contemplation.

"Friends with a chimera?" She smiled.

"You got me there. See you around, water griffin." Denai laughed as she walked off. "I still can't believe that's a thing."

Maluai left her unexpected encounter with Denai and headed back to the island. She couldn't help how elated the meeting made her feel. Her entire life, she feared she would never meet another euman above the surface. With the opportunity to leave home, her laenu feared she'd leave them behind in favor of the allure of adventure. If they had their way, she would enter the challenge, win, and return to Wallai without ever seeing the beauty of the world beyond. She hadn't even made it to the island and the challenge yet, but she had already found a new companion. Someone who would experience the same things she would.

She hoped they were both successful and could meet up after their challenges were done. Denai seemed like an exciting character, and she wanted the opportunity to get to know her without the threat of a curse on their necks.

"I was beginning to think you wouldn't come back." Jeraim sat on the shore when she emerged from the water.

"Sorry. I swam further than I thought I would," Maluai said as her form completed its shift.

"Did you have a good swim?" he asked, peering into the sky at a flock of birds that flew above the water.

"Yes. I swam with some felusian whale pups. Haven't seen a school of them in a while." She paused, considering if she should keep the rest of her adventure to herself, but decided against it. "I also met someone."

"What do you mean, you met someone?" He squinted at her, examining her face. "Someone in the water? Are you okay?"

"Yes. I'm fine. It was a female chimera. Interestingly enough, she's also going into the challenge. I didn't think it would happen so frequently. Is it typical for there to be multiple trials at the same time?"

"There are a lot of species on this planet which leaves a lot of eumen to bend the rules and turn their backs on the ideals of Lunai. When you take that into consideration, it makes sense that it wouldn't be uncommon. I imagine they're always happening."

"Wouldn't we know if they were?" she asked. "Isn't Elderton monitored for this?"

"It used to be. Not anymore, really. No one goes there unless they are being challenged. The only times it's reported to the high council is when a species fails. So technically speaking, they could do the challenge, be successful, and never report it. I imagine most wouldn't want to report it. It means they were doing something they weren't supposed to be doing."

"You're right. Probably a secret they would fight to keep." Maluai pulled back her locs, securing them in a low bun. "Why haven't the griffins had any other challenges? Or have they kept it a secret? I mean, it has been years of things shifting for the

Griffins. The problems we're facing, they aren't brand new, so why is it that now, after all this time, we're finally being challenged?"

"That's a question I can't answer for you. The only one who could answer that is Lunai, and I don't think that she's up for an interview right now." He chuckled.

"Yeah, I guess I just have more questions than answers, but that's not really that uncommon, is it?"

"In life, there are always more questions than answers." He winked at her. "We should feel grateful for the answers that come our way and understand that not all questions can be answered."

"Wow. That was profound. You're really sounding like a mentor, you know that?" She tapped his shoulder. "You're settling into this role well."

"That's good. Maybe that means we'll both actually make it through this alive." He took a deep breath. "Maybe then we can relax."

"Is it really possible for me to die in there?" The question had been lingering in the back of Maluai's mind. "I mean, I know everyone talks about how dangerous this is and the possibilities, but has anyone actually gone into a challenge and not made it back out?"

"Yes," he answered plainly and paused while the word sank in for her before continuing. "It is possible for you to go in and not come back out. And we don't really know what happens to the eumen who don't come back out. No explanation is given, but death is the assumption, because what other reasoning could we possibly give to it? All we know is that anyone who doesn't make it back out fails. Their eumen suffer, and they're given no answers as to why."

"Alright." She clapped her hands, creating a sharp sound. "So, whatever I do, I must make sure I come back out."

"There's something else you have to do before you go in. I know our time here on the island is ending, and you've made significant progress. I'm so proud of you," he said in a moment of warmth that made her stomach tighten.

"What is it?" She held her breath, afraid it would be something terrible.

"Nothing terrible. You can relax." He laughed and pointed to the right side of her face. "Funny how your eye twitches a little when you're worried."

"It does?" She placed her hand on her eye. If it was a normal thing for her, no one had ever pointed it out before.

"Yes." He shook his head. "But the thing you need to do is tradition. It's not mandatory, but it is expected. Each challenger, before entering Elderton, writes a letter to a loved one before they go in. It's a way of leaving a bit of them behind and showing their state of mind. For most, it's a comfort knowing their loved one went in, secure in their decision to compete. It can be an uncomfortable thing to write to someone as if you're not coming back, but for those who don't come back, their letters often give their loved ones some sense of peace."

"And it would be bad if I didn't do this, right?" She chewed her lip.

"I wouldn't say bad. I'm aware of your tendency to challenge traditional ways of thinking, but this is something that's not just for the eumen you leave that letter for. It's for you as well. Take this time, this opportunity, to say all the things you weren't able to say before. And again, I know it will be hard, but you and I have talked about some difficult things while on this island. And now is an opportunity for you to express those things to the ones who may need to hear it most."

"Can I just write you a letter and call it a day?" she asked with a hopeful expression on her face.

"Would you say I'm a loved one?" He raised a brow.

"I... I mean. I mean, I care about you, yeah," she stumbled over her words.

He laughed at her. "You may be ready for this challenge, but you need to practice hiding your emotions better. I'm joking with you."

"Oh." She relaxed her shoulders.

"And though you may want to write me a letter, anything you need to say to me you can say freely, but you can't say that to say your mother or your sisters or whoever else you left behind in your world. Use this time to speak to them, and if you have something you want to say to me, well, I'm all ears."

"How will I get it to them?" she asked. "After I write the letter."

"There are a couple of options. The first is you use the messenger bird." He turned and pointed to the statue of the angry-looking bird with a bag hanging around his neck.

"What the hell is that, and when did it get here?" She frowned, having not seen it before. "I know this has been a stressful time, but I'm sure I would have remembered seeing that thing here."

"It's the Umital bird. It's like a delivery system, and it appears whenever you need it." He shrugged. "I often forget you're not that familiar with the ways of this world."

"No, I'm not." She tiptoed closer to the statue. "And this thing is going to take the letter to whoever I wanted to go to. It will just know?"

"Yes, that's how it works." He nodded.

"It looks so angry." She frowned. "And what's the other way to get the letter to them?"

"We take it there ourselves." He shrugged, as if the answer should have been obvious. "You hand it over, and then you fly away off to your challenge."

"So go back and face my laenu, who hardly believes I can do this?" She stood and shrugged. "Creepy bird statue thing it is."

"I thought you might say that." He laughed, handing her a pen and paper. "Take your time. Figure out what you want your message to be before you write it down. Be honest with yourself and whoever this letter is for. Keep in mind that although we know you will survive this, you may not come back. Think about what you would like to say to that euman in your last words if this was the last time they ever heard from you."

"Nothing somber about that." Maluai took the pen and paper and entered the cabin alone.

She sat on the bed they'd shared the night before and thought about who she wanted to write a letter to. It would be easy to write a letter to her guardian. She could talk about how much they shared in the years since they assigned Seru to look over her and how thankful she was to her for being there to support her decision, but that wasn't something that needed to be said, and she'd already thanked her more times than she could count.

She thought about her mother, the hardest letter she would have to write if she chose to. There were so many things she wanted to say to the queen, so many things that didn't feel right to say through pen and paper. She felt the pen tremble in her hand, and she was struck with an ache in her heart, knowing if she wrote the words, she wouldn't return home. After everything she'd gone through, she wanted to look her mother in the eye and tell her exactly how she felt.

Then she thought of someone else, someone who had the optimism she'd lost over the years. Someone who looked at the world like it was full of amazing and limitless possibilities. And finally, she put pen to paper, and she wrote a letter, one that would keep all her secrets, things that she might never tell the younger girl.

When she exited the cabin, Jeraim sat on the ground in a meditative state. She thought about leaving him to complete the peaceful stance, but when she turned to walk away, his eyes opened.

"Aare you ready to send it?" He looked up at her. "Did you write everything you needed to say?"

"No." She shook her head.

"Do you need more time?" His brow furrowed. "I've heard this can be a difficult thing to do."

"No. I mean, I wrote the letter." She pointed to the statue of the messenger bird. "I don't want to use that weird bird thing. I think I need to go back to Forge and see my mother. It's going to be hard, I know, but I need to place this letter in her hand myself."

"Is a letter for your mother?" He stood from his crossed-legged position on the ground.

"No, I thought I would write it for her, but then I realized the words I wanted to say to her needed to be done face to face, not through a letter. I need to see her face when I tell her what weighs on my heart."

"I understand." He looked at the letter she clutched in her hand. "So, who is it for?"

"The letter is for my sister. I hope I can come back and talk to her about everything in this letter. When I thought about how I may never have the chance to do so, it left me feeling like she was the only euman I was unable to connect with on that level. In my life, I make it a point to tell the eumen in my life just how much they matter to me. But my little sister, we have had little time together." Her voice broke. "If I can't come back, there are things I need to say to her. This letter will never cover it all, but it's something. It's a piece of me, for her to keep always."

"That's very touching, Maluai." Jeraim's voice was a hug his arms did not provide.

"Thanks. It just felt like the right thing to do."

"Alright, looks like we're headed back to Forge." Jeraim spread his wings. "You ready to go?"

Maluai unfolded her wings from her back. "Lead the way, oh mentor."

CHAPTER 15

To the feeling of flying over land. Instead of mimicking Jeraim's path along the air currents, she let intuition guide her while she thought of what she would say to her mother when she finally saw her.

There were so many things she could talk about. All the things she had kept to herself, wishing she had the courage to express them, but this wasn't the time to dump all her trauma onto her mother's lap. She had to be certain of her words before she opened her mouth.

They landed on the island, and Maluai's stomach dropped to see her mother standing and waiting by the shore. Of course, they alerted her to the moment the guards saw the two enter their airspace. She imagined her mother left their underwater city before they could even finish their report.

"Maluai." The queen approached her daughter with gentle eyes but an urgent voice.

"Mother." Maluai embraced her mother.

"Are you okay?" Valuai looked over her daughter, examining her for even the slightest scratch. "We were worried you'd rushed into the challenge, but the Hasking stone never activated."

"Yes, I am," she reassured her. "Nothing bad happened. I'm fine."

"Where did you go?" she asked. "I was so worried. I thought you went to Elderton already."

"Jeraim took me somewhere where we could train without distractions."

"Did that work for you?" she asked, glancing at her mentor, who stood off to the side, giving them privacy to speak. "Was it worth it?"

"It did, and it was. I feel ready for what I have to do now." Maluai looked around them. "I need to talk to you alone."

"Okay." Valuai took a deep breath. "Whatever you need to say, I'm here to listen."

Maluai looked at all the members of the Forge guards who were watching them. This wasn't the place to tell her mother what she needed to say. "In Wallai, please."

"Of course." The queen nodded to her own guards, and they led the way back to the sea.

They shifted from their vanity forms back into their phase forms, calling their tails to show as they dove into the water. The guards doggedly trailed them until they reached the point that they were out of harm's way. The queen followed her daughter, not to their home, not into the populated areas, but to the edge of their territory near the barrier of magic that kept their world hidden.

Maluai swam with her thoughts still spinning as she focused on the message she wanted to give to her mother. She refused to let this conversation turn into a way to tear her mother apart. This wasn't something that was supposed to break their relationship, but hopefully put them on a path to creating one that was healthy for the both of them. She thought of how she would do it, where she would do it, and on the flight from the island back to Forge, she realized the only way to do it was to take her to a place she'd only been to with someone she'd never be able to go there with again.

They swam to the edge of the underwater cliff; the sun glinting off the water and casting a sparkle on the ocean floor. This was a place she shared with her father. He'd take her to take in the water's grandeur, helping her appreciate what lay beyond the boundaries of their home. From there, they could see the Kivari sharks swimming together. It was currently their mating time, and they did a dance that looked both magical and terrifying all at the same time. It wasn't one she was unfamiliar with. Maluai enjoyed watching the sharks in their most chaotic time, when they were both on the greatest guard and yet so vulnerable.

"Why have we come here?" The queen turned to her daughter after watching the sharks in the distance.

"This is where father and I would go whenever I would get so frustrated that my words felt too big to express and my emotions too confusing to understand. This was the place I shared with him and no one else, even though I'm sure the guards knew we were here. I know Seru knew, but when we were here, it was just the two of us. In this space, I could say everything I needed to say without judgment, and I guess part of me is hoping you will give me that same grace he did." She looked around the secret location she shared with her father and over to the little cavern where she once napped on his lap while they waited for the migrating sharks to pass.

"Your father, he brought you here?" Valuai's lips curved into a fleeting smile.

"He did." Maluai nodded. "Getting away from it all helped me clear my mind."

"What is it you need to say?" Her mother looked her in the eye, open to whatever Maluai needed to express to her.

"I was told I had to write a letter to a loved one, something to leave behind. An example of my frame of mind, but I didn't want to do that. Not with you, because what I have to say feels bigger than what a letter can do. I want to go into this knowing I looked you in the eye, and I told you my truth, not thinking of you reading it on the paper and wondering whether your response to it would be."

"I understand." Valuai took a deep breath and sighed. "I'm listening."

"My entire life, you've told me to hide myself from the world. You stopped me from any form of exploration, even within the limits of our own home. Everything I've ever wanted for myself

I had to go without because of your fears. And I don't know if this is what you intended, but over time, your fears became my own. There are great things I feel so incapable of facing now, and no matter how much I tell myself that it isn't my problem, that it's yours, I know the truth.

"You look at me as if I just want to run away, but I'm just trying to not feel afraid. I look at everyone around me, and I see their courage, and I envy their freedom to explore what that means. Because I never had that freedom. And for a long time, I told myself that one day I'd look you in the eye and tell you it's all your fault. The way I fear living. Then I would run away forever, but when the opportunity came, I didn't take it. And I know you think the opportunity is new, but I've had the means for years to leave home, and I haven't. I don't blame you for the way I feel. Maybe you started it. Maybe you're with the root of those feelings, but I've had well over thirty years to come to terms with my feelings, and I haven't done that."

"Maluai." Her mother choked on unshed tears. "I'm so sorry."

"I don't want you to apologize. I just want you to listen." Maluai took another deep breath to calm her edging nerves before she continued. "You tell us, me and my sisters, about how we're supposed to lead, how we're supposed to rule, and how we're supposed to move forward without fear. You want Wallai to become independent in this world away from Forge and the protection it gives us. Your plan is for us to step outside and proudly tell the world who we are.

"When you look at me, you seem to want me to disappear into the shadows of our laenu out of fear that I won't be able to make it in this world on my own. The thing that kept me from blossoming all these years was your fear. I'm done being afraid, Mother. I'm going into this challenge with a clear head and a clear heart. Before I do, I want you to know I forgive you, and I understand why you did what you did, but when I come home, I will not live my life hidden away because you're afraid the world won't accept me."

"I never wanted it to be that way. When you were born, you were just so small and different from anyone else we've ever seen before. The healers didn't know what to think of it, and they told me you were going to die. I had to look at you and hold you in my arms and fear that I could not keep you. And no matter how big you grew, no matter how strong you got, I could not get those words out of my mind. They told me you would not live past a week and yet here you are thirty-five years later. And I guess over the years I told myself the only reason you're still here is because I've held you so close to my heart.

"It wasn't easy, Maluai, knowing you weren't like everyone else. You never shifted. Years after you should have shown your true form, you were still in your vanity form. I thought you were broken, but then it happened, and there was a new fear. It was hard enough thinking you would be sickly. I couldn't imagine other Wallains not accepting you because of how you looked when you were in your true form."

"I understand that, but you can't hold on to me so tightly anymore. It's time for you to let go." Malua looked out at the sharks' mating scene. "All this time it's been father allowing me just enough. Just enough freedom, just enough adventure, just enough life to keep me here. I don't want to leave my home forever. I love Wallai and all the magical things that exist within it, but I will not become its prisoner again."

"I'm sorry it ever felt like one."

"I will go into this challenge, and I will prove that we are ready to stand on our own, and when I come home successful, I expect things to be different. You will treat me as if I'm capable because I am. You will allow me the same freedoms allowed to my sisters. I cannot go back to life as it was."

"Maluai, I still can't believe you're doing this, but I get it now." Her mother reached out to her, and Maluai clutched her hand. "I always knew this day would come. You would stand up and tell me to back off. Honestly, I thought it would be sooner."

"I didn't want to hurt you." Maluai dropped her eyes, then handed the letter to her mother. "This is my letter."

"I thought you said you weren't writing one."

"It's not for you. It's for Naluai." She smiled. "There's so much of me she doesn't know yet. I wanted to make sure she had some part of me to keep close to her heart. Please make sure she gets it?"

"I will." Her mother held the letter to her chest as if it were a priceless treasure.

Maluai turned to swim away but stopped when her mother spoke.

"Are you not going to go home and speak to them before you leave?" Valuai spoke of her other daughters, who she made stay in Wallai after Maluai left.

"No, I think one goodbye is enough." Maluai looked back at her mother, her heart lighter than it was when she arrived. "Just make sure she gets the letter and tell them both I love them, and I will be back."

Maluai left her mother alone on the cliff and swam to the surface. Though they hadn't discussed it before she left him, she knew exactly where she would find her mentor. This time, instead of climbing up the cliff, she flew to the top and found him sitting perched on the edge waiting for her.

"How did it go?" he asked as she landed on the ground next to him, drips of water falling from her wings onto his face.

"Better than I thought it would." Maluai smiled. "She listened. For the first time in possibly my entire life, my mother didn't debate me or tell me I was wrong or try to defend her actions. She listened to me."

"Did you think she wouldn't?" Jeraim's eyes widened in confusion as he asked his question. "Considering what you're facing now, I'd think anyone would listen to you without debate."

"You know, I realized my concern with having that conversation was because I'd never tried to before. Yeah, I had fits whenever she would tell me no, but not once did I ever attempt to talk to her about how I felt. My mom's presence had always seemed like an unbreakable wall between me and what I wanted. I thought she just would push me in a corner and tell me to shut up if I ever fought back." Maluai's shoulders relaxed as she looked up at Jeraim. "She's not an impenetrable force. She's just a mother afraid for a daughter she thought she would lose just days after giving birth. And now, after my father's death, it just makes all that more alarming for her."

"I'm glad you two got to speak." He touched her shoulder. "Looks like you knew exactly what you needed. That's a good sign. You connected with your inner self, found what you needed, and made it happen. Do that when you're in the trials, and you'll have no problem making it out successfully."

"Thanks for that vote of confidence." Maluai smiled, her cheeks flushing as the tension of the pause hung in the air. "I have something I want to say to you as well."

"You know you can tell me anything," he reassured her.

"It's about something I said to my mother. When I come back, I'm coming out of the shadows and into the light. I refuse to live my life hidden away from the world. I want to do all the things I've ever dreamed of knowing I have a home to come back to."

"That sounds like a good plan." He nodded. "Why did you hesitate to tell me? Did you think I would disagree?"

"I want you to go with me, Jeraim," she admitted quickly.

"What?" He swallowed. "You want me to go with you?"

"When I come back here successful, as a champion among the normal eumen." She laughed at the thought of showing off her success.

"I want you by my side. I want you to travel the world with me and show me all the things I have no way of knowing. Like those magical messenger birds. You're the only one, besides Seru, who I would trust to be by my side."

"Well, who am I to deny the wishes of a princess?" He lowered his head.

"I don't want you to do it because I'm a princess. I want you to do it because you want to be there with me. If you don't, I get it, and I will not force the issue. But this isn't an order from a princess, it's an invitation from a friend who cares about you and wants you in her life."

"And this is a friend accepting that invitation. There's nothing else I'd rather do." He looked at her, and that intense pause returned. There was more there, behind his eyes. More he wasn't saying to her. "Just make sure you come back alive."

CHAPTER 16

B efore leaving Forge again, Jeraim and Maluai agreed to take the long way to Elderton. They could have taken the aeroways, a connection of tubing constructed with the currents of air. It used the natural flow of the air to allow for quick traveling across Eldridge and was typically used by those who were without their own wings or had to travel long distances.

They controlled the currents with a combination of science and magic, but the aeroways could still shift if not properly maintained. Riders simply had to walk into the designated points on the ground, and it would lift them up to the cross-webbing that above the ground. While it sounded like an exciting method of travel, Maluai knew if she took that route, it would mean missing out on seeing more of their world.

She promised herself she would remain optimistic about her chances in the trials, but there was a chance she wouldn't survive. She would see as much of Eldridge as she could before then.

"We still have five days until you have to be on Elderton. Plenty of time to explore," Jeraim agreed with her decision, and his wings spread from his back.

"Thank you." She spread her own wings, and the two took flight again.

On their second flight, she dipped beneath the water, rehydrating her flesh once more before their path took them across the expanse of land. This would be the first time she would fly so far away from the water, but Jeraim assured her this was the best path, and he would keep them close to a source of water should she need it.

Two days later, as they flew across the grassy plains, Maluai's thoughts were full of all the things they'd seen. Jeraim kept her away from any other civilizations, but she saw new life. From the rolling landscapes full of flora and fauna, to unidentified creatures like the delpina cat, a small but ferocious feline that lived in the mountains outside Syndelia, home to the lynas. They were deceptively adorable and vain. Jeraim explained that while they loved the attention eumen gave to them because of their enormous green eyes and plump bodies, they turned feral if anyone got too close to them. He warned her not to risk getting too close as their claws were deadly. One scratch would introduce a poison into the bloodstream that would race to the heart and end their victim's life.

They flew over Ravenfalls, a city Jeraim described as a melting pot of Eldritch. Species of all kinds lived within the city, enjoying some of the most advanced technology and boasting the best spots for parties and cultural exploration. And of course, he refused her when she asked to stop there.

"When you're done with the trials, I promise to take you," he called out to her over the air as his massive wings pushed against the current.

"Promise?" she called out to him.

"First stop on the world tour!" He laughed, and they powered forward.

Jeraim was right. Maluai didn't need any other distraction, and if she stopped in a place like Ravenfalls, she wouldn't want to leave.

A few hours after they passed the city, with the sun beating down on her back, Maluai spotted a shadow moving across the ground at speeds she couldn't fathom. A closer look revealed this was no shadow but an euman. One with thick wavy indigo hair that trailed behind her body. Realizing this was a chance to meet someone new without the distractions of the big city, Maluai flew closer to the ground.

Curiosity grew louder than common sense, which screamed at her to reconsider the action. Nothing about the rushing form below her said they were approachable. In fact, had Maluai taken the time to access the situation fully, she would have flown in the opposite direction. Something had to be after the euman for her to move the way she did.

Although they had intended to fly to Elderton without speaking to anyone, she couldn't ignore the urge to connect.

She circled above the euman three times, ignoring the calls of Jeraim before she dove from the sky and dropped onto the ground in front of the stranger who skid to a halt. She planned to introduce herself as she did with Denai and potentially make a new friend in the world she knew nothing about, but her naivety almost cost her her head.

Before she could say anything, before her wings fully retracted into her back, she stumbled back as what once was a small feminine form exploded into a serpent three times her size. The dark blue sari and silk pants dissolved, replaced with metallic blue scales that glinted in the light, ending in bright yellow eyes that shone like beacons as they locked onto Maluai.

Instinct drove her response. For the first time since she was a child, Maluai's body exploded into her true form. Ink-black wings replaced the ones that appeared in her phase form. Blue-tipped feathers stretched the length of them, and talons marked the end of each wing that emerged from her back. She flew backward, landing on all fours, and responded to the serpent's hiss with a thunderous roar.

The two beings, both just modest eumen before, had transformed into powerful creatures, poised for the strike. Just as the serpent pulled back to launch its attack, Jeraim landed on the ground between them, hands outstretched at both of the massive creatures.

"Stop!" His voice was hesitant as he spoke, and she noticed the fear in his eye when he looked at her. Fear flickered across his face before quickly turning to confusion as he slowly turned his back to face the serpent. "We are not here to harm you. Please. Calm yourself."

The serpent hissed once more, eyes darting between the two as she considered the threat. While Jeraim seemed confident he could convince the stranger to return to her more docile form, Maluai refused. She lifted her tail, venom drawn to the sharp tip and ready to pierce the serpent should she try anything.

"Maluai." Jeraim glanced over his shoulder at her, his brow slightly furrowed. "I think you're going to have to make the first move."

Maluai roared again, refusing his request, sure that it was a trap.

"We outnumber her. We need to let her know she can trust us," he said, reasoning with his mentee. "Trust me, please."

Maluai shook her head before looking into Jeraim's eyes. He silently begged for her understanding, and she felt a sense of uncertainty in her heart. When she looked back at the serpent, she cleared her mind of her own fear and finally assessed the situation. Though her presence was menacing, her appearance was an answer to what must have felt like a surprise attack.

Maluai had to trust Jeraim. If she didn't let him guide her in that difficult moment, how would she do it during the trials? She had to rely on him, even if it felt uncomfortable.

If this goes bad, it's on his head, she thought before she breathed through the shift, pulling back her true form to reveal the vanity form.

"Fine," she huffed and pointed at the serpent. "Your turn."

The serpent hesitated a moment longer, and its eyes darted between the two strangers that stood waiting for its choice. Then it shifted. The large body returned to the compact form Maluai originally saw running across the field.

"What are you?" Her voice grew tight with suspicion as she asked the question.

"I'm a griffin," Jeraim said calmly.

"And her?" She pointed to Maluai, her eyes squinting against the light of the sun. "What is she? I can tell she is different."

"I'm a water griffin," Maluai answered for herself.

"A water griffin?" She frowned, suspicious of the answer. "Why are you here? What do you want?"

"We're on our way to Elderton." Jeraim calmly lowered his arms to his sides as he spoke.

"Elderton?" She took a step away from them. "Why? Why are you going there?"

"For the trials," Jeraim answered again, this time glancing at Maluai.

"I'm the challenger for our eumen," Maluai offered.

"Oh."

"Are you okay?" Jeraim asked.

"Yes, I'm just in a hurry." She glanced at a point in the distance where an aeroway base stood.

"Where are you going?" Maluai asked as her eyes followed the tube that lifted into the air. "Somewhere you need to get in a rush."

"To Elderton, actually," she answered her.

"Oh." Maluai brightened. "You're a challenger? What are the odds I would meet another one?"

"Another one?"

"I met another a while ago. She was on her way there as well." Maluai dropped her shoulders. "Seems like the goddess is being generous with the challenges."

"I suspect if eumen were doing right, she wouldn't be," the stranger said. "I can't say it surprised me when our eumen were challenged."

"Yeah. Me neither." Maluai nodded.

"Something is really wrong in our world if this is happening so frequently." Jeraim stepped closer to Maluai, giving the euman more space.

"What are you?" Maluai asked. "We told you what we are."

"She's a naga," Jeraim offered.

"Yes, I am." She nodded, her dark hair moving around her face like a wave of ink. It reminded her of the spill in her home, and her heart ached with thoughts of what it had caused. "Look, I would love to stay here and swap stories about our lives, but I have to get out of here."

"Wait, what's your name?" Maluai asked as the naga headed off toward the aeroway.

"Why?" She looked back at Maluai, confused by her question.

"I mean, maybe when this is all over, we can be friends."

"I don't really see the point in that."

"Oh, okay." Maluai tried to hide her disappointment, but it was written all over her face. "I hope you survive."

"Thanks." She continued running, then skidded to a halt. "I hope you make it out, too. And my name is Nagini."

As Nagini ran to the aeroway, the thunderous noise of the powerful tunnel reverberated as it lifted her from the ground. Maluai desperately hoped the fleeing woman would hear her as her voice echoed through the air, screaming out her own name.

Maluai kept her eyes on the aeroway longer than what felt natural to her because she didn't want to face Jeraim. She knew she would see that look in his eye again. That look of confusion edging on fear. For the first time since they met, he'd seen her exactly as she was. He was the first euman to see her true form since her parents told her to lock that side of her away. The way he looked at her made her think they were right to tell her that.

"Maluai, how long are you going to avoid me?" He finally spoke from behind her, his voice gentle, yet she could hear the nervousness.

"As long as it takes for you to forget what you saw and stop looking at me like that," she said, back still to him. "Do you think you can do that?"

"Please," he started, but she was too afraid to hear what he had to say.

"Jeraim, I'm sorry." She watched the wind tunnel ahead of her.

"Why are you apologizing?" he asked, and she could hear his steps as he moved closer to her.

"Because suddenly I feel like I tricked you," she admitted.

"Tricked me?" he asked. "Why are you saying that?"

"My griffin is different from anything you've seen before, right?" she asked.

"Well, yes." He paused. "Your face and tail are different, so are your wings. You're—"

"I'm a freak. I know," she cut him off.

"No, you're just different. Unique." He placed his hand on her shoulder. "It was just surprising to see. I mean, do you know why you're different?"

"If I knew the answer, I would tell you, but I have no clue." She sighed and thought of the warmth of his hand on her shoulder before she pulled away from him. "I've always been this way. It's why, in all my life, they never allowed me to show anyone my true form. My parents were worried eumen would look at me the way you just looked at me. And they would have questions I have no answers for. When eumen find a mystery, they want to dissect it. They would do the same with me."

"I understand." His voice was low and kind, but he spoke with hesitancy.

Maluai took a deep breath before she turned to him. When she looked into his eyes, she hoped to find the same warmth and acceptance that had always been there. She hoped he would remain the same euman she had grown close to over the last year, but when their eyes met, it crushed her heart.

"Don't look at me like that." She looked away from him. "Don't look at me like I'm different."

"I'm just surprised, is all," he tried to explain. "I'm trying to process this."

"You're trying to process it because you don't see me the same way anymore." She shook her head. "Suddenly, I'm not your friend, but a puzzle you have to figure out."

"That's not true." Jeraim reached out to her, but she pulled back. "Can you just give me a moment to process this?"

"Take all the time you need. We should really get going. Time is running out." She looked away from him.

"Maluai," Jeraim pleaded. "Please, talk to me. I get that this is a difficult thing for you, but maybe if we talk about it, we can both benefit from it."

"Look, maybe we should take the aeroways. Cut this short. I'm drying out, anyway."

"We don't have to do this." He looked around them. "We can still take our time. You said you wanted to see more of the world before you began the trials."

"No, I think it's for the best," Maluai reasoned. "I'll have plenty of time to explore when I make it out."

With a sigh of resignation, he said, "Okay. Whatever you say."

"How does this work?" Maluai stood in front of the platform that connected to the aeroways.

The vertical shaft of air spun with energy, creating a distinct buzzing sound as it shot up into the air. Its grandeur was breathtaking, but also somewhat intimidating.

"There are two ways to access the aeroways. The first is through the inner knowing that comes with tapping into the primordial magic that created them. In simple terms, you think of where you want to go, picture it in your mind, and the aeroways take you there."

"And if you can't do that?"

"That's when the second option comes into play." Jeraim pointed to the side of the platform where a small console stood. "You dial in the coordinates of the location you want to go. Once inside, a pod of air will form around us and navigate the way to the island."

"Then it just spits us out on the other side?"

"Yes." A soft chuckle escaped his lips. "It's not as intense as that."

"How many of these are around the world?"

"Hundreds, maybe more." He shrugged.

"That many?" She looked up the length of the shaft. "That's a lot."

"Well, they're accessible to everyone, and with more areas developing, they're being used more often. The phoenixes installed the consoles for those who weren't able to connect to the magic of the tunnels."

"That was nice of them."

"Yes, it was." He touched her shoulder and frowned when she pulled away. "Let's go. Just stick close to me inside the shafts. I'll make sure we get where we need to."

He stepped in first, and she followed, feeling the cool air of the shaft on her skin. Jeraim pulled her close to him, wrapping his arm around her waist and holding her so tightly she couldn't pull away. She told herself it was because they needed to stay close like he said, but the gentle pressure of his hand on her waist and the electricity of his gaze as he looked into her eyes said there was something more behind the hold.

A moment later, after a deep breath filled her chest, they lifted from the ground and shot through the tunnels. Gone were the thoughts of the crack in their relationship. Maluai watched the lands rush beneath them. It was difficult to decipher the changes between the landscapes. Soon, the rush of trees turned into mountains, then into vast plains, ending at the water's edge. Before she knew it, they were landing just beyond the entrance to Elderton.

"That was amazing," Maluai spoke, her words punctuated by jagged breaths. "Almost better than flying. If only it didn't move so fast."

"Definitely faster." He released her reluctantly as they stepped out of the shaft. "I prefer to fly, take in the scenery, and feel the fresh air. Things get stale in those shafts."

"So, this is it?" Maluai looked at the enormous gates that marked the entrance to the island. The wall of interlocking trees spread from either side of the gates, their thick canopy blocking out any view of the inner island. The wet, salty smell of the ocean air mixed with the sound of the water crashing against the shore made her mind race.

"Yes, this is where I have to leave you." His words came out strained, a hint of unease in his voice.

"Maybe I should take a swim before I go inside," she hesitated, her feet rooted to the ground as she stared at the looming gates. "My skin is a little dry."

"Of course." He waved to the open water. "Take your time."

Maluai spent an hour swimming around the edge of the island. Her mind rushed with thoughts about everything from her laenu to the trials and the mentor who waited for her. When they talked now, there was a tangible tension in the air, and she didn't want to risk feeling the sting of rejection by talking to him about her true form.

When she got out of the water, he was still there, waiting for her, and the panic of their conversation bubbled to the surface again.

"So, I just go through the gates now?" she asked as soon as she stepped out of the water to avoid talking about anything else.

"Yes, this is as far as I can go," he said. "The gates only open for challengers."

"Okay." She took a deep breath. "Well, I guess this is where we say goodbye."

"Are you sure you're okay?" he asked.

"Yes, I'm fine." She looked him in the eye. "I signed up for this. I trained, and thanks to you, I'm ready. All that's left to do is walk through the gates."

"Well, I'll leave you alone. You don't need me watching you." He reached out to touch her shoulder in a moment of encouragement, but pulled back. "You got this."

As Jeraim took flight, his wings created a gust of wind that brushed against her skin. She looked up at him, her eyes wide, as he gracefully flew in circles above her head, the sound of his wings beating in the air. She only hoped she would see him again.

As he moved out of view, Maluai turned to the gates. She took several deep breaths before she walked toward them. When she made it within a few feet, the gates opened, and on the other side, there was darkness. She squinted her eyes as something came into view. As the image of the euman in front of her took shape, a sharp pain pierced her heart, and a soft sob escaped her l ips.

Maluai whispered. "Father?"

CHAPTER 17

He stood in front of her with a soft smile on his lips. As soon as she saw the euman whom she thought she would never lay eyes on again, all the effort she had put into getting ready suddenly became insignificant, and in an instant, she lost all her composure. She couldn't stop the tears from streaming down her face, and for a moment, she felt like they would never cease. Although she wanted to stay there and look at the euman from afar, she knew she had to keep going and continue with her journey.

"Father?" Her voice reverberated as she carefully walked across the ground, the darkness outlining his shape, illuminated by an unknown light source. "Is that really you?"

"Maluai," he spoke, and again, her heart felt like it would break after hearing her name in his voice again. She had to draw upon every ounce of her inner strength to keep from shattering into pieces. If she were to fail her test before getting through the gates, she would never forgive herself.

"What is this? It's just some kind of mind game?" She tiptoed closer, keeping enough distance between them just in case she needed to run away from the apparition.

"It is no mind game." He reached out to her. "I'm here to give you a message."

"A message?" She looked around as if expecting to be ambushed, but nothing happened. This wasn't something that her mentor prepared her for, but she considered he hadn't known. Was this something his uncle would have kept secret from him? Maybe it was against the rules to tell new challengers about how they might have to come face to face with someone they thought was dead and gone.

"I have a message that I need to tell you, and it is by the grace of our goddess that I am standing in front of you right now," he explained. "Each challenger receives a message from her upon entrance to Elderton."

"I can't believe this is actually real. Are you really here?" She pushed past her apprehension and reached out to her father. When her fingers found his flesh, she openly sobbed again. "I can feel you. How is this real?"

"This is as real as anything else could be. We can question all things, but those are metaphysical questions we don't have time for right now. Just know I am your father, the same father who carried you on my shoulders when you were still no taller than my knee, and I am here to give you a message."

"It really is you." She tried to stifle the sob growing in her throat, taking a deep breath as she swallowed it. "What's the message?"

"You think this challenge is something for everyone in Wallai. You've convinced yourself that it's about saving your eumen. What you face in there will not be about everyone else. It will be about you. The trails will focus on the thing you struggle with the most, and even in your training, you haven't fully come to accept."

"I don't know what that means. I faced everything I've been neglecting, and I've delved into my reasoning for coming here. What else was I meant to do? I even spoke to Mom before I left home. You would have been proud of me. I finally told her how I feel about everything."

"That's wonderful."

"Wonderful, right. And yet, what did I go through all that for if you're telling me I was wrong?" Maluai's heart raced with a new panic that felt as though it would choke her. "All that time training, centering myself, and it was the wrong thing? That means I'm completely unprepared for what I'm about to face. This is terrible."

"You're not completely unprepared. Your training will help you, but you must understand this challenge isn't solely about saving others. Going into this thinking about that won't help you. It's about the things that drive you, the things that make you who you are. And my daughter, there are a lot of things that comprise the recipe that is you."

"Things I apparently don't understand."

"Although you have shown strength, courage, and determination, you also still feel fear, and you have recognized the essence of fear, but you have not identified the source. I know you think you understand it, but in this challenge, it would be up to you to learn and understand every facet of your fear. It doesn't start and end with your mother."

"My mother isn't the root of my fear?"

"No, she isn't." His voice trailed off as he there were thoughts he couldn't express.

"Okay." With her lip caught between her teeth, she anxiously attempted to comprehend the meaning of his words. "Is that your full message? Do you have anything else to say to me?"

"Unfortunately, yes, it is."

"Here, I hoped your last words would be about us." She sighed. "Will I ever see you again?"

"That is not a question I can answer, but know I am always with you, whether you see me or not. I love you now and forever. From the moment you were born, you've been the light in my life right along with your sisters. You are all my heart, and as long as you exist in this world, so will I."

He touched her cheek, and though she could feel his hand, it wasn't the same. She felt an edge of static between their flesh that reminded her he wasn't here to stay. Maluai stood there, her heart sinking as she watched her father become a silhouette in the distance. Soon, he faded away completely.

The light that shone on him dimmed, and a stillness descended, the silence so thick she could feel it. She thought about his words. There was a root to her fear she hadn't tapped into. Despite hours of meditation and self-reflection, she was still avoiding something deep within herself that she was afraid to confront. How would she do it? How could she come to grips with something that had become so deeply ingrained in her she hadn't even noticed it?

She heard the rusty creak of the gates as they slowly closed behind her, and suddenly, the area filled with light. The warmth of the sun stretched across her face and body, reminding her that even though her father was no longer alive, she was. She walked forward, her hands trembling from her shaken confidence, but her resolve still strong, knowing the importance of what she was about to do. So, the challenge wasn't all about her eumen, but her succeeding would help them in a way she could only dream of. That was enough for her.

Just beyond the gates, she saw rows of tents and campfires. Jeraim explained to her that some challengers wouldn't go directly to their houses to begin the trials. Instead, they would rest and take the time to sit and think about their challenge before entering the house. That didn't feel right for her. Sitting around and thinking about things hadn't helped her before. All that meditation she did, and it didn't help. She was no closer to understanding what she needed to do to win this.

Instead of sitting around the campfire and waiting to find a friend to talk to, she marched forward past remnant embers of fires recently burned. Past the tented structure and through the tall blades of grass that led to the rows of houses. Just as he said, they were all unique.

She could see the intricate statues and markers of each species proudly displayed on the houses. She recognized that of the phoenix and that of the wolf. And as she continued walking, something internally guiding her to the house that belonged to her.

When she walked by the house of the dragons, her jaw dropped open to see the structure burned to the ground. That was what happened when a challenger failed. Their house, the structure that represented their eumen in the eyes of the goddess, burned to the ground. And it would remain that way for the duration of their curse. She'd heard nothing of the dragon's failure, so she assumed it was recent, and she hoped their eumen would survive their curse.

As she approached the house that belonged to her, she noticed the two massive golden griffin statues with jeweled eyes towered above the entrance of the walkway. She noticed something was off, and the air around the griffin statue seemed to hum with energy. This was the house of the griffin, and yet, on some level, it didn't feel like it belonged to her. The grandeur of it, all the windows and gilded accents, made her uncomfortable. She realized the house was more a representation of Forge than Wallai. It was an echo of the greed that consumed the lan d griffins.

She took a step toward the entrance but froze in her tracks as her mind filled with a flurry of thoughts. She was deep in thought about her need for self-expression when she felt the angry gaze of the statue of the little messenger bird, and alongside it, a pen and paper. And so, she sat and she wrote the letter. She knew she couldn't move forward with the trials until she had spoken her truth to the one who needed to hear it. He told her not to write to him, but he had to hear what she had to say.

Jeraim,

I know you said I didn't need to write to you. That I could say whatever I needed to say to your face. While you may have been willing to listen, there were just things I couldn't put into words. The distance of a letter seems easier, and there are things about myself I want to share with you. This challenge comes with uncertainty, and I couldn't begin it without telling you the truth.

First, I want to say I'm sorry I kept so much of myself hidden from you. In the time we've gotten to know each other, I've kept so many secrets, and it was not fair to you or to the friendship we were building. To be honest, I'm fearful the secrecy I have maintained has ruined the bond between us.

I haven't even started the trials yet, and I've already learned something about myself. There is a core issue, something about myself I need to deal with, only I don't know what it is. All I can do now is to be as honest with myself as possible and hope that's enough. And that honesty begins with you.

In the last year of our secret meetings, you've come to mean so much to me. And now that I am here facing having to live a life without you by my side, it worries me. I hadn't realized just how much I was hoping for us to take on the world together until I was forced to face the realization that you may not want that after truly knowing me.

I want to fix that and give you the chance to know everything about me, but I realize things may be different now that you've seen my true form. Just know I won't hold it against you if you decide to part ways when the trials are over.

I'm writing this now because I know there's a chance I won't remember you when I cross the threshold. As you said, the letters are a statement of the challenger's state of being, a testimony to their mindset before entering the trials.

I've learned that this challenge is going to make me face my greatest fears, and while this is not one of my core fears, it is one I'm at least aware of. My fear is that I will never know you in the way I've hoped to know you and that you'll never see me without the mask I've worn my entire life. I wish that once this is all over, I can take off the disguise and show you my authentic self. And I hope you will accept me. All of me.

See you on the other side.

Maluai.

As she handed her letter to the statue, she heard a rustling sound as the bird came to life, and its stone casing crumbled away. The sight of the bird with its dazzling plumage was enough to make her mouth drop open in surprise. It still contorted its face into an angry scowl, and it glared at her as though she had woken it from a deep slumber. Despite its clear annoyance with her, it still took her letter, and it flew off into the sunset.

As the Umital bird flew away, Maluai considered her options. She could go directly into the home, or she could take her time. She still had two days until she absolutely had to begin the trials, but two days was too much time. When she thought about it, all she wanted was one last sunset. One last opportunity to watch the sky change its colors above the water. She glanced up at the horizon, and the warm breeze turned to a chill as the sun dipped.

Maluai walked around the premises of the home and found a bench in the backyard that gave her the perfect view of the sunset. Her thoughts were of her father, her mentor, her mother, and herself. As the last rays of light disappeared from the sky, she felt a deep inner peace, a meditative state of being. When she came out of it, listening to the crash of distant waves, she knew it was time.

Moments after the sun disappeared, she returned to the front of the house and climbed to the top of the steps. She noticed again that the Griffin shifted. The bird she saw differed from what she'd imagined; its feathers dulled, and its lifeless eyes held a vacant stare. But there was only so much analyses she could do. Whatever the meaning, she would learn it later.

Putting her hand on the door, she could feel a tingle in her palm as she slowly twisted the handle and opened the door.

She took one step, carrying her across the threshold, and she fell into the ocean.

CHAPTER 18

Her eyes opened to the soft colors of the coral that covered the ceiling above her bed. A gift implanted by her father. The memory of him putting it there seemed broken, but she held on to it for the warmth it gave her. Maluai rolled around in her bed, sure that she could stretch the moments beneath the weighted blanket. The authoritative knock on her door shattered her hopes for a peaceful and relaxed day.

"Time to move, Princess," Seru called from the other side of the door.

"Fine!" she huffed and threw the blanket across the bed. Her body floated up from the bed, and she sighed.

While she hated the wake-up call, she knew it was necessary. If not for the authoritative voice calling from the other side of her door, she would stay in her bed for hours on end, and it would mean irritating her mother. Things were good with her laenu, and she didn't want to be the euman to ruin their good streak. So, she got up from bed and prepared herself for the routine of meetings at court and lessons on how to be a proper princess.

You'd think that after thirty years of lessons, she would know what she was doing, but according to her mother and her guardian, she was not as refined as she should be. As much as she hated it, she reminded herself that it was only a small part of her life and took comfort in knowing the day would not be a typical one. It was a day her father would take her and her sisters out into the world. It was one of the few times her mother wouldn't lecture them about leaving their home because they would be together as they present themselves to the Wallai natives.

Things were good. Maluai repeated the thought, her hands gliding over her hair as she stared into her reflection in the mirror. She primped her hair and made sure she perfectly styled it before she opened the door and saw her guardian standing there.

"There's a busy day ahead of you." Seru gave her an approving nod after she quickly accessed her appearance. "Are you sure you're ready for this?"

"As ready as I'll ever be. I know this is an important day. You don't have to worry about me." Maluai smiled and adjusted her crown. "Did my mother tell you to pay extra attention to me? Is she afraid I'll mess things up?"

"Your mother is nervous, but trust me, she's proud of all that you've done, and she knows you're ready for this and more responsibilities." Seru always tried to squash any doubt Maluai had about her mother, but it was never enough. There were always the lingering thoughts about disappointing the queen.

"You're right. I am ready." Maluai lifted her chin and pushed her shoulders back, correcting her posture. "This is only the beginning, Seru. I'll show my mother that I can do this without issue. Then she will have to let me have more independence."

"You know you haven't shown your true form in quite a while. Your audience will expect to see it."

"And they will see it." Maluai lifted a brow at the skeptical look on her guardian's face. "You don't think I can do it, do you? I don't know how many times I have to tell eumen I prefer my tail. Besides, my dresses are so much prettier when they're not stretched out over my true form."

"We can get you new dresses." Seru smirked at the sentiment.

"That is not the point," Maluai huffed. "I'm allowed to present how I want to. Just like everyone else."

"Yes, you are." Seru nodded and gestured for the princess to head down the hall.

"Thank you." Chin lifted, Maluai swam forward.

"Lucky for you, they likely won't expect to see it again for another ten to fifteen years, so you have plenty of time to fix your wardrobe."

"Doesn't this feel archaic to you, having to parade around our true forms for the eumen?" Maluai asked as they swam past two aides who dropped their heads as if afraid to look at her. She frowned at their reaction, but continued swimming.

"It is tradition. You are of the royal bloodline, and the eumen need to know your connection to your true form is still intact. Unfortunately, there are those of us who have lost that connection, and this demonstration reassures Wallains that the right eumen are leading us. I wish they could go off faith alone, but they need to see evidence."

"I get it. I do, Seru. But you know how doing things simply because tradition calls for it makes me itch." Maluai peered over her shoulder, glimpsing her guardian's rigid face.

"Well, scratch that itch, and let's get going, please."

The Presenting was a ceremony the royals performed when anyone of their bloodline came of age. As Seru explained, it was a way to prove that those in power hadn't lost their way. Above everything else, their eumen valued the connection to the goddess, and with the water griffin, those who moved away from the ways of Lunai lost the ability to show their true form.

Naluai was the youngest of their bloodline and had just come to maturity. It was time for her to show her true self. In a show of support for her sister as she held her parade, Maluai and Kaluai would stand by her side also in their true forms. This show would strengthen the message that the royals were still solid in their pledge to the goddess.

Those who still had a connection to their true form were tethered to the mystical energy that had created their eumen. In a time when they were considering splitting from the land griffins, faith was good, but evidence was better. They would need to protect themselves from anyone in the world who would threaten their standings. This potentially included the land griffins.

Maluai understood the importance of the ceremony, and though she had shown her form before, it made her nervous, but she couldn't understand why. This presenting ceremony wasn't about her, it was about her sister, the youngest. She and Kaluai were really just there to support their youngest sister, as this would be her first time presenting her true form to their eumen, but she hadn't shown hers since her presenting ceremony. Whenever anyone asked about it, she made excuses about her preference, but there was something more to it. Something she couldn't quite understand.

Still, there was this feeling in the pit of her stomach that she was making a mistake. If she was to go out there and show her form something would go horribly wrong. But she followed her guardian down the hall, head held high, as they moved to the court where they would talk about the ceremony and the festival of the lights that would happen afterward.

This was a day to be celebrated. This was the day for her sister. When her sister would become accepted by their eumen without question, and yet, she couldn't shake the feeling that something was wrong.

She sat through the meetings, listening as intently as she could about the ceremony. It was all the same. They would transport the princesses under cover to the edge of their territory, and then, once revealed, would swim along the path to the front of their palace. Along the way, Wallains would gather to witness Naluai's true form.

The aides assisted them in putting on the regal presenting gowns. The special fabric would part and move with them as they shifted, and then, when they returned to their phase form, it would gracefully cover them like a flowing gown.

Once dressed, the aides loaded the sisters into the caravan. They drew the curtains to muffle any noise and keep them hidden from prying eyes.

"How do you feel?" Kaluai pulled her youngest sister's hand into hers. "You look a little shaken."

"I'm nervous," Naluai admitted. "There's so much pressure. What if I mess up?"

"Don't think like that. You'll do great." She turned to Maluai. "Won't she?"

"Huh?" Maluai was so preoccupied by the growing fear of her true form she didn't even notice the two speaking.

"Are you alright?" Naluai reached out to her. "You look nervous yourself."

"Oh, yeah. I'm fine. Sorry, my mind is preoccupied."

"Right, well..." Kal raised a brow and nudged her in the side. "Tell our sister she will do fine."

"Of course you will, Nal." Maluai smiled. "You've done this plenty of times in private. Now you get to show off your beautiful self. Eumen are going to be so jealous of your coloring."

"You think so?" Naluai beamed.

"Absolutely. I mean, I wish I had that rainbow effect," Maluai complimented her sister. "It's so rare. You're going to show them how special you are, and they are going to love you."

"Okay, I can do this." Naluai smiled at her older sisters. "I got you two by my side. I can do anything."

"Awesome." Kaluai touched her cheek. "Well, it's time, and I'm up first. I'll see you out there."

The two youngest watched as the oldest shed her phase form to reveal her true form. Her tail unraveled into a dual ended tail, a marker of a truly powerful water griffin. Wings with scale-like feathers stretched from her back, and her hands shifted, fingers elongating to end in pointed claws. The last thing to change was her face. Where there were once the soft features, a powerful beak appeared. When her shift concluded with a soft tremble that ran across her body, she winked at her sisters and exited their covering.

Kaluai stepped out, and the crowd erupted into a chorus of cheers, clapping and whistling.

Maluai hugged her sister, kissed her cheek, and moved away from her. She took several deep breaths and allowed her true form to appear. And it did. Her back stretched, her tail grew to twice its length, with a split tail just like her sister. Her true form appeared like any other, but the feeling of wrongness was palpable to her. It was like standing inside a shell, one that didn't connect with her at all. Her breathing became labored with growing panic, yet she held her emotions in check. She would get through this for her sister.

As she presented herself, another wave of cheers erupted across the crowd. She glanced at her sister, who nodded to her, then they both turned to watch the curtained doorway. With the rest of Wallai, they waited on bated breath for the youngest royal to emerge.

Just as they predicted, Naluai emerged, and the cheer went absolutely nuts. She swam forward, first acknowledging her sisters, and then moved past them to show the crowd her true form. And as she moved, the light bounced off her scaling, creating a mesmerizing rainbow effect. The crowd pointed and whispered their admiration of her coloring as they swam the path from the convoy to their home.

As they arrived at the palace, the music began. A fanfare that marked the beginning of the festival. It was time to celebrate the successful continuation of the royal bloodline.

"This day couldn't have gone any better." Her father put his arm around her shoulder as they looked out over the festival. The music still pumped, eumen danced, ate, and sang the songs of their goddess. "I'm proud of you and your sisters."

"Thanks." She smiled at him, but her smile faded when her eyes met his. The life she knew, the vibrancy, was no longer there. It was like staring into a void. "Are you okay?" she asked.

Before her father could answer her question, her mother appeared, calling her attention away from her concern for her father.

"Maluai," the queen addressed her with a warm smile.

"Mother." Maluai lowered her head slightly to her mother.

"You did excellent today," her mother praised her.

"Thank you." Maluai smiled. "Just wanted to make sure it was a good day for Naluai."

"And you did." She paused, glancing at her husband before returning her attention to the princess. "Your father and I have been discussing something I think will interest you. As we move to gain our independence, we will need to perform outreach to the rest of the world. We think it would be good if you, alongside Kaluai, led this effort."

"Really?" Her eyes widened. "You're trusting us with this?"

"Yes. We believe it is time for you to take more responsibility for Wallai. It would mean more freedom for you. As long as you show you can handle it."

"Oh, thank you!" Maluai cheered. "This is going to be amazing. I promise I won't let you down."

"I'm sure you won't." Her father squeezed her shoulder before letting her go and reaching out to his wife.

"Maybe we can go to our secret place," she whispered to her father after her mother swam away.

"What's that?"

"Our place, where the Kivari sharks mate." She frowned. "It's been a while since we've gone, but I know you haven't forgotten."

"Huh." He scratched his chin. "It's been a long day. Perhaps you need rest."

"What? How could you forget?"

"I have to go, Maluai. My time here is ending."

"What?" She shook her head. "What do you mean?"

"I'm the king. I can't hide away in the corners." He smiled, and again, his expression was a hollow marker that made her stomach twist.

"Are you okay?"

"Of course I am," he snapped. "Enjoy the party. Stop asking so many questions. Things are just as you've wanted them. Be happy."

"I... okay." As he turned and swam off to join his wife, she nodded and watched, a sense of dread settling in her stomach.

"Mal," her oldest sister called out to her. "Did you hear the news?"

"Yeah." Maluai turned to her sister, who swam up to her. "I did. She just told me."

"It's amazing, right? I mean, finally we can do more than sit around here attending meetings," Kaluai cheered, then frowned when her sister didn't reciprocate her excitement. "What's wrong?"

"Nothing, it's just..." Maluai held her thoughts, unsure if her sister would be open to them.

"Mal, tell me. What is it?" Kaluai insisted.

"Does something seem off to you about father?" Maluai asked. "Like when you look in his eyes. Something is different."

"What?" Kaluai frowned. "You're making things up in your mind."

"Maybe, but he doesn't seem like himself. I'm worried."

"Don't ruin this. Everything is exactly how we wanted it to be," she echoed her father's sentiments. "You should be happy right now. Just be happy, Mal. Don't question it. Let us be happy this time."

"This time? What do you mean this time?" Maluai asked. "Was there another time?"

"You should go rest. It's been a long day," Kaluai changed the topic. "You look tired."

"Why does everyone want me to go rest?" Maluai huffed. "I'm fine. I'm not tired."

"Clearly, something is wrong. You're confused, and you've been looking weird all day. I think you just need rest." Kaluai lowered her voice, her eyes darkening as she spoke. "Go rest, Maluai."

Maluai backed away from her sister. When she looked at her, really looked, she realized something was off about her as well.

"Yeah, I think I will go rest," she conceded for no other reason than to get away from her sister.

She swam through the crowd, and Seru appeared in her shadows.

"Princess, where are you going?" her guardian called out from behind her.

"To rest," she said without looking back. She didn't want to see that vacant expression on another euman's face.

She made it back to her room without issue. No one stopped her as she swam. Most eumen, including the workers who usually swam the halls of the palace, were at the festival.

Back in her room, she closed the door behind her and leaned against it, taking calming breaths. Maybe the others were right.

Maybe she just needed to rest. After considering whether her laenu could be right about her, she swam to the mirror to remove the jewels and gown the aids adorned her with.

Before she could begin undressing, she noticed it. Her own eyes were different. When she should have been excited, there was sadness staring back at her. She felt hollow, and all she could think about was the side of herself that she refused. Her words replayed in her mind. She preferred her phase form, her tail. That wasn't the truth. She could lie to the others, but she couldn't lie to herself.

"Why am I so afraid of you?" She peered at her reflection and spoke to the side of herself she rarely showed. "You're a part of me. If I'm going to go out into the world, they're going to want to see my true form. I can't keep you hidden anymore."

She took another calming breath, and once again, brought her true form to the surface. Maluai forced herself to stare at her reflection.

"This is okay. I'm okay," she whispered as she took a count of her tail, clawed hands, and large beak. As she embraced the feeling of calm, her reflection in the mirror quivered, and the newfound confidence that filled her faded away.

The mirror shook, reverberating against the wall, and in the reflection, she saw glimpses of something else. As she looked in the mirror, she saw a completely different reflection of herself. Staring for what seemed like an eternity, the two images started to blend and swirl, as if they were battling for her attention.

She reached out for the mirror, and just as her finger touched it, the glass cracked. From the point of her finger, each broken pane showed a different reflection.

"This isn't right." She pulled her hand back, shaking her head as memories clashed in her mind.

Thoughts that made her realize her reality wasn't real. She cried as she looked at the ceiling above her bed, and the gentle memory of her father installing the coral faded and the colorful formation dissolved.

Her reflection shifted again, and she saw the true form. The one she was told to hide. Four powerful legs, no tail. Her flesh was without scales but covered in silver webbing. In an instant, a lifetime of fear slammed into her.

"This isn't my life. This isn't my truth."

She touched her face. Despite the pain, she dug her claws into her own flesh and ripped away the lie. The beak fell to the floor, pieces of flesh floating around it as she looked up at her reflection again to find the shortened feline face. A mixture of anger and panic drove her actions, and Maluai ripped away more of the skin. Each painful pull punctuated by her own screams of agony.

She heard loud screaming and forceful banging outside her door as the guards desperately tried to reach her, yet an unseen and powerful force kept the door firmly shut.

One last scream, and the last of her fake form fell away. She stood in the mirror and cried as she accepted the form that appeared to her.

JESSICA CAGE

"This is me," she sobbed. "This is really me."

Her ears ached with the sound of rushing water, and in the broken reflection of the mirror, she saw it appear behind her. A large doorway stood out against the wall; its frame intricately carved from bright coral where the door should be. She felt a tugging sensation, drawing her ever closer to the swirling vortex of water.

"What is happening?" Maluai sobbed, but her instinct told her to walk through it, and she did.

CHAPTER 19

M aluai's body was awash with adrenaline as she felt her chest burn from the extended effort of swimming fast. Her mind spun as the memories of her broken facade faded, blending with the images of her current reality. Soon, she forgot all about the confusion of moments before she crossed through the portal.

As her vision settled, the fuzz of her memories easing, she locked in on the sight of her best friend. Genuve whipped her tail, propelling her forward. The mermaid glanced over her shoulder just long enough to make sure Maluai was still behind her.

"Swim faster, or you're going to get your tail chomped off!"

She looked back and saw the group of sharks, their fins slicing through the water, and the adrenaline rushed through her body faster and stronger. She pushed her tail, sending a flurry of bubbles into the water as she tried to keep up with her mermaid friend in front of her.

Racing around a rocky outcropping, they made it just in time as the sharks swam past, the sound of their fins cutting through the water. Maluai gasped for air, her breath coming in shallow, rapid bursts.

"Shezia! That was close!" Genuve laughed. "I thought I was going to lose you there."

"What happened?" Maluai pressed her hand against her head to ease the spinning sensation. "What am I doing here?"

"Oh, don't back out on me now. You've always said you wanted adventure." Genuve swam in circles, letting her arms flail out around her. "After all these years, I finally bust you out of that place. We're going to enjoy this! A little run-in with sharks will not stop us."

"I'm sorry. I feel like I blacked out for a minute. That was intense!" Maluai's breath calmed, and her head cleared.

"Blacked out? Are you okay?" Genuve swam closer to her and peered into her eyes. "You look a little grey around the gills."

"I don't have gills." Maluai frowned.

"Well, there's proof you still got some sense about yourself." Genuve laughed. "It's the thrill of it all. You'll be okay."

"Yeah. I'm fine. I just... I don't know what happened."

Just after the words crossed her lips, a rush of images flooded her mind. Broken memories of the moments she lost fused into place. She saw herself swimming from the palace and making it just beyond the border of her home before the alarms sounded. They could hear the guards yelling after them from a distance but pressed forward.

Whenever she felt like she would tire out, her mermaid best friend encouraged her to keep moving. They made it beyond the reef, a marker of the end of the magic that hid her home from the rest of the world. It wouldn't be long before the guardians caught up with them, and they would punish her for what she did, but she was excited and proud of herself for finally taking the risk.

"Did I actually do that? Genuve, I left home! My mother must be losing her mind right now." Maluai was close to a state of panic. "Can you imagine how much trouble I'll be in for this?"

"Think of the trouble when we get back. For now, adventure is this way." Genuve pointed in their intended direction. "If we stop now, it won't be worth it at all. Let's go!"

"You're right. I'm already out here. I might as well enjoy it!" She shrugged. "So, where are we going?"

"You'll see when we get there."

Her enthusiastic friend led her through various underwater tunnels and passages. They swim deeper and farther away from the typical paths of travel than Maluai had ever imagined going. Genuve said it would make it harder for the guards to find them. They wouldn't assume the princess would ever take a path so dangerous.

They pushed forward, and even though she had plenty of questions, the thrill was too much for her to stop. Maluai felt a tingle of anticipation as they set off on this journey, curious about what wonders it would bring. All her life she had wished for the chance to explore the world with no rules to hold her back, and now, that moment had finally arrived.

Maluai followed her friend, and the sound of mermaids' laughter and music filled her ears, causing her to feel a fresh wave of excitement. When they rounded the bend of the narrow passage, a vast, still expanse of water welcomed them. Just beneath them, tucked away in a corner of the ocean floor, was an underwater festival.

It surprised her to see that there were more than just colorful mermaid tails at the party. There were creatures of all sorts, including water dragons, kinokos, and spirtuses.

"Are you ready? Because this is a moment you will never forget," Genuve hyped her up before she swam ahead.

Maluai watched as Genuve swam through a group of spirtuses, creatures that resembled seahorses with wings. The creatures were three times the size of anyone in Wallai and temperamental. She remembered her father telling her that his cousin once tried to ride one and ended up unconscious for four days. Maluai made a note not to even look like she wanted to ride them, though their colorful bodies made it so tempting.

"Come on!" Genuve called out to her, and every head of the spirtus group looked her way with wide eyes.

This was it. She couldn't hide anymore. This was the adventure and the life that she wanted, and because of her friend, she had the opportunity to experience it. She took a deep breath for courage and swam forward, and it wasn't nearly as overwhelming as she thought it might be. Genuve Introduced her to everyone they passed. Maluai always knew her friend was out-going, but she didn't know just how well known the mermaid was in the underwater world. It made sense, though. Genuve was always reporting the wildest adventures to her. Of course, she would have made countless acquaintances along the way.

The drinks were flowing, and she sampled strange, bubble drinks and exotic foods she had never tried before. Everything was delicious, and she drank this weird green liquid. Genuve handed her the third bubble fitted with a straw to sample the milky green liquid inside. She took two sips before her head spun. Maluai attempted to keep up with Genuve, but soon, she felt herself getting lost in a sea of unfamiliar bodies.

As she searched for her friend, she passed a group of water dragons and kinokos. The underwater fairies were both chilling and captivating, the gentle sway of their wings like a lullaby. Each had three pairs of wings, layered like armor, and extending from the tip of their head to the end of their tail. Long wisps of translucent flesh hung from their legs and arms. Spiraled ridges that blended with the blue and greens of their flesh covered their legs, chest, and arms. Their heads were small compared to their bodies, but they had wide eyes that made them appear like babies. A part of their charm that often got eumen mixed up in deadly games with the kinokos. What terrified her most about them were their hands. Their fingers were loose webbing. They could fuse the webs into any form, and if they wanted to shoot them off their body like spears, only to form more moments later.

She watched as they played minots. A game of chance involving three shells and a pearl. The player tossed the four items, and they tallied the scores based on the position of the shells and the pearl. Shell face up was worth five points, and shell face down was worth ten points. If the shell landed on its edge, standing, it was worth thirty points. If the pearl touched any of the shells, it tripled its point value.

"Genuve!" Maluai called out as she got a glimpse of her friend, but when she looked back, there was a dark glint in her eye.

Genuve swam away from Maluai, despite her urgent calls.

Maluai, refusing to lose sight of her friend again, pushed through the crowd. Just as she was making progress, a loud clap startled her and caused her to turn around.

"Honor!" the kinoko's shrill voice called out. "Honor!"

Its long fingers shifted, fusing, and separating as it pointed to the water dragon opposite the playing field.

"I won fair and square, ma hezi!" the dragon responded and pointed to the playing field. "You all saw it. Pay up!"

"I will do no such thing. You deceived me!" the kinoko screamed. "Honor!"

"Honor my ass. You think you're going to cheat me and use this dramatic show to distract me?" The water dragon whipped his tail through the water, causing the crowd to scatter as his body expanded. "You owe me a scart head, and I'm giving you one minute to pay up."

A moment later, there was a loud, ferocious roar, as the dragon and the kinoko clashed in battle. Everyone was frantically swimming away from the escalating fight as more dragons and kinokos roared and clashed. Soon, the festive gathering turned bloody, and unfortunately, that was when the milky green drink kicked in.

Maluai's head spun as the dangerous images shifted to a dizzying array of clashing colors. She felt like she was in a world where the colors were so bold, they almost hurt, and the sounds were so loud, they echoed in her ears. A dragon flew past her, knocked away by a kinoko, and she pressed her finger to her lips, shushing it, completely unaware of the blood spilling from its slacked jaw.

Despite her inebriated state, something inside the princess made her heart hammer with a warning about the danger of her situation. It screamed at her to get away from the situation. She felt a force inside her push away the veil of her intoxication, and the truth of her reality flooded her senses. Maluai shook her head, trying to sober up as she swam away from the growing battle, but something stopped her. The call of a familiar voice.

She turned to the sound but saw nothing. Again, determined to get away, she swam in the direction she spotted Genuve, but the voice called to her again. This time, when she turned, she saw her. Sitting in the middle of the playing field amid the battle between the dragons and the kinokos. Naluai.

Maluai found it impossible to move. It wasn't fear that arrested her limbs; it was indecision. Maluai couldn't believe the thoughts that rushed through her mind. Could she actually consider leaving her sister there? And for what? The promise of more excitement? What if her sister got hurt? Part of her was screaming for her to run away from the danger, but she knew she couldn't leave her sister there. It wasn't right. She would never forgive herself if Naluai was hurt, or worse.

It took longer than she thought it ever would, but eventually, she pushed past her selfish thoughts and whipped her tail to push her back through the frantic crowd toward her sister. A hand wrapped around her wrist and her back. She turned, ready to fight off whatever creature had dared touch her, but relieved to find her friend holding on to her.

"Thank the goddess, it's you. I need your help." She pointed to the playing field where her sister sat screaming out with eyes full of terror. "It's Naluai. we have to get her out of here."

"Don't be silly." Genuve laughed as if they weren't in the middle of a battlefield. "There's no way we can go back now."

"What are you talking about?" Maluai pulled away from Genuve, but the mermaid refused to let her go. "We can't just leave her here."

"Girl, adventure is awaiting and we'll miss our chance! If you stop now, if you go back now, you'll never be free again. They'll lock you away and never let you go. You don't want that, do you?" Genuve spoke with an addict-like urgency. Her eyes darted around them as if fearful of something Maluai couldn't see.

"I don't care about any of that. Besides, if I don't save my sister, they will do a lot worse to me when they find me. She doesn't deserve to get hurt. It's our fault she's here. She probably followed us here. Why else would she be here? I can't leave her like this."

"But what about other things you want for yourself? What about freedom and adventure? What about love?" Genuve's voice deepened as she spoke. "Don't you want all those things? If you go back now, you'll never get them."

"Genuve, let me go!" Maluai tried again to pull away from her, but the mermaid pulled back with more force than Maluai thought possible.

"No, I helped you get out of there, and I'm not letting you go back. All the years we dreamed of adventure and of freedom! All my years of coming back to that stupid place to see you! You owe me this."

"My sister is more important to me than any wild adventure you could dream up, so if you think I'd ever abandon her for something like that, you don't know me at all. I'm only gonna ask you one more time to let me go."

"No." Genuve's gaze narrowed, and her eyes turned dark.

Maluai's mouth dropped open in surprise as she looked at her friend and noticed the transformation. The mermaid she once knew, the girl with soft features and a sarcastic tongue but a good heart, turned into something ugly. Something she had no name for.

Her tail split into six ends, each of which reached out to grab hold of her limbs. Maluai listened in horror as Genuve's joints creaked as her arms bulged with muscles too large for her petite frame. Her skin lit with the embers of fire, her flesh becoming warm, so warm that Maluai thought it would burn her. Genuve grinned and showed rows of spiked teeth. This was not the friend she thought it was, and Maluai questioned her own sanity. What had she allowed to lure her away from home?

Geneve's hand expanded. Her fingers turned to tendrils that stretched the length of Maluai's. Each time she pulled to free herself from the hold, it tightened until Maluai felt like she would lose all feeling in the arm. Her sister screamed again, and she looked back to find a kinoko narrowing in on the small girl.

Maluai thought the only thing she could do was shift to her true form. It would give her enough strength to get away from the creature and save her sister. She quickly called her griffin to the surface, but nothing happened. She tried again, each attempt echoed by her sister's panicked cries, but each time she failed. Something blocked her true form from her.

She had to break free on her own, but how?

A sudden rush of water brushed past her face, accompanied by the loud whoosh of a dark form shooting by. The spear, formerly the fused hand of a kinoko, stood from the ground. She seized the opportunity; this was her chance. She reached for the spear, her fingers barely reaching it but still ripped it from the ground. With a swift movement, Maluai stabbed it at the beast that held her. Despite her own speed, the beast knocked it away, then slammed its massive fist into Maluai's jaw.

Dazed and confused, she fell back, but the creature still held on to her. Naluai's cries grew louder, ringing in her ears until they drowned out all other sounds.

As the beast reared its head back, its six tails spread out around it. Maluai knew she only had moments left. Behind her, the kinoko moved closer to Naluai. She only has a moment left to save her. Maluai spotted another spear. This time, she had to make it count. She ripped the weapon from the back of the dragon's head and turned it on the monster. That time, with all her anger fueling her strike, the spear pierced the chest of the beast.

It cried out. Its monstrous voice echoing across the current before it shifted, turning from horror to melody. Maluai became transfixed, her eyes widening, and her voice caught in her throat, as she watched the monster at the end of her blade transformed back into her friend. Slowly, it shifted, and the hideous mask of a beast became the delicate features of a frightened mermaid.

"Genuve," Maluai sobbed as blood spilled from her friend's lips. "Oh, no. I'm so sorry."

"Get out of here," Genuve choked. "You aren't safe here."

Maluai nodded, mouthing her apology again as she released her hold on the spear. With it, her friend fell to the floor as Maluai turned and swam away.

She dodged the kinoko's grasp as she swam past and scooped her sister from the playing field. Naluai cried and buried her head into her sister's shoulder as Maluai continued to swim. She didn't look back. She couldn't. She was too afraid the kinoko would be on her tail, or worse, another beast like the one that took over her friend.

"I'm here. You're okay. I got you," Maluai repeated to her sister. "You're safe."

A structure made of coral glimmered in the sunlight ahead of them. She saw the whirling motion of the water in the opening. Maluai felt inexplicably drawn to the place, as though some unseen force was pulling her in. She accepted it without hesitation. She swam through the opening, feeling the cool water against her skin and the electric current pulsing around her as she held her sister tightly.

Chapter 20

M aluai came out of the other side of the portal, bursting through a door, stumbling. She clutched her arms to her chest, trying to hold on to her sister, and heard her own heart racing as the small girl was no longer in her hold. Disoriented, she scanned the area for her sister, then felt a wave of dizziness as the seascape changed. She was no longer in the ocean's expanse but back at home. Inside the court in the palace. Soon, the sound of her older sister yelling filled her ears, and she turned around to see the angry face of her eldest sister.

"I can't do this anymore. I swear, no matter what I do. It's never enough for her. I'm done!" Kaluai yelled in frustration. "Time and time again I try to prove myself, and she just shoots me down!"

"What are you talking about? What's going on?" Maluai struggled to make sense of things, as once again, the memories of the prior moments shifted and faded from her mind.

"I have been the perfect daughter all my life. I've done exactly what our mother wanted. And now that is time for me to take over, for me to move into my power, she refuses." Kaluai swam in circles as she vented her frustrations. "She says I still need to learn. I still need to do more. I don't know what more I can do. Our father passed away so long ago, and yet, she still refuses to relinquish her reign. What more could she possibly want? That's it. I don't care. I'm done. I'm leaving."

"Leaving?" Maluai shook her hands in her sister's face. "No, no... wait. What are you talking about? You're leaving?"

"There's so much more I want for myself, and I've always turned away from it because of responsibility. Because of my duty to this laenu. I can't do it anymore. I'm relinquishing my title."

"I know you want to lead, but Mother doesn't have to give up her reign. It's tradition, yes, but she gets to do it in her own time." Maluai shook her head. "This doesn't sound like you. What happened? Whatever it is, we can figure it out as a laenu."

"No, I'm sorry." Kaluai pulled the crown from her head and pulled the weighted beading from her locs. "I know you don't want this, and with me gone, everything falls to you, and I'm so sorry about that, but I can't do this anymore."

"Me? What do you mean, everything falls to me? You're next in line to rule Wallai, not me. Whatever is going on between you and mother can be resolved," Maluai pleaded with her sister. "You will have your time. You just need to be patient."

"There's a whole other layer to it, something I can't figure out. I wish I could have the same assurance you have, but I just can't seem to find it. Not anymore. I've given up life, adventure, and love time and time again." She paused, her voice trailing out. "Love. You can't fathom how many things I've had to give up just to keep our eumen going, and yet she looks at me with a critical eye, despite the fact that I'm not asking her to quit entirely. I just want more responsibility. I want to feel like I'm not wasting my life waiting for her to decide when I'm ready to lea d."

Maluai thought about her sister's words because it was exactly how she felt. She had said the same words to her sister years ago, but the roles were now reversed. She didn't know what was going on to inspire such a reaction from her sister, but she would figure it out. Kaluai couldn't leave their home. Wallai needed her.

"Do nothing. Not yet. Let me talk to Mother. Give me a chance to figure out what's going on here." Maluai moved to the door, hopeful her sister would comply, but Kaluai refused.

"I'm only coming here to talk to you, to tell you I'm leaving, but I won't be back," her sister announced.

"Leaving? Stop saying that. You're not leaving us. This is just a rash reaction to whatever argument you had with our mother. We can fix this!"

"I love you, Maluai. I really do, but I'm done now. You can be the dutiful daughter, and I can be the one who disappoints her. At least now she will have a reason to feel that way."

"Where is she?" Maluai swam into the queen's quarters and found her guardian outside the main doors to her bedroom.

"Princess, please wait." Kianna swam to Maluai, hoping to stop her advance.

"I need to talk to my mother. Now," Maluai demanded. "Whatever happened between her and my sister, I need to help make it right."

"I'm afraid the queen is ill." Kianna's voice trembled as she spoke. "She is in no condition to talk now."

"What?" Maluai choked. "What do you mean, she's ill? How can this be?"

"I am not sure, but it came on quickly." Kianna glanced over her shoulder at the closed door. "The healers are with her, but it doesn't look good."

"I have to get in there." Maluai moved for the door, but Kianna slid in front of her, blocking her path again.

"I think it's best you stay out here."

"I don't remember asking you what you thought was best. Move aside, and let me in," Maluai insisted, and Kianna moved away from the door.

Kianna averted her gaze from the princess and lowered her head in reverence. The guardian wouldn't defy the princess. She moved away from the door. Kianna moved away from the door, allowing Maluai to enter her mother's room. As she stepped across the threshold, her chest tightened, and her mouth felt like it was filled with cotton. She watched as the healers and aides moved around the queen, and Maluai's heart sank at the sight; it reminded her of the last time she saw a parent in such a fragile state. Her father, on his deathbed. Hollow, dying. The queen looked the same.

"Mother?" Maluai felt like a child again, calling out to her mother and hoping she would answer with fortitude and love.

The queen looked at her, coughed weakly, then closed her eyes. She said nothing. She didn't have the strength.

"What happened?" Maluai asked, her eyes focused on her mother's shallow breaths.

The aide gave an explanation Maluai couldn't hear over her own thoughts. Her mind was too busy racing through the many scenarios of how things could turn out. She had to hurry to find her sister. Kaluai couldn't have known her mother was sick. There was no way she would have threatened to leave if she knew.

As she turned to leave the room, her head spun, and she had flashes of memories implanted in her mind. For years, her mother's health had been fading more and more because of residual damage from the spill. The healers did all they could to keep the queen strong. This was why Kaluai was so upset. It wasn't just because she wanted to lead. It was because their mother was overworking herself toward an even earlier grave.

Maluai swam to her sister's room. She assumed Kaluai would be there, packing her things. Instead of the stern face of a stubborn sister, she found two letters. One with her name, and one with their youngest sister's name. Maluai's heart fell to the pit of her stomach. Kaluai was gone. Her mother was dying. Her world was falling apart.

It was only a matter of hours before the bells rang. Five bells. Each one struck her heart like lightning as she sat alone in her sister's room clutching the unopened letters.

The queen was dead.

Life was a blur of motion. The bells. Naluai's tears. The ceremony. A search for a sister who no one could find. Kaluai was gone. A week later, Maluai stood at the head of the court in front of the council members, who looked at her to take the place of their leader. She could barely hold herself together, and they wanted her to take up the crown. One that was never meant to be hers.

"I want to start by saying I appreciate the grace you all have given me during this time," she spoke, her eyes locked on her sister, who sat at the head of the court by her side. "This has been a difficult time for our eumen and for the royal laenu. With Kaluai gone, you feel I should lead. It would be a failure on my part should I not admit I do not believe I am the right person for the role."

The council members and attending guards looked around, their eyes wide, and their whispers frantic as they tried to understand the confusion.

"I know this doesn't give you the best confidence in my abilities. You must understand that after our mother, Kaluai was to lead."

"Princess," Fituen, the councilman, moved forward. "Might I interject?"

"Please." Maluai gave him the floor.

"I think it is best we all look at this with clear heads. The princess is showing us honesty, a value we have always appreciated in the royal laenu. None of us in this room have been blinded to the fact that Maluai rebels against tradition. It has never been in her path or in her plans to rule the citizens of Wallai," Fituen addressed the room, his voice booming with confidence as he spoke. "Weighing the present conditions, I think it is prudent to contemplate alternative possibilities for the heads of our eumen."

"And who would you have lead us, if not the royals?" Hasik spoke, her eyes narrowing on Fituen. "They are the ones connected to Lunai. They are the ones are eumen believe in."

"Our eumen also believe in the council. We are just as connected to the goddess as the royals." Fituen had the answer ready before it was asked. "Together, we could form a new leadership for Wallai."

"You want to eliminate the royal laenu?" Maluai's heart raced. No, she didn't want to lead them, but she also didn't want to erase the history of her laenu. They'd already been through enough.

"Not eliminate. No, princess, but to introduce a temporary replacement while you figure out what it is you really want to do. I think we can allow you the grace to do so, and perhaps, your sister will return, and she will take her rightful place as the queen, but if you are unsure about your position here, it is unfair of us to ask you to sit on that throne. We need a leader who is sure. We need a leader who will not falter. Can you tell us that is you?"

"No, I cannot," she answered honestly.

"Well then, I suggest we put it to vote." Fituen glanced around the room. "Those who are in favor of this temporary change of leadership, please speak now."

The other members of the council were reluctant, but eventually, they each gave their approval of his plan.

"There you have it, Princess. So long as you agree, you will have your time to figure out what you want, and we will allow it. In the meantime, we, the council, will sit role and decide what is best for our eumen."

"How long does she have?" Naluai spoke up for the first time.

"I'm sorry?" Fituen frowned.

"I understand my sister doesn't want to sit in that position, and I am not yet of age for the role, but how long does she have to make this decision? If we do not set the time frame, she could very well be gone for a day and come back, and you can say it's too late." Naluai lifted her chin when Fituen narrowed his eyes at her. "We should give my sister the opportunity to decide what she wants for her life. I agree with this, but I but I do not agree with going forward with this without setting the expectations clearly."

"Very well." He looked at Maluai. "Princess, how long would you suggest we have until you decide?"

"A month," she answered, unsure of how long it would take her. "Maybe two?"

"Let's say three months. Three months to decide what you want to do. We will honor whatever choice you make in that time." He turned to Naluai. "Does that appease you?"

"Yes, it does." The young princess nodded.

"Then it's settled," Fituen announced with more of that confidence that leaked from him like a toxin. "We will adjourn for today and spread the word about our temporary solution."

The guards and the council members left the court, leaving the two sisters alone, and as soon as they were alone, Naluai swam close to her sister and spoke in a hushed voice.

"I don't like this. I want you to be okay, but I do not trust him. You know he's always had something out for us. This is a power grab. You know that, right?"

"Yes, I understand it, but..." Maluai shook her head as she tried to clear her thoughts of the noise.

"But this isn't the life you ever wanted." Naluai placed her hand on her sister's shoulder. "I know, and I don't want you to make a choice that would make you unhappy, but we have to think of our eumen. We have to think of Wallai. We even have to think of our sister."

"Our sister? You can't be serious." Maluai scoffed and pulled away from Naluai's touch. "Our sister who left us here alone, knowing she was next in line to rule. Our sister, who knew our mother was sick and still ran away because she couldn't have her way! You want me to think of our sister? Where is she now? Do you honestly expect me to think that in all the oceans she hasn't heard about our mother? What could possibly be keeping her away?"

"I don't know. I never thought she would leave us like that. She was always telling me it would get better. That Mother was hurting because of losing Father. That the only reason she was being hard on us was because she was so unhappy. I didn't know it was that bad. If anyone was to run away, I thought it would be you."

"Yeah, me too. Look, I will take my time and consider this. I won't make this choice without careful thought, but I have to do what's right for me," Maluai promised her sister.

"Even if it's not right for our eumen?"

"I don't know." Maluai took a deep breath. "You could always come with me."

"No." Naluai sighed and looked at the doors of the courtroom. "I can't."

"I don't want to leave you alone," Maluai said. "Not after losing our mother and sister."

"I'm not alone. All the guards and aides here will keep me company. Besides, someone has to keep an eye on Fituen while you figure out what you want to do." Naluai gave a mature response. "What you have to do now, it's not about me. It can't be about me."

"I love you." Maluai pulled her sister into her arms.

"I know." Naluai hugged her back. "Just please be safe out there and come back to me."

"I will."

Maluai swam to her room. She thought she would find Seru along the way, but her guardian was nowhere to be found. Instead, standing outside her door was the councilman, Fituen.

"What are you doing here?" She hesitated to open her door with the councilman there.

"I just wanted to speak to you alone," he spoke calmly.

"About what?" There wasn't anything more to say. She would leave, figure out what she wanted, then return and let them know. What more could he possibly have to say to her?

"I wanted to reassure you I will take care of everything in your absence." His smile was troubling.

Maluai narrowed her gaze. "You? Don't you mean the council?"

"Yes." He chuckled. "Of course. I just want to make sure you understand things will be good here until you return. I will watch over our eumen and your sister."

She felt a knot in her stomach, an uneasiness that something was off. He was always the one combating her mother's decisions. He was the one always wanting to challenge their decisions, but this was her way of escape. Though she knew she shouldn't, the small voice of warning in the back of her mind couldn't quell the fear that made her want to run.

Maluai ended their conversation and left the councilman standing in the hall alone as she went into her room. She quickly gathered her things, just a few items she would need to make it out in the world on her own. As she hurried around her room, she noticed something along the wall that wasn't there before. It looked almost like a doorway forming with pieces of coral. She ran her hand along the surface, squinting at it, and it felt familiar, but she didn't know why. Afraid this was a way to distract her, something put in place to keep her home, she turned her back on the mystery, and she left her home behind.

Eighty-seven days later, Maluai swam through the waters with the dumi whales. She'd explored the oceans and was returning home to give her decision, but when she reached the edge of Wallai, she panicked because she knew her choice would disappoint so many eumen. She nearly turned away, but heard a familiar voice call out to her.

"Maluai?" the voice of her guardian called out, and Maluai's heart jumped.

"Seru?" Eyes wide, Maluai swam to her guardian and embraced her. "It's so good to see you."

"Where have you been?" Seru asked in an urgent tone. "We've searched everywhere for you."

"What do you mean?" Maluai frowned. "I wasn't exactly in hiding."

"It is no matter. We must get you to the palace and reinstated. Kaluai is still missing. They have locked away your sister in the palace for months. The guardians can't get in."

"What?" Maluai panicked. "No, Fituen and the council members have taken care of everything. That was the deal."

"Fituen has made a play for power. Hasik is ill, and Limua just agrees with everything Fituen says. I think she's afraid of him," Seru reported.

"Naluai?"

"She is okay. The aides have reported that she isn't hurt, but we haven't seen her since you left home."

"I—" the pangs of guilt filled Maluai's stomach. "This can't be right. Fituen said he would take care of everything. He would keep everyone safe."

"I understand this is shocking, and I wish I could welcome you home with better news, but this is the reality we face now."

"No, this isn't right." Maluai turned from Seru. "This isn't right." She swam away, her guardian's desperate screams of her name echoing in the water around her.

Maluai swam to the surface as fast as she could to get away from her guardian. Her guilt was far too strong for her to stay in the water, so she emerged on the shore beneath a cliff. As she looked up at the peak, she felt connected to the place. Though she searched her memories and could not remember being there, it felt familiar to her. She followed the urge in her heart and climbed to the top, despite not being able to recall why it felt so familiar.

As she made it to the peak, a man's voice reverberated through the area. She scanned the area, trying to find him, but there was no one. She stopped her search when she heard another voice engaging in conversation with him. It was her own. The sound of her voice speaking words she couldn't remember every saying, and she realized she wasn't hearing someone who was there currently but memories of conversations she'd had with him.

Maluai clutched the sides of her head, and her eyes slammed shut as she tried to remember something she had clearly forgotten. This voice, this person, the sound of his voice, made her feel things she hadn't felt for anyone. And yet she couldn't remember him.

As the wind kicked up, bringing the blended smell of flowers and ocean. She got a picture of a face. She saw his dark skin and the silver markings that stretched across his left eye. She saw the way he looked at her, the hints of love and concern. The voice was there again, and when he said her name, she knew there was more there more than she could ever understand.

"Who are you?" she spoke aloud, though he was not there. "Please, tell me your name. Who are you?"

Maluai felt like she was going insane. Speaking to eumen who were not there, avoiding problems that seemed too big for her to face. Could this really be the way she lived her life? Could she really be so fragile that she couldn't face the truths, no matter how simple or difficult they were?

"Meditate," his voice spoke, and the words resonated with her in a way she didn't understand. "Center yourself. Meditate. Find me."

Maluai's first thought was to challenge the words, but her instincts screamed louder than her own stubbornness. She sat down on the cliff and crossed her legs. Her breathing quickly fell into a rhythm, and with each release of air, she felt more of her troubles fall away.

Exhale. She released the concern for the palace.

Exhale. She dropped her worries of disappointing her parents.

Exhale. She left the fears of her eumen in Wallai suffering.

Exhale. Her sister's expectations fell away like an anchor holding her ship steady.

And with the next breath, he appeared. A distant figure in a foggy expression of her mind. But she knew it was him, this nameless male.

"Who are you?" she called out. "Why do I know your face and your voice? Who are you?"

"None of that matters. What matters is I'm here to help you," he answered.

"Help me. What do you need to help me with? Why are you in my head?"

"Maluai, you have lost your way, but you can find yourself back. It's not too late."

"Lost my way? I'm not lost. I'm home. What do you mean?"

"You have a purpose there, and you're not fulfilling it. I can feel your indecisiveness, your worry, your concern. Something is wrong. What is it?"

"I think I made the wrong choice," Maluai's voice trembled as she admitted her truth.

"What do you mean?" he asked.

"My mother died. My sister left. Everyone expected me to be queen. I could have done it. I could have said yes, but they gave me a choice not to, and I did." She swallowed the lump in her throat. "I ran away. And it was everything I wanted it to be. I came back to tell them I would give up my position in the royal laenu for good, but things aren't okay."

"Is it too late for you to fix things?" he asked. "You haven't made that declaration yet, have you?"

"No, but—"

"You're hesitating, why?"

"This isn't what I want for myself." She looked at him and felt her heart aching.

"Dig deeper," he urged her.

"What?" She frowned, feeling the familiarity in his words. "What do you mean?"

"That's a surface answer. Dig deeper," he said. "What is the true motivation behind your choice?"

Maluai took a deep breath to center herself. "I don't know."

"Come on. You know yourself. If you can't be honest with anyone else in the world, you must be honest with yourself. Accept your truth, Maluai. What is really holding you back?"

"I want adventure... freedom."

"Do you think the queen of your home has no freedom?"

"No, but—"

"But what?"

"What if I'm not good at it? I mean, my entire life I've gone against tradition. I've never wanted to be in the role, and I didn't take it seriously because Kaluai was supposed to be next."

"But she's not now. You are."

"This isn't right. This isn't how it's supposed to be going."

"Life doesn't care about the paths we carve out for ourselves. What you wanted may not have been the right way for you. Fate has corrected your course, and you must accept it."

"So, I just don't get a choice?"

"Of course you do, but you must know your choice may negatively impact others. If that is something you can live with, go for it."

"I don't want anyone to suffer, but I'm afraid I'm not the right person for this." Tears streamed down her face. "What am I supposed to do if I mess everything up? What if I make things worse for our eumen than they already are? I'm alone! My mother and father are gone. My sister is gone. It's just me. What if I mess it up?"

"And how are they now? How are things? Where are the eumen right now? Now that you've gone away. Now that you've stepped aside and let someone else take over. How are they now?"

"I don't know, but it doesn't sound good." She sighed. "I can tell it's not good. I've been trying to ignore it, but I feel it. My eumen suffer because I left them under the tyranny of someone who thinks he knows best, but every decision he makes takes us further away from the goddess."

"And you would stand aside and let that happen?"

"What am I supposed to do? Tell me what to do," she pleaded.

"I cannot make your choices for you, but something tells me you already know what to do." His voice faded from her mind, and though she tried to keep him there, her eyes opened to the setting sun.

CHAPTER 21

M aluai sat on the edge of the cliff and watched the sky.
It was always something about the sunset, something
that made her mind mellow and her heart calm. And when the
sun was gone and the two moons began their dance, she found
herself filled with a new strength. One that she'd lost a lot of the
day her father died, and the rest the day her mother died.

That was the thing. Maluai was afraid. And that fear, the
feeling she tried to deny, kept her mind racing with thoughts of
unavoidable failure and excuses of why she couldn't do what she
needed to do. She felt weak without them, without their loving
hold, their stern voices, and even their judgmental ideals. They
were her parents, and they were gone, and though she was an
adult, she felt completely lost without them.

But when she was honest with herself, the fear of disappointing them, even though they were no longer around, was what
drove her to run away. But she couldn't do that anymore. Her
eumen needed her. Her sisters needed her, and if she didn't step

in, Fituen would destroy everything her laenu spent centuries building.

So, she watched one last sunset. She gave herself one last sunset before she would return home and claim her rightful place as Queen of Wallai.

She dove beneath the water, her tail appearing to propel her forward, and headed back to the place where she saw Seru at the edge of their territory. As predicted, her guardian was there, waiting for her return.

"I thought you were leaving." Seru smirked as she greeted the princess.

"I just needed to clear my head." Maluai smiled. "You know me."

"I do. I'm glad you're back, Princess. Wallai needs you."

"So, fill me in," Maluai said as Seru turned to swim. "How are things, really?"

"I wish I could give you better news, but things are not well."

"What do you mean?" Maluai's heart sank as she followed her guardian. She frowned when she realized they weren't heading for the principal city, but further into the outskirts of their territory. "What happened?"

"The first few weeks after you left, things were well. The council members made few changes, and it was as if they were holding true to their word and waiting for you to return to give to give your decision, and then things changed. Fituen suddenly wanted to change a lot of things. He started speaking about freedom and power. And the more his rants went on, the more we realized he wanted war with the Forge."

"War? Why?" Maluai believed in the separation of Wallai and Forge, but she, like her laenu, wanted it to be a peaceful transition.

"He believes it will establish our place in the world. He is unhinged, Princess. Of course, the other council members refused his request. They didn't believe this was the way for us to find the freedom we search for, but the more they denied him, the more impatient he became. Soon, Hasik fell ill, and the healers realized this was no normal illness. This was inflicted on her. When we realized what was going on, I took Hasik with some of the other guards and fled the palace, but by doing so, cannot go back. There are still guards and guardians within the walls, some who are on our side, and some who are not. They keep an eye on your sister, alongside her aides, while we remain out here protecting our eumen from Fituen's rage."

"Rage?" Maluai felt her own anger rising. "What do you mean, rage? Has he turned on our own eumen?"

"Fituen does not have the most loyal supporters like he thought he would have. Most Wallains don't agree with what he wants, but he made it very clear that anyone who doesn't agree is at risk. The guards who follow him turned their weapons on their own eumen at his command. And we have been here protecting them, taking them somewhere safe where they are free from harm."

"I can't believe this is happening. He promised he will take care of things while I was gone," Maluai spoke. "I should have known this would happen."

"He said exactly what he needed to make you feel more comfortable with your decision to leave." Seru stopped and looked at the princess. "It was a strategic move."

"And it worked. I should have stayed. I should not have run away like that."

"The important thing is that you're back now. You did what you needed to do to make sure you were sure of your decision. And your return, we'll speak wonders to our eumen. No one thought you would abandon us. We didn't think you would come back with two days to spare," she joked. "But we never thought you would leave us forever."

"Thank you. For keeping watch over my sister and our eumen. For believing in me, even when I didn't."

"Of course, Princess. They're right through here."

Seru guided Maluai through a winding, dark corridor, leading them to a cavern deep beneath the surface of the ocean. She recognized it as one of her father's hideouts. Few knew about them, but the guardians, those most loyal to the royal laenu did. There were several hideouts, some close to home, others further away. If anything should happen, they were to bring the royals to these locations.

When they rounded the corner, she felt a chill run up her spine as she saw what was waiting ahead. Her eumen huddled together like terrified babies. And her heart broke because the weight of her guilt tripled with the sight. And no matter what anyone said, she knew this was the truth. When she left, she abandoned her eumen and left them to suffer under Fituen's control.

"Is this everyone?" Maluai took stock of the eumen in the space. They were of all ages, from infants to elders, who should have been home being cared for by their loved ones. Instead, they huddled together in a dark corner underneath the ocean floor. This was not okay.

"No, there are others in the other hideouts. Soon, we will run out of space," Seru spoke. "We've done everything we can, but things are escalating. We now have reports of Wallains who are going missing or suffering the same illness as Hasik."

"Fituen is calling for war on our own eumen. I will not stand for this," Maluai whispered. "I have to do something."

"I agree." Seru nodded.

Maluai swam forward to the center of the room, and as she did, the scared eyes locked on her, and there was an instant shift. There was hope. She could hear their hushed tones as they discussed her return, and when the whispers died down, she spoke up.

"You know, I have never had to do one of these speeches. I've never had to stand in front of a group and rally their spirits. That's always been my mother, or before her, my father. A part of me thinks I should take inspiration in their words, and maybe even channel their messages, but I don't want to be disingenuous. I need to speak to you in a way that is authentically me.

"I abandoned you all, foolishly placing you in the care of someone who didn't prioritize your wellbeing. And I did that out of fear. Fear that I could not be the queen you all deserve. The idea of being your queen filled me with a dread that I would let down my parents and all the generations that had come before them. But, out of fear, and being too intimidated to confront a seemingly unconquerable challenge, I did the exact thing I wanted to avoid. I failed you.

"I will not stand here and make a stirring speech about how we can fight our way out of this. Because honestly, I don't know what's coming next. But I need to do something much more important. To begin, I want to apologize for not facing my fears and running away from you. I'm here, and I'm standing firm in my decision to stay. That is my promise to you. What Fituen has done here is not okay, and I will do everything in my power to fix it. But I understand that simply by being here, I cannot take away the pain and the fear he has caused. I only hope that I can someday restore your faith in the royal laenu.

"It has been a rough time since my father's passing. From what I hear of the reports of things that have happened since my departure, we have tough times ahead. Because there is no way to move forward without addressing what Fituen has done, and any ripple effects his actions caused. I hope you can find it within you to forgive my naivety for leaving and to stand beside me as I fight to bring us back to what we once were.

"One euman connected with Lunai. That is a vow I make to you right now. I am back, and I have no intention of ever leaving you again."

After she finished speaking, the room was still and quiet. An elder with grey hair and a wrinkled face swam toward her, his movements graceful and strong. Out of respect, Maluai held still as he looked into her face, searching for something unstated. Moments later, after a heavy pause, he saluted her in the Wallain way. And the others in the room slowly repeated his action. Showing the princess they forgave her and would follow her as she reclaimed her place as queen.

A wave of emotion surged through her chest, and she lifted her head in acknowledgement of her eumen. She returned the gesture to the elder. The waves of emotion were almost too much to bear, yet the feeling of being in the right place was undeniable. Maluai felt a wave of clarity wash over her as she realized what she had to do.

"Seru." She turned to her guardian. "Please gather the guards. Let anyone who is on our side know. At first light, we head to the palace. I'm taking back what belongs to me."

Seru worked quickly to engage their network of communication. Soon, their allies gathered at the edge of their territory. Maluai swam to meet them and was happy to find there were far more eumen there than she thought would be. She hadn't lost their loyalty.

"Before we head to the palace, I want you to know this will be a fight. But my plan is not to incite war between our own. This is a fight, but it's between me and the traitor, Fituen. From what I hear, he will not give up control easily, so I must do this in the ways of tradition. I will challenge him. I will fight him. And I will reclaim our home!"

The crowd cheered as she turned, and with Seru and Emixi by her side, she led their eumen to the gates of her familial home.

As they approached, Fituen's guards formed a barrier of armor and shields, blocking the entrance. Maluai called her followers to a halt, leaving twenty feet of space between the two sides. She looked up at her home and felt the sorrow of the place. It always felt alive with energy, but that was gone now as it mourned the loss of the royal laenu.

"This is your princess," Emixi spoke, her voice reverberating through the water. "Move aside and let her through."

They were like statues, not stirring even a single inch. When Emixi moved forward, prepared to levy her power over them, the opposing guards drew their weapons.

"This fight is not one for you to fight." Maluai swam forward as she spoke. "I am here for one thing, and that is to challenge Fituen! If he wants the throne, if he wants to lead our eumen into the future, he will fight for the right. I am still the intended queen, and as promised, I have returned to give my choice. I have chosen to take up the crown and ascend to the throne. Will you stand here and let Fituen avoid the traditions of Wallai?"

"You abandoned your eumen, and you talk about tradition?" Fituen's voice boomed from behind the guards as he swam into view, positioning himself above the others.

"I made a deal with you." Maluai swam to his level, refusing to allow him to look down on her. "To take the time to consider my place here and return with a decision. I held up my end of that deal."

"Why should our eumen accept a queen who wasn't sure just months ago that she was fit for the role?" Fituen laughed condescendingly. "I have never doubted what my place should be here for. For too long, we've accepted the complacency of your laenu, and it's time for a change. It is my promise to usher in that change. And anyone who doesn't agree with me will suffer for it."

"Is this the leader you want?" Maluai jumped at the chance to use his words against him and turned to their eumen. "Do you want someone who would make you suffer for disagreeing? Do you want to follow a leader who places so little value on your input? I am not here to hold my power over anyone. I am here to act as a representative for the eumen of Wallai. The same way those in my laenu have always done." She turned back to Fituen. "Regardless of what you have decided is right for you, there is a way this is done. I am back. I am the head of the royal laenu.

And if you aim to prove that you are the right leader for Wallai, then you will fight for it. And anyone who follows you should disagree with my challenge is following a coward."

"I do not have to stand here for this. Guards, do your job. Get these traitors off the steps of my home," he ordered.

"Look at that. Too afraid to fight your own battles. Instead of proving yourself, you would have them turn on their laenu and their friends. Proclaiming to be a king, yet you cower in fear. You're a liar, and you're a thief of the throne. If you think you can take the crown without a fight, you're dead wrong." She looked at the guards, who stood on Fituen's side. "Is this the leader you want, or do you want someone who will fight for you? Because I can tell you now, he will do what is best for himself. And when you no longer serve that purpose, he will betray your trust and toss you aside with the rest of our eumen."

The guards looked at her, and then the head guard lowered his weapon and swam to the side. And soon, the other guards did too, leaving Fituen standing with no one by his side.

"This is your chance to prove to your eumen that you are their rightful leader. Fight for the position or tuck your tail and swim away." Maluai issued her challenge again.

"If you must embarrass yourself further, I accept your challenge," Fituen announced, and before Maluai could respond, he attacked.

His massive wing smacked her before he pummeled her body with ten powerful blows of his fist. Maluai's body jerked with every hit, and when his last punch landed, she fell to the ocean floor. As she fell, she heard the small, terrified voice of her sister.

"Maluai!" Naluai's voice screamed, and she looked over to see the youngest princess standing in a window of the palace.

Maluai's heart ached more than any of the physical wounds inflicted on her by the councilman. Time slowed as she watched two arms pull her sister back. The guardian would protect her. Lavi's protective instincts kicked in, and he refused to let Naluai take any chances with her safety. Maluai was thankful to the loyal guardian, and she took that view, the image of her sister being held back, and she called to her true form.

No one had seen it. Her entire life, her laenu kept it secret, despite what they expected of the royals. She'd somehow skirted around the topic because of their combined fear that the eumen of Wallai wouldn't accept her. But she knew in this fight she would have to show them who she really was.

Her back hit the ocean floor, and in the swell of dust that exploded around her, Maluai's form shifted, out of view of the eumen who followed her.

"Look at her, so weak," Fituen boasted. "Weak. Barely put up a fight! But she wants to be your queen!"

A collective gasp of surprise rippled through the crowd, causing Fituen to pause his premature lean into announcing his own victory. He turned to follow the gazes of the eumen around him to the settling dust where Maluai's body fell.

He slowly spun around to find her standing there. The dust settled, creating a fog around her body. Maluai stepped forward, and a distinct energy surged through the water as she appeared in her true form. The palpable shock was tangible as everyone gasped in unison. She was not at all the water griffin they had imagined.

As she swam, using four legs to push her through the water instead of a tail, Fituen realized her true form was far more dangerous than his. He felt the weight of her power and backed away. But the disapproving faces of the eumen around him stopped him, and he took another course of action.

"Look at her. She is nothing like us. How can she be our queen?" he tried to discredit her claim. "She is not one of us!"

"You're a coward," she said and looked at her eumen, her own fear of their acceptance causing her heart to race. "I am different. How could I possibly deny that? I mean, look at me. But I am one of you. You saw my mother carry me. You were here for the announcement of my birth. I don't know why, but this is the way I was born. My parents kept this a secret, and I allowed it. I could have defied them and revealed myself to you long ago, but I was just as afraid as they were. I made a promise to you all to be authentic. This is me, authentically. And I'm here to fight for you."

"You would stand behind this abomination?" Fituen tried to swim away, but those who stood on his side blocked his path.

"Fight or flee," Emixi called out as the guards and guardians formed a circle around them. "If you cannot defend your position, you will never be our king!"

"Fine, if this is what you want. To follow an abomination. Feel free." Fituen dropped his hands to his side. "Who am I to stop you? You claim you want to be close to Lunai, and yet you accept this thing. She is not of us!"

Fituen feigned defeat, then as the guards parted to let him through, he spun around and unleashed a flurry of attacks against Maluai. Only this time, she was ready for him. She dodged his blows, but he was faster than she thought he would be. The underestimation of his power resulted in brutal injuries for the princess.

Maluai screamed out as his beak stabbed into her shoulder. She fell back, leaving her chest exposed, and he took the opening. His claws sliced across her chest and created a cut that bled out into the water.

As she fell, a warmth enveloped her, reminding her of the love of her parents. It was more than their love. It was their acceptance, and their encouragement to keep going. Her father's words echoed in her mind. *You will find echoes of my love for as long as you live, and even after you're gone from this world and join me in the next.* He was there with her, and so was her mother.

Instead of falling on her back, she flipped in the water, her feet landing firmly on the ocean floor and propelling her back up. She was in pain, but she pushed through and took the opportunity. She planted her claws in his back, ripping through his wings, then spun the traitor around to face her. He screamed out in pain, but the sound cut off as she opened her wide mouth, and her sharp teeth plummeting into his shoulder, returning the favor.

She bit his shoulder, severing the nerves, and her paw struck his face, cutting his eye with her claw. Fituen's body went limp, and his wide eyes stared up at her in fear as her tail appeared above her head. The sharp tip pointed to his chest, and a moment later, she stabbed it through his heart.

Fituen's life ended the moment she stabbed him, but Maluai knew she had to finish it in the way of their eumen. With her eumen looking on, she opened her mouth again, and in a bloody move, ripped Fituen's head from his shoulder. The crunch was the worst of it, the feeling of her teeth passing through his flesh and bone. And when she spit his head away, and it fell to the ground, the onlooking guards and citizens cheered.

This was their queen, their fearless leader.

With Fituen dead and her sister safe, Maluai swam to the top of the palace. She looked out over the Wallains and their home, which still had touches of the damages that resulted in their father's death. In the distance, in the rays of sunlight that reached down from above, creating a rainbow above their home, she saw them. Her mother and father, together in their new life, and tears fell from her eyes.

And then, as she watched the image of her parents fade away, everything froze. The sound of her eumen muted, and just a few feet in front of her, an arch of coral appeared. The same one she saw before. In the center, there was a swirl of lights beckoning her forward. Maluai knew it was meant for her, and it brought her a sense of peace. Her eumen would be okay. She made sure o f it.

She swam through the opening, the wash of energy moved over her body, and on the other side, she saw him again. That cool voice in her mind. The one who made her feel things she never thought she would.

CHAPTER 22

His arms wrapped around her as she fell into his chest, her chest burning as she caught her breath. His labored laughter filled her ears, and she looked up to see his sweat covered face smiling down at her.

"You're getting faster." He kissed her forehead. "Soon, you'll be able to catch me."

"You have the advantage above water. Come down below and see how you fair." She poked him in the chest, and he kissed her again before letting her go.

"Stay with me." He grabbed her hand and pulled it to his lips for a soft kiss.

"I can't." She frowned, and her heart dropped when his eyes turned down. "Apparently, tonight is a very important night, and I will be in a lot of trouble if I miss it."

"A quote from the queen?" He raised a brow, and she nodded. "I could come with you."

"Jeraim," she started, but he dropped her hand and stepped back.

"I know." He sighed. "You don't have to say it. I'm not invited to that part of your life."

"I'm sorry."

"No, don't apologize. You don't have to." He looked her in the eye. "I know what I signed up for."

"Soon, things will be different." She moved closer to him.

"You've said that for months," he responded, the sadness in his voice ringing clear.

"At least we get to spend time together now."

"Because I'm your *trainer*," he groaned. "Do you know how difficult it is to have to tell everyone I'm just your trainer?"

"Would you like some other hunky land griffin to train me?" she joked to ease the tension between them. "I could choose someone else to run around out here getting me acclimated to the land griffin ways. It would mean spending less time together, but you wouldn't have to tell anyone you're my trainer anymore."

"No. Of course not," he growled. "No one else gets to see you sweat but me."

"I know this isn't ideal, but it's a step toward something better." She reached up, caressing his face. "Besides, I will be above land tonight. Dinner with the royals of Forge. Some big announcement. I'll meet you right here, in our spot, before I return home. Deal?"

"I'll be here." He turned to her and kissed the inside of her palm.

As soon as Maluai returned home from her training, Seru ushered her to her room where the aides waited. They immediately went to work cleaning up the princess and dressing her in the wardrobe her mother chose for the night. Maluai was the obedient doll, and when the aides finally left her, she looked in the mirror. Usually, she hated to get so dressed up, but she thought about her plans to rendezvous with Jeraim after dinner and couldn't help but be excited for him to see her without the sweaty sheen from their workouts.

A knock on the door drew her attention away from her reflection.

"Yes?" Maluai shouted as she adjusted a skewed jewel on her necklace.

"It's me," her older sister called out from the other side of the door.

"Come in, Kal," she called back.

Maluai turned to see her sister enter wearing clothing far less impressive than her own, and her mouth fell open.

"Is that what you're wearing?" she asked her sister.

"Yes." Kaluai frowned, then compared her outfit to her sister's. "Why are you so dressed up?"

"The aides came and said mother wanted me to wear this tonight." She shook her head. "At least I look nice, I guess."

"Huh." Kaluai shrugged. "She's been acting really weird lately."

"Maybe she's still trying to process our father's death," Maluai suggested as she glanced at her reflection once more.

"It's been two years, Mal. I know it's difficult, but how long does it last?"

"Grief is hard, Kal," Maluai defended her mother. "Especially when it was someone who was your other half. Our parents were so deeply in love. That can't be easy to move on from."

"I guess. It would just be nice to move forward." Kal sighed. "I feel like we'll be stuck in that moment with her forever. I miss him too, but I need more for my life."

"Is that why you're here? To talk about moving forward?" Maluai sensed there was more to her sister's visit.

"Mal," Kaluai started with a deep breath.

"Yes?" Maluai gave her sister her full attention. "What's wrong?"

"I need to tell you something," Kaluai said. "I've been debating keeping it to myself, but I can't anymore."

"I'm here for you." Maluai touched her stomach to help calm the pang her sister's words inspired. "What is it? Are you okay?"

"Nothing bad. At least, I hope you won't think so." Her large brown eyes looked up to Maluai and relayed something far more promising than her heavy words.

"Okay, tell me." Maluai took a deep breath. "I'm ready. I can take it."

"I'm in love," Kaluai announced. "I'm in undeniable love."

"You are?" The smile stretched across Maluai's face.

"Yes." Kaluai brushed the braids over her shoulder. "I tried to deny it. You don't know how hard I tried to ignore this. I just can't do it anymore."

"Wait, with who?" Maluai asked with excitement to find out all the details of her sister's secret affair. "When did you find time to fall in love?"

"In Forge." she bit her lip.

"A land griffin?"

"Yes." Kal nodded. "Do you think it's terrible?"

"Of course not!" Maluai took her sister's hands into her own. "Who is it?"

"Cairaix," she admitted with a small smile playing on her lips.

"The princess! Oh, my goddess!" Maluai smacked her sister's arm playfully. "Kal!"

"I know." Kaluai laughed. "But we've spent so much time together these last years as we worked on the new treaty between our eumen. At first, I thought it was just me, you know. I thought it was in my head. But it wasn't. There was this intense attraction, and she felt it too!"

"That's wonderful, Kal." Maluai felt her heart swell with joy for her sister.

"Isn't it? I mean, you really think so, right? Because I can't get her out of my head. I've been calling for extra meetings just to see her more."

"Are you going to tell mother?" Maluai asked.

"Are you going to tell her about yours?" she asked knowingly.

"I don't know what you mean." Maluai moved away from her sister. "We're talking about you, not me."

"Sure." Kaluai pointed at her and squinted her eyes. "I see it on you because I recognize it. It's the same thing I see when I look in the mirror. New love."

"Is it that obvious?" Maluai looked at the door, then to the window as if someone would be there spying on their conversation.

"Let me guess." Kaluai swam in a circle, then stopped with her finger pointed at Maluai again. "The trainer?"

"How did you know?" Maluai asked, shocked at her sister's accuracy.

"Please! Who gets that giddy about running around and sweating all day? Most days, when you have training, you're up and out of here before Seru can knock on your door."

"Shezia! I didn't think I was that transparent. It's just so hard, you know? Keeping the excitement bottled up when I really just want to shout it out."

"Trust me, I get it. Don't worry. Mother thinks it's just because you're still trying to be free of the laenu. I don't think she realizes it yet."

"How long do you think that will work?" Maluai asked but continued speaking before her sister could answer. "I want to be with him, but I don't know how she would respond."

"I'll make a deal with you. You tell her first, and if she responds well, I'll tell her my thing." Kaluai laughed.

"Oh right, make me the sacrificial guppy."

"I'd love you forever for it." Kaluai batted her lashes before she turned for the door.

"You'll love me, anyway." Maluai smacked her on the butt. "But you can find someone else to toss into the gauntlet for you!"

They arrived at the planned dinner, the smell of freshly cooked food wafting through the air. They had spread an abundance of delicious food across the massive table set up with at least twenty seats. From the sight of the dishes to the sounds of conversation, this wasn't a typical dinner. The sudden pit of nerves in Maluai's stomach only got worse when she noticed her mother gazing at her with a look of undeniable love in her eyes.

The crowd was much larger than expected, including both the water and land council members. Everyone was looking at her with a mix of confusion and curiosity, like they all knew a secret she wasn't privy to.

"What is going on?" Kaluai whispered in her ear as their younger sister moved ahead with their mother.

"Okay, I'm not the only one who notices it. I thought I was going crazy," Maluai whispered back.

"Did you also notice the uppity prince staring at you?"

"What?" Kal pointed at the prince, who stood near the head of the table next to his mother. His eyes locked on Maluai like she was a treasure he was about to add to his collection.

"What is that about? Go get your future husband!" Maluai joked.

"The way he's looking at you, I'd think he wants to be yours!"

"Not funny."

"Oh look, they're calling this to order. I guess we should take our seats." Kaluai walked ahead, prepared to take the seat next to her mother as always, but her mother pointed to one seat further down.

"You sit there today." She nodded.

"Okay." Kaluai wouldn't question her mother, not in public.

"Maluai, please." Queen Valuai addressed her middle child. "Next to me today."

Maluai looked at her sister, and suddenly, their joking energy faded away as the rest of the dinner party sat down. And then, as if the awkwardness couldn't get worse, Queen Helena stood at the head of the table calling everyone to attention.

"Before we enjoy this beautiful meal prepared by the talented cooks in our kitchen, I would like to thank Queen Valuai and her beautiful daughters for joining us here tonight. And to announce what I believe you all have suspected." She looked at her son and then at Maluai.

Maluai's stomach sank as the world seemed to move slower around her in her heightened emotional state. She watched intently as the queen's lips moved, forming the words that would shape her future. Her eyes swept the room, taking in the smiling faces of the guests who offered their congratulations through claps and cheers. Maluai felt a chill run down her spine as the queen's words finally resonated with her much later than they should have.

"I'm sorry, what?" She stood from the table, interrupting the queen's speech about the future of their eumen and the strength the marriage would give them. "Marriage? Since when am I set to marry Marruk?"

"Maluai, please."

"No, Mother. Not this time," she screamed. "You promised my hand in marriage in some deal with Forge and didn't think it was important to tell me?"

"Why are you being this way? I've told you my plans for establishing a new relationship with Forge."

"Yes, between Wallai and Forge. You said nothing about me having to marry someone I don't love or even know."

"You will get to know him better in time."

"You're out of your mind." Maluai turned and walked away from her mother.

"Maluai, get back here, now!" the queen shouted after her, but she ignored her mother's call.

With sounds of murmurs filling the room, Maluai came face to face with her guardian at the door. Seru didn't stop her. One look into the princess's eyes, and she stepped aside and allowed her to flee from the palace.

She took a deep breath, closed her eyes, and called on her wings, which responded with a soft rustling sound. The massive wings spread from her back, ripping her dress. Maluai planned to do it more gracefully when she headed to see him. She planned to pull the shoulder straps down to save them and then land, adjust herself, and reveal herself. She wanted to witness the sparkle in his eyes as he saw her beneath the moonlight. Without the layer of sweat and grime from their training. Instead, she landed in front of him, dress ripped in the back, one shoulder barely holding on and tears streaming down her face.

"What happened?" He rushed over to her. "I wasn't expecting you for a while. Are you okay?"

"No, I'm not okay." She shook her head, nearly hyperventilating as she spoke. "My mother. I never knew she could be so heartless."

"Maluai, you need to breathe, please." He placed a hand on each of her shoulders. "Slow down. Tell me what happened."

"She promised I would marry Prince Marruk!" Maluai blurted out the words, then hated herself for the harsh delivery when the pain spread through his expression.

"What?" he asked. "What do you mean?"

"Yes, behind my back. My mother sat with your queen and promised my future to Forge."

"I know this sounds too big for us to face, but I promise you, it isn't. We will get through this. We'll find a way." Jeraim pulled her close and kissed her. When their kiss ended, she laid her head on his shoulder, and out of the corner of her eye, she saw something. A glint of a jewel in the moonlight, but when she turned to look, it was gone.

She stayed with him only for a moment before she raced home and locked herself in her room, refusing to face her mother.

The next day, before the sun rose, she returned to Forge and waited for Jeraim on their training grounds. But he never arrived. Two hours after their scheduled meeting time, she still sat there, alone. Just as she was about to give up and go home, she heard the flap of wings from above, but when she looked up, hopeful of finding him, it wasn't him.

Peliak landed in front of him, his red locks wild around his head.

"Where is he?" Maluai questioned Jeraim's friend.

"He's in holding," Peliak reported. "I debated coming to tell you, but I figured you should know. He's not coming."

"What?" she asked frantically. "Why? He's done nothing wrong."

"They found out about you," Peliak answered her with what he clearly thought was the obvious answer. "I was with him last night, after you two met, and the guard came bursting into his place and drug him off for acts against the queen's wishes."

"I don't understand." She shook her head. "How could they have known? He doesn't deserve to be punished for loving me!"

"The queen will not let him ruin her plans," Peliak answered. "It's too important to her."

She called her wings and took the sky, determined to save Jeraim from Helena's wrath. As she flew, rehearsing her demands in her mind, something distracted her. The same glint, the jewel, hung from the neck of a female land griffin. Cloaked in blue, the griffin turned and flew in a direction opposite the palace. Maluai followed her because she knew the truth.

"You did this!" Maluai yelled as she landed on the ground behind the stranger. "I saw you last night, watching us. You told them about us! Why would you do this?"

"Of course, I did." She rolled her eyes.

"Who are you? Why would you do this?" Maluai asked.

"My name is Wintia. I am the one intended to be with Jeraim," she huffed. "I wasn't going to let you steal him! Besides, you can't be together. You know our kind don't mix. How could you think I would stand aside and let you break the rules?"

"Those rules are archaic!" Maluai's emotions swelled. "And because of your actions, Jeraim is in trouble now."

"You're a princess!" Wintia yelled, her afro bouncing around her face. "You're supposed to be a good example for your eumen. Lead with honor. Is this honorable?"

"What is really your problem? This isn't about me or my position."

"I told you." Wintia narrowed her gaze. "Jeraim is mine!"

"You're delusional." Maluai turned her back. "I'm getting him out of there, and we will be together."

"No!" Wintia charged Maluai from behind, but thanks to her training, she was quick to counter the sneak attack.

Maluai brought her true form to surface, and her enormous paws knocked the weaker griffin to the ground and pressed into her chest. She leaned into her until the whimper crossed her lips. Maluai growled, revealing teeth that could easily end the euman's life.

"This is the last time I will entertain your foolishness. You claim to love him so much, yet you put his life at risk, and for what? Even if I walk away from him, he will never be with you. He doesn't even know you exist!"

"I love him," Wintia sobbed.

"Get over it!" Maluai growled again. "Get in my way again, and it will be the last thing you do!"

Maluai left Wintia on the ground, sobbing over her broken relationship with the euman who had never cared for her. She flew forward, her wings beating against the air with a sound like thunder, her determination clear. She would face the queen of Forge and demand she set him free.

As soon as she landed on the ground, she tucked her wings back into her. Maluai held her head high and strode forward, determined to make her way into the palace and demand to have an audience with Queen Helena. But before she could move forward, she heard her mother's and sister's voices calling to her.

"Maluai." Her mother stepped in her path.

"I'm not here to see you." Maluai looked past her mother. "I have to set something right."

"We have to talk," her mother said urgently. "You can't do this."

"Now you want to talk to me? I didn't think that was necessary for you. What is it? Do you want my input on the floral arrangements for the big day?" She scowled at her mother. "Move."

"You would disrespect me like this?" Her mother's voice turned hard with her disbelief.

"I show you the same amount of respect you showed me." It hurt Maluai to speak to her mother like that, but she had to make her point. "And now, because you went behind my back and signed my life away with no input from me, an innocent euman suffers."

"What are you talking about?"

Maluai glanced at her sister, who nodded in support.

"I'm in love. I've been in love, and if you weren't so lost in your own grief, you may have noticed. Here I was worried that you would be upset because of who I chose, because of what he is, and you chose someone like him. Only they couldn't be any more different." She dropped her head back. "Marruk, Mother, really? You chose Marruk for me? In what world does that work?"

"I chose the best match for—"

"Don't. Don't lie to me! You chose what was best for Wallai, not for me. I know you're the queen, and you must protect the future of our euman, but what about me? You are my mother, and you signed me away to be married to a self-important narcissist." She felt tears swelling in her eyes. "To him, I would be nothing more than another superficial trophy to add to his collection. Do you really think he could ever love me? Or is it not important to you that I ever know true love?"

"I—" Valuai looked at her daughter, and for the first time, the queen was lost for words.

"I love him. And because I love him, Queen Helena had him locked up. Because my love for him interferes with your plans for the future of two eumen who you claimed to want to separate. What happened to that plan? Why are you now forging a stronger alliance through marriage? When did I lose view of your grand plans for Wallai? When did you?"

With a loud creak, the doors to the palace opened, and the Forge guards marched out. Queen Helena stepped between them; her lips pressed into a thin line of displeasure. She knew why Maluai was there and wasn't trying to hide it.

Valuai looked at her daughter still, her back to the Queen of Forge. As she looked at Maluai, the sorrow that had been weighing on her heart suddenly dissolved, lifting the veil that had been clouding her vision. She saw the love her daughter had for someone whose name she had yet to share, but she knew exactly who it was.

"How could I have missed it?" she whispered. "It's written all over your face. You hurry to see him, and you never object to the demanding trainings, despite having complained about every formal training your entire life. Jeraim. It's him, isn't it?"

Maluai nodded. "It is, Mother. I love him."

329

"You withheld this information from me instead of coming to me. How could you imprison him, knowing she loves him?" Valuai turned to Helena. "Why would you do this?"

"Are you as naïve as your daughter? I took the necessary steps to ensure your promise was upheld. Besides, I assumed you knew. Why else would you have made the commitment? I saw a problem, and I took care of it. Was that supposed to know you don't talk to your children?"

"I will ignore your insult for now." Valuai narrowed her gaze. "This marriage will not happen. You will release Jeraim at once. We have to call this off. I'm sorry."

"Called it off? There is no calling it off." Helena moved forward, and her guards shadowed her advance. But they stopped cold when Valuai's guards appeared, landing at her side, Emixi at the head. Helena narrowed her eyes. "Are you going to be a queen of your word? We had a deal."

"It's not as if your son would care if I married him or not," Maluai spoke up. "He's not even interested in me. Never has been."

"That boy isn't interested in anything, but your interests are of no concern to me," Helena snapped. "This new treaty, this bond between our eumen, that is the only thing I care about."

"There will be no marriage between us," Maluai said firmly. "How can you expect me to give up my life, my freedom, and spend it in a loveless marriage with a euman who doesn't care if I live or die? I will experience the warmth of love radiating through my life. I refuse to be restricted by societal expectations, and I will make my own decision about who I will love. It may be difficult for you to hear this, but your son does not fit the bill."

"The absolute disrespect you spew out of your face is unnerving! I don't care how your mother allows you to talk to her. You're in my home now, and you will show me respect." Helena stepped toward Maluai, her finger pointed in her face, but Valuai moved in between them.

"Move against my daughter again, and there will be war. I know this is what the treaty is about. Or do you take me for a fool, Helena? You boast about how you want to protect both sides. We both know good and well Wallai is stronger on her own. It is Forge who needs *us*." Valuai looked over at her daughter to make sure she was okay.

Maluai nodded, keeping her thoughts to herself as her mother continued speaking.

"I admit my mistake here. My grief and determination to pave a better way for my eumen blinded me to truths others would have seen obvious, but I did it wrong, and I'm just happy I can correct my mistake before I lose my daughter's love forever." She turned back to Helena. "But do not take my ability to admit my mistakes as a sign of weakness. You are the ones who need us. You are the ones who are no longer connected to your magic. Isn't that why you're so uncompromising about this now? You realized the risk of the target being placed on your head if the rest of the world finds out you've lost your connection to Lunai. So, we will find another way to solidify this new treaty. If you want to deny my decision here, if you want to take action against my daughter, know it means you are taking action against Wallai. Know that it means war. Know it is a war you will lose."

"No one wants war. Is the only alternative to my marrying an uninterested prince a devastating war?" Maluai asked. "There has to be a better way to resolve this."

"No one has to suffer being married to my boring brother for this to happen," Cairaix's voice, strong and melodic, carried on the wind as her wings moved powerfully, carrying her through the sky. As she landed, the princess of Forge's grey wings rustled in the breeze, providing a majestic backdrop to her body.

"Daughter, this is no place for you," Helena addressed her.

"I am the next queen of my eumen. This is exactly my place," Cairaix said firmly, and when her mother shot her a look of disbelief, she didn't falter. "You know, in the last years, I've listened to Maluai and her sisters. Unlike you, Mother, I value their opinion, and I agree with them. We've stuck to traditional ways for far too long, and we've allowed those of us who have lost sight of our true purpose to guide us.

"But one day, when you all are gone from this world, it would be ours to repair from your debauchery. You want a new alliance between our eumen, and you want that to happen through marriage. Fine. We will give you what you want one last time. And then, you will step aside and listen to the future of our eumen instead of clinging to the skeletons of the past. I propose it is still possible. Maybe not with the marriage you thought, but with one with one that is loving, nurturing, and wanted on both s ides."

"What are you talking about?" Helena asked. "This is not the time for you to choose to defy me."

"I'm inspired by your action here today," she said to Maluai. "And now, I must take action of my own. A proclamation I have been hesitant to make. I am in love, and I would like to declare that love with the promise of marriage."

The princess opened her wings, taking to the sky with a whoosh of air, and flew in circles above Kaluai's head. It was the mating circle, and both queens looked like they would faint as they watched her. Kaluai, however, looked as if she would float off the ground. After slowly circling Kaluai, each loop growing more intimate, she finally landed next to her, and the two embraced tightly.

"Cairaix," her mother whispered.

"This is who I love, and I will be with her," Cairaix declared with an air of authority.

Valuai looked at Kaluai, and the corners of her lips lifted as she witnessed their budding love. "I accept your offer, Cairaix. I would be glad to have you as a new daughter." She turned to Helena, who, of course, had no option but to accept the compromise. Still, she stood in her stubbornness.

"Mother," Cairaix said. "Let it go."

Helena pursed her lips, then turned to her guard. "Have Jeraim released."

Maluai smiled as she left her laenu, knowing she'd done the right thing. And she felt lighter without the weight of her secret. The overwhelming desire to be reunited with her love drove her to go to the place they shared. She knew he would be there. The place where she first heard his voice saying he loved her. She landed on the cliff and was greeted by the salty ocean breeze as she waited for him.

"You told them?" He landed behind her with a soft thud.

"Yes." She turned to face him, and her heart smiled when the corners of his lips lifted after hearing her confirmation.

"What about your concerns?" he asked. "You were worried they wouldn't accept us."

"Jeraim, their acceptance is not worth more than your life or our love. I always planned to tell them. I just wanted to find the right time and way to do it. If I could go back, I would tell my mother right away and avoid all of this. "

"There is no need. We can be together now, right? Truly."

"Yes." She smiled, and he kissed her before he took off into the sky.

As Jeraim performed his mating dance above her, something called Maluai's attention away from him. An archway of intertwined coral and tree branches appeared, casting a soft, pink hue over the area. Maluai looked at the forming doorway, and the feeling of sorrow overwhelmed her when she lifted her gaze to her love, and she knew she had to leave him behind. She only hoped he would understand.

As he flew above, she crossed the threshold and awakened to the sounds of explosions.

CHAPTER 23

A t first, the feeling of being jolted from her dream was
almost imperceptible, yet it gradually grew stronger. She
clung to the dream that held all the promises of a life she so
longed for. Maluai fought to remain asleep until the shaking
grew so violent, she couldn't help but awaken. Following the
violent shakes was an orchestra of screams of pain from her
eumen. Her eyes sprung open, and moments later, the walls
around her bed shook.

The princess hopped out of bed, her heart pounding with
fear as she swam over to the window to take in the dreadful
sight outside her room. Balls of flames plummeted through the
water, landing on the ocean floor and setting her home ablaze.
She smacked her hand over her mouth, silencing a gasp as she
watched one of her eumen be swallowed up in the flames as they
tried to escape.

"How is this happening?" She gawked at the underwater fire.
It made no sense, but she knew her eyes were not lying to her.
Her home was burning.

Maluai backed away from the window and then became frozen in her own fear as a series of troublesome questions rang through her mind. What could she do? Why was this happening? Was her laenu okay?

As she questioned her current reality, a different version of her life blended into chaotic flashes in her mind. Maluai remembered things that were not clear to her just moments before. She remembered her mother's decree of their freedom, and Queen Helena's blatant disregard for what was right for the eumen of Wallai. She remembered months of agonizing debates and meetings that led to only more disagreement about the future of her eumen. And then she remembered just the night before, before she laid her head on her bed on her pillow, she spoke with her mother.

"I cannot promise you that this will not turn ugly." Queen Valuai sat across from her daughter, a gentle yet serious expression on her face. But *"but I want you to know that it was never what I wanted."*

"I know that." Maluai reached out to her mother and held her hand. *"I know your intentions have always been for a peaceful transition."*

"I wish I could understand what drives these responses we get from Forge, and I guess, on some level, I do. They are afraid that without us, they will suffer. That fear is so strong that it blinds them to the fact that their actions are harming both sides. To them, it's worth it if it means even the slightest chance of preserving some sense of ill-gotten pride for them.

But I want you to know I will always do what I feel is best for our eumen and our laenu. You and your sisters come first, but there may be a time when we are not together. There may be a time when all of this means we have to part ways. Kaluai will not want to do this. She will oppose me. Naluai will be too afraid either way it goes. She's young, but she looks up to you. If the time should come when I need you all to get away, I need you to be the one to make sure your sisters do as I ask. Your youngest sister will follow you. Your older sister will go to protect you. Promise me."

"You say this as if it's written in stone." Maluai chuckled nervously, but frowned when her mother's face remained serious. "Is just a hypothetical, right?"

"There are no hypotheticals. We do not operate in hypothetical thinking. We plan for the possibilities. I'm telling you, this is a genuine possibility. One that you must be prepared to act on. Promise me."

"Okay, I promise."

The thud of the door slamming into the wall behind her startled Maluai and brought her attention to the unexpected guest. She turned to find Seru, who carried a bag in one hand and her spear in the other. She swam around the room quickly before pulling Maluai further from the window and potential danger.

"What's going on?" Maluai asked as she watched Seru make sure the room was secure. "Why is this happening?"

"Forge has attacked. We are going to war," Seru explained as she handed her the bag she carried in with her. "Princess, I need you to get dressed. Now. We have to go. These are special protective gear. They will protect you."

"Protect me? Won't you be there for that?" Maluai took the bag and opened it, quickly pulling the armored gown around her.

"Should we part ways, this is just a contingency plan." Seru touched her shoulder and looked at her with a serious expression.

"Right," Maluai said nervously. "Is there a chance of that happening?"

"The others are waiting for us," Seru avoided answering her question. "Your sisters and the queen are also preparing to move. We must meet them."

"Okay." Maluai nodded and finished dressing before following Seru out the door.

They swam down to the center of the palace just beneath the court, where they built a hidden bunker with secret tunnels that led out to various bunkers. As they approached, the guards opened the door, revealing the group that had already gathered. Her mother was with her sisters in the center of the space while the council members and guards gathered in the corners having hushed conversations.

"Maluai." Her mother sighed in relief when she saw her. "Thank the goddess, you're okay."

"Yes, I'm fine." She embraced her mother, then her sisters. "What are we going to do?"

The queen looked around the room at the eumen, who looked to her for guidance. She took a deep breath and then turned to Kianna, nodded, and then addressed the room.

"While this is not what we wanted to happen, we knew it was a possibility that Forge would not take our separation with grace. They are testing us now. This attack is a test of Wallai's strength and determination to stand on her own. And we will not fail! The guards are in position, our eumen are being evacuated. But we will stand and protect our home."

"We?" Kaluai asked.

"Your guardians will escort you to you to safety."

"No." Kaluai moved forward. "We will not leave you. We will stand and fight this together."

"Kaluai." Their mother swam to the princesses and placed her hand on her oldest daughter's face. "Your fate is intertwined with the fate of Wallai. I am determined to preserve our home. However, I must, by any means necessary, secure the future of this laenu and Wallai. We must protect you and your sisters to guarantee a thriving future for our eumen."

"What are you talking about? The future of Wallai? There is no future without its queen!" Kaluai insisted.

"I think we should go," Maluai said, making eye contact with her mother. "Mother is right. There is a time to fight and a time to be strategic. This is the best move to make."

"Really?" Naluai looked up at her with wide and fearful eyes. It was just like the queen said it would be.

"Yes." Maluai nodded, though she didn't truly believe her words. It was what she promised her mother. "I will go as mother asks."

"Then I will go with you." Naluai held her hand. "You shouldn't be alone."

They both looked at Kaluai, who huffed. "This is the wrong decision. I just want you all to know that. We should stay together."

"Kaluai, my daughter, please trust me," Valuai pleaded.

"I do trust you, Mother. I do."

"Good." The sounds of war battling on reached them from above, and the Queen signaled the guardians to move. "Then it's time for you to go."

The three sisters hugged their mother one last time. As soon as their embrace ended, their guardians, flanked by the lower guards, ushered them through the secret passage away from the palace.

"Do you agree with this?" Kaluai asked her sister as they were ushered through the underground. "Do you honestly believe this is the best way?"

"Kal," Maluai started to ask her sister to back off.

"I really want to know. Why are you walking away? We're the future for our eumen, right? Shouldn't we be on the same page?"

"Fine." Maluai turned to her sister, halting their progress.

"Princess, we really should keep moving," Seru said, but Maluai held her hand up.

"No, Kaluai. If you must know," Maluai admitted. "I don't think this is the right thing to do."

"So, why are we going?" she asked. "Why did you agree?"

"Because I promised," Maluai blurted out. "I made a promise, and I can't go back on my word."

"Promised?" Kaluai frowned. "Who did you promise?"

"Mother." She sighed, rubbing the kink forming in her neck. "Before bed, she called me to her room and asked me to make sure you left because she knew you wouldn't."

"How could you agree to that?" Naluai moved in front of her sister.

"What?" Maluai frowned. "What do you mean?"

"How could you say yes to that?" Naluai shook her head. "Knowing it wasn't what you really believed in, you still said yes?"

"I don't know, I just—"

"You chickened out," Naluai finished the thought Maluai couldn't.

"Naluai."

"No. You took the easy route." She looked at her in disbelief. "Like you always do."

"Nal," Maluai started. "Please. You don't understand."

"No. I understand perfectly. I came here with you because I thought you believed it was the right thing to do, but you're just running again. Running from the hard things. When will you ever stop that?"

"I—" Maluai tried to speak, but vivid memories overwhelmed her thoughts, causing her to choke on a sudden wave of emotion. His face was like a dream, and the sight of it made her heart melt. As she heard his voice, memories of his name suddenly flooded her mind. As the flashes continued, growing more intense, she could almost feel the man's hand in hers. Somehow, despite having no solid evidence that this he was real, she knew he was there for her.

"Jeraim," she said his name aloud. "I need you."

"What?" Naluai grabbed her hand. "Who is Jeraim? Are you okay?"

As her thoughts sped up, she felt the room spin around her and heard the faint echo of a whirring sound. The guards and her sister's faces were indistinguishable to her, blending together as one. They twisted and morphed with each other until everything went dark. Eyes slid shut, Maluai's body sunk to the floor of the passageway as if weighed down by the overload of emotions.

Despite her dramatic passage into an unconscious state, she felt an internal calmness. The surrounding area grew brighter, and she stood atop a grassy hill, looking out at the sea. After that, she spotted him. The euman from the memories she couldn't be sure were hers. He walked across the grassy hill toward her, and her heart raced as she watched him.

"Jeraim?" she repeated the name that echoed to her.

"You remembered me." He nodded. "That's good."

"Yes." She frowned. "Though I'm not sure why I remember you."

"What's wrong?" He continued walking toward her, but didn't appear to get any closer.

"Why did I call you? Who are you? Why do I know you?" She lifted her voice because he appeared to get further away, though still walking toward her.

"That's not what you really need to know," he spoke in an even tone that reached her ears without faltering, despite the distance. "I'm here to help. That's what matters. Now, tell me what's wrong."

"I... I don't know." Maluai struggled to pick through the blend of memories that fought to the surface in her mind. "I mean, we're under attack."

"Wallai?" he asked. "Are you hurt?"

"Yes, Forge has attacked." She looked over her body as if she couldn't remember the physical state of her being. "I'm fine, I think. No, they did not hurt me."

"Good, you're safe." He sighed. "Are you not sure how to defend yourself?"

"My mother asked us, my sisters and me, to leave," she explained. "And I promised her I would make sure we did."

"You held up your word?"

"Yes, but I'm not sure it's the right thing to do." She shook her head. "I'm struggling with the choice now."

"Why is that?"

"Because we're a laenu. We're supposed to be together, right? I mean, with everything going on, we should be together." Maluai frantically worked through her reasoning. "The royals of Forge won't be separating right now. They will fight together. We should do the same thing."

"Did you tell your mother that?" Jeraim calmly asked, but she felt like he'd twisted a knife in her stomach.

"No," she snapped. "I didn't."

"Why not?" Even though she became agitated, he remained cool.

"She insisted we leave at the first sign of danger. It was like she knew it was coming. She said it was best for the future of our eumen, and I chose to believe her because I wanted to have hope. My sisters will be safer this way."

"Is this about your sisters or is it about you?" he challenged her explanation.

"Excuse me?" She frowned. "You think I'm a liar?"

"No. I do not think you're a liar. I know you to be many things, but dishonest is not one." He continued walking toward her. "Here's what I believe. Things got tough, scary. You saw a way out, and you took it. You once told me you run when things are hard. It's how we met. You were escaping something difficult. It caused a lot of discord between you and your laenu and made them believe you would leave them behind the first opportunity you got."

"That's what Naluai said. She said I was taking the easy way out." She dropped her head back to look at the sky. "It's true.

It's what I do. I even did it when our father passed away. I left them to face losing him without me. And now our mother faces losing Wallai without us there."

"Is that what you're doing? When you're honest with yourself about how you feel, is that what this is? Are you leaving to protect your sisters, or are you doing it so you won't have to face something that may not end the way you want it to?"

"I don't want to lose anyone else. We've already lost our father, our king. If this keeps them safe, then it's the best thing to do. Right?" She looked at him, but he appeared further away than before.

"That's not a question for me to answer." Jeraim smiled. "You know the answer. Because it's your opinion of the situation, no one else's."

Maluai breathed in deeply, the salt of the ocean air tickling her nose, and considered her options. The fear of losing them was so strong, she willingly sacrificed her beliefs, though in the end, she'd still have to go through the pain of losing someone. She could only hope her mother would survive in their absence.

"We have to go back," she said firmly. "We can't leave her there."

"Did you really need me to help you realize that?" He raised a brow. "It feels like you could have gotten to that understanding on your own."

"I'm not sure. I'm not even really sure who you are." She let out a soft, stifled laugh, her mouth creasing in a slight frown. "There is something inside of me that is drawn to memories

345

of you and of things I don't know I experienced. And looking at you makes my heart do this fluttering thing I've never felt before. It's all so confusing, but if I'm honest, I like that you're here, in my mind, to offer what feels like an outside perspective. Hopefully, that doesn't make me insane."

"Sanity is subjective," he said before he stopped walking and then faded away.

The sun had been high in the sky, but suddenly, it started its descent, painting the sky with a spectrum of vibrant colors and creating a warm, orange glow. She felt a wave of serenity wash over her as she accepted that what felt right in her heart was the right thing to do.

"Are you okay?" Kaluai asked as her eyes opened to the sight of six faces leaning into her like spectators at a shark race.

"Yes." She adjusted herself, and the others backed away to give her space. "I'm okay."

"You just passed out. Are you sure?" Naluai asked. "That's not normal."

"I'm okay, I promise." She looked between her sisters. "We have to go back."

"What?" Kaluai placed her hand on Maluai's forehead. "Are you sure you're okay?"

"We are a laenu. We will not leave our mother behind to fight this alone." She turned to Naluai. "You're right. I always run from the hard stuff. Not anymore. I'm done running."

"What about your promise?" her younger sister asked.

"Technically, I promised we would leave." Maluai shrugged. "We left. And now we're going back."

"So, back to the palace?" Seru asked, looking over her sister's head.

"Yes, unless you don't want to join us," Maluai said. "I understand you have to follow orders."

Seru looked at the other guardians, who all nodded. "We thought you'd never ask."

"You want to go back?" Naluai gasped.

"It's as much our home to defend as it is yours." Seru moved aside and gestured for the princesses to swim back the way they came.

Before they could move, they heard more explosions above them.

"I don't think we have time to take the long way." Kaluai looked at the carved ceiling above their heads.

"You're right."

Seru twisted the shaft of the spear in her hand, and the head of the weapon spun, creating a bright light as it moved. A soft whirring sound emitted from the tip as it sped up. The other guardians pushed the princesses back to a safe distance as Seru took aim. A moment later, when the sound reached its highest pitch, a blast of power ripped through the weapon and created a hole in the ceiling big enough to swim through.

They rushed through the fresh opening and started a direct course back to the palace. The guardians and guards positioned themselves around the princesses, their vigilant eyes scanning the surroundings for potential threats as they moved. Along the way, they witnessed more devastation. They had to move swiftly to avoid the fireballs that sizzled through the water, smashing into the ocean floor.

Just outside the palace, Maluai spotted their mother. Flanked by her own guardian and a sizeable group of guards, she headed for the surface.

"There!" Maluai pointed to her mother. "She's going to the surface."

"Then so are we." Kaluai shifted her course, and the group followed without question.

By the time they broke the surface of the water, they could hear the roar of the crowd and the clashing of weapons. Maluai's eyes darted around the area, taking in every detail. Her mother was already confronting the enemy on the land while some guards soared through the air with a loud whoosh. She recognized their target, the massive golden cannons that shot the flames into the water. They'd taken two out, but there were still three active shooters.

"Seru!" Maluai called to her guardian and pointed to the cannons, which were revving up to shoot more flames. "We need to take those out."

"On it." Seru shot from the water, with three other guards, their wings quickly drying to carry them through the sky.

She watched as the guardian fired her own shot from her spear and smelled the sulfur in the air as the blast destroyed one cannon. As Seru moved on to her next target, Maluai returned her attention to the flight on the ground.

"Mal," Naluai shouted. "We need to help Mother!"

The princesses made their move, simultaneously leaping from the water, their wings carrying them forward. Their moment of heroic uniformity was broken by Fralim's attack. The Prince of Forge slammed into Naluai, knocking her back into the water. Maluai gasped, ready to defend her sister, but the youngest princess quickly recovered and returned her own blow to the prince. She kicked him in the stomach, knocking the prince directly into the hands of Lavi.

Feeling reassured that Naluai could protect herself, she proceeded on her way to help her mother. Ahead of her, Emixi and Kaluai moved gracefully, in perfect harmony. Every time an offense was made in their direction, they countered it with ease, the sound of clashing swords ringing through the air. Emixi's movements were a perfect mirror image of Kaluai's. When Kaluai dipped, Emixi rose. When the princess launched a hit, Emixi was there to follow it up with an equally powerful blow. In their wake, the guards of Forge dropped lifelessly into the ocean.

They made it to the grounds where her mother fought.

"What are you doing here? I told you to leave," the queen addressed her daughters, not missing a step as she continued her fight.

"Yeah, well, your daughters are as stubborn as you." Maluai shrugged before dodging the blow of a sword, punching the guard out and taking the weapon for herself. "Deal with it."

"We'll discuss this later," the queen said as the fight continued.

The three weaved through each other's steps, the motion coming together to create a stunning synchronized dance of death that was only enhanced when Naluai joined in.

"Fralim?" Kaluai asked the youngest princess.

"Gone," Naluai confirmed.

"That's not going to make things better," Maluai muttered.

"You're right about that." Kaluai pointed to the sky, where the Queen of Forge appeared.

In mid-flight, Queen Helena shifted from vanity form to true form. A sorrowful cry pierced the air, reverberating through the sky as the queen mourned her son. And then everything moved too quickly for Maluai to process. Soon, Naluai was down, injured, with her guardian protecting her. Kaluai and Emixi were in the sky fighting Marruk as a bloodied Cairaix fell to the ground. But what was worse was the sight of her own mother, surrounded by the guards of Forge. She saw Helena making her move and refused to let this be the end.

"Seru!" Maluai cried out, and her guardian understood. Maluai shifted into her true form and bulldozed her way through the guardians who surrounded her mother while Seru went for the queen. Opposite Maluai's guardian was the head of the queen's guard, Kianna. Kianna's blow landed, knocking the queen of forge from the sky, but not before she removed Seru's head from her shoulders.

Maluai's heart broke as she watched Seru's limp body slam into the ground just a few feet from her. The distraction was enough. The guards of Forge surrounded her, taking their attention from the injured queen.

"You killed my son!" Queen Helena screamed as she approached Queen Valuai. "I will take everything from you!"

"You've already taken everything from me! My husband is dead because of your actions, my eumen suffer, and now you know but a taste of the pain we have endured." Valuai stood, shifting to her true form. "You want to take Wallai down? You'll have to take me out first."

She felt the tension in the air as everything around her slowed down. Every second was marked by the sound of her breath, the feeling of her heart beating, and the warmth of her tears. The two queens clashed, but Helena overestimated Valuai's injuries, and the queen of Wallai played it perfectly. With a surge of confidence, Helena thought she had the advantage—until Valuai grabbed a Forge blade, a weapon of their enemies, and thrust it forward. It moved effortlessly through the flesh and bone of Helena's neck. When her head fell to the ground opposite her body, the fight ended.

With every blink, Maluai was transported to a new, vibrant world of sights and sounds. Forge's solemn surrender. The memorial for the fallen guards and guardians. Seru's face being hung in a portrait among those to be honored. The freedom of Wallai solidified in stone. And then her mother and sisters, standing proudly among the other eumen of Eldritch. Quick succession, the success of their eumen, and then darkness. Cold, empty, frightening darkness.

She didn't question it when the passage appeared. She sighed at the beautiful coral structure and stepped forward, only hesitating for a moment when she felt the deep sadness radiating from the other side. But if she had learned anything at all, it was that she had to face the hard stuff; she had to keep moving forward.

CHAPTER 24

The darkness lingered, engulfing everything in its oppressive silence. With each step, she desperately hoped the end of the journey would come, but all she could hear was her own footsteps echoing as she walked through the endless void. Until a soft cough cut through the silence. At first, she couldn't distinguish what it was, but then it became more discernible. The deep gurgling sounds. The sound of life slowly fading away, like a gentle whisper. These were the chaotic coughs of death's last call.

As the sound grew clearer, she grasped exactly what it was. The markers of an end of a life. The life of someone whose memory she had held so close to her heart. Someone she thought she'd never see again, and yet she had to come to face him once more. She continued walking, hoping her assumptions were wrong, but then at the end of the long, dark corridor, were the doors to a room she knew. The room where her father d ied.

Maluai stood outside the doors, contemplating what to do. Her options were limited. She felt trapped, with no other options in sight. As she turned, she saw the walls inching ever closer, their shadows looming over her as they advanced. She felt an irresistible pull to go in. Of all the things she thought she'd have to face in her life, of all the things she encouraged herself to prepare for, this was not one of them. This was a thing of her past. She couldn't comprehend why she was back, but she felt an undeniable tugging in her soul that told her she had to move forward. She had to face the hard things.

She pushed the doors open, expecting to see the healers working diligently to keep their king alive, but there was no one inside the room. All she saw was a bed with a frail figure lying beneath weighted covers. The door slammed behind her, the sound almost deafening, but she remained still, unable to move forward. It smelled. The room smelled of death, of decaying flesh, of singed wounds, and rot.

Maluai had a feeling she needed to get closer, but she couldn't move. She stayed close to the door, pressing her back against the hard surface.

"I can't do this," she whispered to herself and tried to leave the room, but when she turned to the door, it had no knob.

Maluai stepped back, looking for a way out, but the more she examined the door, the more it faded away until it was nothing but a flat surface. Another wall restricting her access to the outside world. When she looked around the room, everything faded. The windows and the secondary door disappeared.

There she was, trapped in darkness with the one thing she never wanted to face. Then the room filled with water, and as it did, her legs shifted into a tail.

Despite knowing she would be alright; the water was her home; she panicked. Her breathing quickened, and her heart raced, and then her mind forced her back to a memory. A memory of him when he was happy, healthy, and alive.

"Move gently, not just your actions, but your spirit as well. Calm your energy, Maluai. You must be careful. These are tiny little fish who startle easily, but if you're careful, if you're gentle, they will stay, and then you'll see something wonderful," her father instructed her to remain as still as possible as the little fish school exited the hutch they hid in and began a beautiful dance of colors.

"This is the sign for feeding," he whispered. "It not only gives coverage for the younger fish in their colony, but it distracted any predators, because from afar, they would look larger. If we were to swim away and watch them from above, we might mistake them for a whale."

"It's beautiful," her youthful voice whispered as she watched.

"It's more than that." He pointed. "See how they change position? The ones who have already fed take the place of those who haven't. It is a fascinating system these simple creatures have come up with."

"Why are you showing me this?" Maluai could hear the change in his voice, the sound of the intended passing of wisdom.

"There is a lesson in this for you. One of patience. If you are patient enough, beautiful things will happen, and you will see the world open to you. If you try to make things move in your own time, it will be impossible to experience all the things this world has for you."

"How can you say that to me when I'm not even allowed to leave our home?" she huffed, but kept her voice in a whisper. "The world doesn't have that much for me. The world has what lies within the borders of our home, and while it is beautiful, it is not without limits."

"And if you keep thinking that way, it will remain limited." He lifted his daughter's chin to look her in the eye. "I promise you there is so much more out there for you, and this time of restriction is but a drop in the well of what life has in store for you."

Maluai gasped as the vision faded away, and she was once again in the room with the stench of approaching death. She felt a deep sorrow inside as she saw the emaciated figure in the bed, her vision blurred by tears. The struggled rise and fall of labor breathing taunted her, and again, she tried to look for an exit, but the walls were bare, and the only light in the room came from an orb that sat at his bedside. There was no way out, there was no option left. She clenched her fists and prepared to confront this.

Her heart pounded in her chest as she weighed the only choice given to her. She wanted to turn away but couldn't bring herself to look away from his suffering. Like an internal emergency exit, her mind pushed away from the moment. She flashed again to another memory from another lifetime.

They raced through the rooms, swimming above and beneath and through the obstacles they put together. Maluai's laughter filled the hallway. She was the fastest of them all.

"You couldn't beat me even if you had a jet on your plu's!" she screamed as she zoomed through the hall and skidded into the dining room. The sounds of her sisters echoed through the halls behind her, and Maluai came face to face with her father, who sat at the dining table.

She smacked her hands over her mouth, her wide eyes full of regret. The word she used was unfit for a princess, and she expected her father to scold her, but he laughed. His laugh was so big it echoed through the room. She remained still, confused, as his body quivered with each boom of his laughter. He smacked the table and held his side; the laughter growing louder until he was wincing from pain.

"Father?" She considered running. Maybe this was an unchecked response before he would finally put her in her place about her foul language. "Are you okay?"

"You know, if your mother heard you talking like that, you would be in huge trouble," he spoke as his laughter finally calmed. "But the look on your face!"

"I know. I'm sorry."

"Don't be sorry." He winked at her after looking over his shoulder to make sure his wife wasn't there. "Be careful."

"Are you not angry?" she asked nervously.

"Angry? Why would I be?"

"My language."

"There are worse things you could do. Besides, as a future ruler of your eumen, you'll learn that your position may cause for you to say worse things than that."

"I don't want to do worse than that." She looked mortified. It was fun to curse when there were no consequences, but she didn't want to do it as a princess when her words held meaning.

"Though no one desires these moments, life may sometimes put us in situations of distress, and we have to find a way to cope and move forward. Sometimes that means saying or doing things we otherwise wouldn't."

"Even cursing?"

"Even that." He laughed before pointing to the door she came through. *"Now, I believe you're losing your race. If you lose, you'll never hear the end of it."*

Once again, the memory ended, and Maluai returned to her present moment. The lesson her father taught her felt like a force pushing her. She had to have the patience to let life work and the courage to face whatever it presented her with. Running was not an option. So, she took a deep breath, and she spoke. She let her truth pour out of her, no matter the consequences of the words.

"I don't know if you can hear me. I think you can, but I'm not sure. This isn't the first time I've had to live through this moment. The moment of your death. Only this time is different. This time I can't run away. That's what I did last time. I ran."

Her voice shook with a mixture of sorrow and fear. "I couldn't face it. I ran because it was too hard and because you told me it was okay to do what came naturally to me. But it wasn't okay. I know that now. Leaving my mother and my sisters to lose you without me was not okay.

"I told myself it was because I was with our eumen. I was taking care of Wallai the way you would have been, but that was a cop out because I should have been by your side, and I know that." Tears welled, causing her voice to tremble. "The problem is, knowing the right thing to do doesn't make it any easier. I couldn't face losing you then, and I don't want to face losing you now. And I don't know why I'm made to relive this moment.

"You were everything to me. You were my lifeline. In a world that often felt too dark to navigate, you brought light. Even with the limitation set on my life. You are the reason I look for adventure instead of wallowing in my despair. How could I ever have faced losing you? How could you possibly expect me to face it now?

"My eyes are your eyes. You know that? Not like my sisters. When I look into their eyes, I see my mother. I see her soul and her warmth, but every time I look in the mirror, in these wide eyes of my own, I see you. I see my father staring back at me, and I hear your words echoing around me, telling me you will always be here with me, but you are not. Yes, I feel your presence, I do, but I rather have you here... really here.

"Even now, with the opportunity to lay eyes on your face, I am afraid because I know it is not real. I tell myself to move forward, and yet I'm stuck here. Wall against my back, hoping this will all go away, and I won't have to face what I couldn't before. Losing you. I don't want to lose you. Not again. There is nothing in this cold, dark, decaying space that makes me believe there is any way you will survive this. I knew it then, and I know it now."

Death is inevitable.

The words came rapidly and from all directions, filling the air with a cacophony of sound. Each time she heard the words spoken, it was a different person giving voice to them.

Her mother. Death is inevitable.

Her sisters. Death is inevitable.

Her guardian. Death is inevitable.

Her mentor. Death is inevitable.

Her father. Death is inevitable.

Death is inevitable.

And then, as if given a life of its own, the room took away her choice. The walls slowly moved in, creating a creaking noise as they did. This wasn't something she could avoid forever. She looked ahead. She had to face him.

At the last moment, when she thought it would force her to do it, it gave her a choice. The wall to the left of the bed opened, revealing the ocean, a free and clear patch away from her problems. And she almost swam through it. But his words flooded her mind.

"In your heart. You will find echoes of my love for as long as you live, and even after you're gone from this world and join me in the next."

She had to face him. She turned her back to the easy path, the path of avoidance, and she swam to her father's side.

He was just as frail as she imagined. A lost echo of the euman she once knew, but it was him. Her father. His eyes opened to her face, and there was a glint of life there, a sparkle of joy at seeing his daughter by his side. She pulled his hand into her, heart breaking at the feel of his bones against her palm, and pulled his hand to her lips.

"I'm here," she whispered. "And I will carry you in my heart, through this life and the next, and the next, until we meet again."

As tears fell from her eyes, his lips curved into a gentle smile before his chest lifted for the last time. The last pull of air. And then he gave in to death's call.

The king, her father, breathed his last breath, and she collapsed over the bed, pulled him into her arms, and sobbed. She closed her eyes tightly, not wanting to see him without life of his own, but when she opened her eyes, it wasn't her father she held.

In her hands was a stone.

She frowned, and then a rush of memories slammed into her mind. Everything before she entered the house, every challenge she faced, and the one she failed, all of it. And then, as the swirl of thoughts stopped, she opened her eyes again, and she was standing outside a house on a remote island.

A winner of the Eldritch Trials.

CHAPTER 25

The warmth of the sun embraced her back as her cries filled the air with a somber melody. Maluai's tears ran down her face as her body adapted to the change in her environment, giving her two legs to walk with. The stone she held in her hands was gone, but her shoulder stung. When she pulled away her shirt, the tattooed symbol of Mother Goddess, two trees embraced at their roots and circled by swirling chains, was revealed on her flesh. As the truth of it all sank in, she felt her chest tighten, and a faint gasp escaped her lips. She'd completed the Eldritch Trials, and the marking of Lunai was a badge of honor she could take home to her eumen.

Despite her happiness about having proven herself, the echoes of her mourning were still there. Her father was dead, and despite having faced several versions of him before and during her challenge, she understood she'd never see him again. Yet she couldn't get past the sensation of holding him and feeling the bones of his frail fingers in her hand.

She sat on the steps of the house, the sound of her quiet sobs echoing in the morning air. Maluai let her body tremble with emotion as she finally allowed all her pent-up tears to flow. Until she heard the bone shaking sound of bricks crumbling and crashing, accompanied by a deafening thud.

Maluai looked up at the confusing sight, and her head spun. The house she entered, the structure with the changing statues and weird ambiance, stood in front of her.

"What?" she asked as she walked down the steps, eyes locked on the gilded griffins. If that was the house she entered, where had she come out?

She turned, and her heart soared as she saw the structure standing proud, not a stone out of place. The new home was resplendent with the vibrant hues of coral, giving the illusion of scales of the underwater creatures. This was their home; this was a representation of Lunai's acceptance of their independence. In the eyes of Mother Goddess, Wallai stood on its own.

"Yes!" she shouted as she called her wings to appear and took to the sky. Just before she flew away from Elderton, she watched the griffin statues outside of the house of Forge collapse.

She flew from the island of Elderton to Forge; the wind whistling through her feathers as she glided through the air. Her long silhouette was visible in the sky for miles before her feet contacted the ground. When her feet touched the ground, they met her with a wave of hostility instead of the applause she had expected.

"What happened?" Queen Helena stomped toward her, face twisted in anger and voice raised several octaves. "How could you fail?"

"Excuse me?" Maluai frowned.

"The Hasking stone disappeared. The Iris is still active, and you are back. Which means you failed." She pointed to the center of the island where the fountain was. "When a challenger is victorious, the Iris displays their face and then returns to its slumber. That didn't happen."

"Back off, Helena." Queen Valuai landed, her own guards and two guardians by her side.

Maluai sighed, relieved to see Seru with her mother. She knew the things she'd seen during her challenge weren't real. Still, that didn't change the way they felt. Maluai didn't think she would ever recover from watching her guardian die in such a heartless way.

"Your daughter took this challenge. It was her choice. No one forced her, and she failed us all! Our eumen will suffer a curse because of her failure. So, no, I will not back off. We will all suffer because of her!"

"You will suffer because of your own doing," Valuai corrected the upset queen. "Maluai isn't the reason the goddess challenged Forge, and you know it."

"I didn't fail," Maluai spoke up, and the two queens snapped their attention to her.

"What?" Helena's mouth dropped. "Surely you did or the fountain—"

Maluai pulled down her shirt collar, revealing the intricate lines of her new tattoo. She knew the mark was undeniable evidence that spoke louder than words. Helena was determined to find a way to lay the blame on Maluai, regardless of whether it was warranted.

"How is this possible?" Helena looked as if she would pass out.

"Mother." Maluai looked at the queen of Wallai. "Lunai has granted our independence. We have our own home in Elderton now."

"What?" Valuai stepped to her daughter and pulled her hands into hers. "Are you sure?"

"Yes, I entered the house of Forge, but I came out on the steps of our own." Maluai smiled. "We are no longer bonded to the land griffins."

"That is impossible," Helena snapped! "We have a treaty!"

"I don't think Lunai is concerned with written treaties from eumen of the past," Maluai said proudly.

Without warning, a rumbling shook the earth beneath their feet. Forge shook with the thunderous sound of collapsing buildings, and the ground trembled beneath her feet. The island suddenly shifted, as if it was being moved aside by an invisible force. As they braced themselves, they watched as the old island slowly shifted from the location it had sat for eons. And a new one with the unmistakable markings of coral appeared in its place. Wallai rose from the ocean to sit partially submerged in the water. A new home for the water griffins.

"Wallai stands on her own," Valuai said proudly, pulling her daughter into her arms as they watched their eumen rejoice on their new island. "That is our home now."

A strange sense of peace surrounded them as they stood on the disheveled island, the sounds of distress ringing out in the air. The chaos of Forge was not theirs to calm. Maluai embraced her mother, her warmth radiating through her arms. Just before they were about to go home, the ever-watchful Beltan, the monk who guarded the temple of Lunai, landed next to them.

"Queen Helena," he huffed as his wings folded around him.

"What is it?" The queen, who suddenly looked like she would lose all the contents in her stomach, turned to him.

"Lunai calls for another challenger," Beltan announced. "Forge must face the Eldritch Trials without the help of Wallai."

"This can't be happening." Helena looked at Valuai and her daughter with disgust. "This is your fault!"

"She's already chosen her challenger," he stumbled over his words. "This is unprecedented."

"Who is it?" Queen Helena asked urgently.

Beltan's words felt like a death sentence to Maluai. His voice echoed in her ears as he spoke the challenger's name, her heart aching and her stomach plummeting.

"You volunteered to be the challenger?" Maluai asked as she landed on the cliff behind Jeraim, who looked out over the changed landscapes of their homes.

"Yes, I did." He turned to her. "Though there wasn't a long line of eumen in front of me."

"I just got back, and you're leaving." She sighed. "I wanted it to be a lie, but it's true. You're going to Elderton."

"You succeeded," Jeraim changed the topic. "That's what we should talk about right now. You're a champion, Maluai. How does it feel?"

"It would feel a lot better if you weren't about to go into the challenge." She moved closer to him, looking up into his dark eyes. "And it would feel even better if I hadn't just lived through it, and if I didn't know exactly what you're going to face when you're in there."

"Maluai," his deep voice reached her in a gentle caress that aimed to calm her rising emotions.

"Why?" she asked. "Why did you put your name in?"

"The same reason you did. I had to do it because it felt like the right thing to do. When you left, a stillness descended upon my life. I had vivid dreams of my uncle, and I saw strange images of you. I could see you conquering your challenge and envisioning a future that we could build together. It was both alarming and comforting, and I struggled to keep up with the emotions." His words were clear and steady as he looked deeply into her eyes.

"After the first night, an inexplicable urge to go to the fountain overcame me, and I couldn't ignore it. I told myself first that it was just my longing to give you strength, that I wanted to provide you with more support than I could out here, but when I got there, it was different. I felt a strange force compel me forward, and the next thing I knew, I was watching my blood pool into the fountain. I could feel the stillness of the water, and I knew its message without having to look. Lanai chose me just as she chose you, just as she chose my uncle."

"And now you have to go in there." She swallowed the knot in her throat. "And I guess that means I have to be your mentor?"

"No." He chuckled. "You will not be my mentor. I'm choosing to do this alone."

"That's an option?" She frowned. "Why wasn't that an option for me?"

"Would you have gone with that option?" He frowned.

"Maybe." She scrunched her nose. "So, you're going."

"Yes. I waited for you to get back because I wanted to see you and congratulate you because I knew you would be successful, and I was right. And I can see how much stronger you have become since the last time I saw you. You did it! You should feel proud. Through your actions, you have shown Lunai and your eumen what you are capable of, and now you can build a new life."

"But you are supposed to be a part of that," she whispered. "You're supposed to be a part of my new life, remember?"

"Maluai."

"I can imagine the shock you felt when you saw me in my true form, or the confusion that might have caused you. I wanted to say something, but nothing I could think of felt adequate. Just please know, even this, standing here with you now, is testing my limits. I've been shielding myself for so long, but that challenge revealed to me I can't keep doing that. More than that, I realized I have a specific vision for my life, Jeraim, and you're in it."

"Maluai," he said her name again, and again, she interrupted him.

"If you're going to reject me, can you do it after you get back?" She frowned. "At least let me hold on to the fantasy until I know you're safe."

"Reject you?" He narrowed his eyes at her. "Why the hell would I ever reject you?"

"I'm a water griffin," she stated the obvious. "Not only that, but I am also a unique water griffin. You and I are not supposed to be together. It's against the rules."

"I got your letter. And I read it. Every single word, time and time again. Let me tell you one thing, I don't give a damn about the rules." He stepped closer to her and wrapped his arms around her waist, pulling her close to his chest. "I told you I chose someone, but she didn't know. You told me I should make damn sure she did. And here I was, standing here and telling myself I should wait until I get back. That I didn't want you waiting for something if I should fail, but I realize now you need to know before I go in there. I love you. You have my heart, and you've had it since the moment I've met you. Maluai, Princess of Wallai, champion of the Eldritch Trials, I would break any rule and cross any world to be with you. Know that when I'm in there, I'm fighting for you. I'll be fighting to get back here to you to live the life you imagined for us."

"You love me?" As she spoke, her question trembled, stuck in her throat like a lump of fear.

"Yes, I do." He smiled. "I love you, Maluai."

"Even though I'm different?" She squinted against the sun that shined brightly from behind his hand.

"Especially because you're different." He pressed his forehead against hers. "I love you as you are. I love you for who you are and for who you will become. Every version of you."

"You better survive this," she whispered. "And you better come home to me."

"I will." He looked over her head at the new island. "In the meantime, it looks like you have a lot of work to do."

"I can't believe I did it." She turned in his arms to face the new Wallai. "We're free, and it's so weird to say that because really, we always were. The elders were just afraid, but now Lunai has given us the chance to live in this world and really to be a part of it as we never have before."

"And I can't wait to see all the wonderful things you do." He tightened his arms around her.

"You're leaving now, aren't you?" Maluai couldn't ignore the obvious. It was why he waited for her there, away from everyone else. Jeraim wanted to say goodbye.

"Yes, I don't want the fanfare, and I don't want the political dramas surrounding my departure. I know what to expect. I know it will be difficult, but knowing I have someone to come home to is enough to get me through it."

"Just make sure you don't forget me while you're in there?" She turned back to him.

"Did you forget me?" He raised a brow.

"Let's talk about all that when you get back." She laughed.

Jeraim looked into her eyes, and their noses brushed as he leaned in. The moment was serene, but her stomach fluttered with anxiety. Before he left her for a challenge that could take him away forever, he kissed her softly, as if he was memorizing her lips.

"I'll be back for you," Jeraim whispered against her lips.

He unfolded his wings, and the sound of their beating filled the air as he rose into the sky. Jeraim flew above her head, his wings beating the air, and then he descended. The tips of his wing brushed against her cheek with a soft caress as he marked her as his mate before he flew off to face his own test.

CHAPTER 26

NEW WALLAI

Maluai prepared for her new life. Her aides moved around her in quick succession, chattering about the coming events. This was a time for celebration, and yet the princess, the champion, found little reason to be cheerful. Her mind drifted to the euman who she felt should be by her side in the celebration. It had been two days since he left. From what they told her, the challenge took her nine. She told herself there was no way it would take him longer than that.

In a matter of hours, Wallai would celebrate their newfound independence and the champion who secured it for them. And thinking about it brought a fresh wave of nerves, because during the celebration, Maluai would present herself to them, her true self.

She discussed it with her mother the night prior and stood firm in her decision.

"I have to do this," Maluai expressed her feelings. "I don't want to continue living in fear. That is something I learned through all of this. I can't keep hiding in the shadows. I want to live in this new world, in this new phase of my life, as authentically as possible."

"I just worry about you."

"I know it. But if I can't be myself when I am at home, I'll have no reason to stay here. I don't want to leave, not forever, but you have to let me exist the way I feel is best for me."

"You are so much like him. Your father." Queen Valuai sighed. "Who am I to argue with Lunai's champion? Do what you feel is right."

Maluai hugged her mother tightly, happy to receive her support. "Thank you."

It was the council members who caused the biggest point of contention, particularly one very vocal member. Despite Maluai's success, Fituen remained resolute in his determination to challenge the queen. During the three brief meetings since Maluai's return, he scrutinized every decision the queen made regarding the future of their eumen. Maluai reflected on Fituen's actions during her challenge and realized the false events may have revealed the council member's true nature and motivations. She considered speaking to her mother about it, but chose instead to wait and see how things played out. Besides, she couldn't very well accuse him based on things he hadn't actually done.

Her aides led her out through the halls of the palace, which was now above water. It was an unusual experience to walk on two legs instead of swimming in the comfort of her own home. As she walked, the hall filled with the echo of her mother's voice. Soon, she would join her out on the deck that overlooked thousands of Wallains. This was the first official address of the queen after their home gained its new foundation in their world.

"My pledge to you, my eumen, is to lead with a pure heart and to keep us grounded in the mystical power of Lunai." With a championing voice, the queen spoke, inspiring all who listened. "The purity and strength of the royal bloodline are undeniable, as proven by your princess and the latest Eldritch Trials champion, Maluai!"

Maluai stood in the hall, feeling the vibrations of the eumen's cheers as her mother spoke from the balcony. Then there was a pause. Her mother's voice ceased, and she understood that was her cue to go out.

"Princess," the guard near the double doors greeted her. "Are you ready?"

"Yes." Maluai nodded, and then he opened the doors.

As Maluai stepped out, the sheer magnitude of what lay before her overwhelmed her. Looking out over the sea of faces of Wallains, she shivered with excitement. Some stood on the new grounds of their home. Some swam in the ocean, waving up at her, while others flew in the sky. She stood there, taking in the moment of freedom, savoring the power of choice to be themselves, to exist as they pleased.

"This is your time." Her mother turned to her, crown poised perfectly on her head. "Show them who you are."

Maluai had never unveiled her true self to anyone. Her parents had always prevented her from doing it, offering creative excuses and reasons to squash any suspicions. It was time for her to embrace her true self, no matter the consequences. She was desperate to learn her eumen's true feelings toward her. She had been hiding her true self for too long and was ready to let the world see who she really was.

Maluai stood silently in front of the cheering crowd and transformed into her true form.

As she closed her eyes, she felt her chest rise and fall, her breath growing deeper and fuller. Her limbs changed, her chest expanded, and her posture shifted as she moved. Her tail exploded behind her, sending a burst of energy up her back, and her wings followed suit. The sudden silence from the crowd was deafening. Maluai hesitated for a moment before opening her eyes, and when she did, she saw the Wallains staring at her with wide eyes, clearly shocked.

Their reaction embarrassed the princess, who was ready to flee, but then a fantastic thing happened. The crowd exploded into cheer. She could feel the thunderous sound reverberating through her chest. Her heart was racing, and with each cheer from the crowd, she felt more and more inspired to let out a triumphant roar. The sound was so powerful that the audience could feel it shaking the ground, but it only made them cheer louder.

Maluai's mother turned toward her and gently caressed her face before revealing her true form. Suddenly, her sisters Valuai and Naluai appeared, soaring into view in their true forms. This was their presentation to their eumen. Lunai had chosen the royal bloodline for their unwavering devotion and strong connection to her divine powers. And despite everything, that connection was stronger than ever.

TROUBLE IN FORGE

"What's the cause for such alarm?" Queen Valuai addressed the council as she took her seat on the throne. Kaluai sat in the position next to her, where her father once sat.

"There are troubling reports about Forge," Hasik reported. She stepped to the head of the room, nodding at Maluai as she passed.

"There are?" the queen questioned. "Why is the first time I'm hearing of this?"

"We wanted to wait until we were sure. No one has heard from the king in all this time," Hasik explained. "Now that

Wallai is known, those who hold power expect him to at least make a statement about what is going on here."

"What about Queen Helena?" Valuai asked.

"She isn't responding to requests from the council members," Limua reported the news. "Queen Valuai, we have exhausted our resources. You will need to step in."

"What else do we know?" The queen squared her shoulders. "What are we dealing with, really?"

"There are rumors, unsettling ones," Limua continued.

"And they are?" Kaluai leaned forward.

"There are some who believe King Lequad is dead," Fituen said in an indifferent tone.

"Where did these rumors start?" the queen asked. "We cannot act on unfounded rumors."

"Word comes from the royal staff," Hasik answered. "The queen has prohibited anyone but two healers to enter the room. Healers, we are told, are inexperienced."

"We can't rush in there accusing their queen of hiding something like this. We must be careful."

"I agree. We won't rush to judgement or accusation, but we will address it. Wallai needs to be on good footing. The loss of Forge's king could look bad for us. If we do not get ahead of this, it may look as if we have something to do with it." The queen turned to her guardian, Kianna. "Get a small group together. We will head to Forge in two hours."

"I will prepare," Fituen spoke.

"No, not the council," the queen rejected his offer. "This will be a simple social visit, royal laenu to royal laenu. This cannot look like an ambush. If we bring the council members, that is exactly what it will look like."

"Queen Valuai, with all due respect," Fituen began, but a forceful voice cut his unsolicited commentary short.

"Fituen, with as much respect as is deserved for your continued interruption of the queen, this is not up for debate," Maluai interrupted him, and the council member backed down. "We will proceed as my mother wishes."

Filled with pride, the queen gave her daughter a nod of approval. "I'm calling this meeting to an end unless there is other business to attend to."

"That is all," Limua confirmed.

"Great. We will prepare to leave." The Queen stood, and the others filed out of the room.

MEETING OF THE ROYALS

Maluai and her laenu landed just outside the Forge palace walls and were welcomed by the guards and eldest princess. Cairaix stood on the steps of her home, her face a painted mask of worry. Still, she kept her poise and greeted the unexpected guests.

"Queen Valuai, princesses, it's so good to see you again," Cairaix welcomed them.

"It's great to see you as well," Valuai responded and quickly glanced at her eldest daughter, who blushed. "Thank you for accepting our visit."

"Of course, please come inside." Cairaix turned to walk into the palace, and the Wallain royals followed her.

"Where is the queen?" Valuai asked as the guards ushered them into the greeting chambers where they would spend their visit.

"She will be here shortly. We've sent word of your arrival." Cairaix nodded with a small but worried smile. "As you can imagine, we were unprepared for this visit."

"Yes, I apologize for that. I meant to send word ahead. I know things have been chaotic, but it's important for us to come together and socialize in this new space. It is my intention to make sure our eumen maintain a healthy relationship."

"I agree." Cairaix nodded. "We should keep things peaceful."

"Do you?" Queen Helena stood at the entrance, hair and clothes disheveled. She looked as if she'd been soaking in an alcoholic bath. "You agree with those who abandoned us?"

"Mother," Cairaix started, but her mother refused to hear her.

"Valuai, you can understand my confusion about having you in my home." Helena continued her dramatic entrance. "I'd think you have nothing else to say to us. You got what you wanted."

"Helena, I never intended to abandon Forge entirely," Valuai responded.

"Yes, intentions, fleeting things," Helena brushed her off. "We intend one thing, we do another. Intentions are for babies who understand no consequences of actions."

"Are you feeling well?" Cairaix moved to her mother's side.

"Yes, perhaps we can move this visit to another day," Kaluai suggested.

"I'm fine!" Helena protested, stamping her foot like the babies she'd just spoken of. "Sorry I'm not as put together as you are right now. As you can imagine, it has been a stressful time."

"We didn't come to add to your stress," Valuai said.

"And yet, here my stress level has risen." Helena shook her finger at Valuai. "There are those fleeting intentions again."

"Mother." Cairaix grabbed her mother's hand.

"Cairaix, please." Helena pulled away from her daughter. "Alert the staff. We have guests!"

"Will the king be joining us?" Valuai asked what they'd come for.

"Excuse me?" Helena looked as if she'd been kicked in the stomach.

"Your husband, the king. Will he be joining us?" Valuai repeated her question.

"I—" she froze, then spoke in a frantic cadence. "The king, yes. The king is busy. Important things to handle."

"Right." Valuai nodded, suspicious of the response.

"Why are you always asking about the king?" Helena narrowed her gaze.

"What do you mean?" Valuai squared her shoulders, and the Wallain guards shifted slightly closer to her.

"Every time you come, you're asking about the king." Helena pointed at Valuai. "Why are you so concerned with my husband?"

"It's customary for the king to at least show his face when there are guests, is it not?" Valuai spat back.

"Yes, when the guests announce themselves before they appear, perhaps," Helena spoke through gritted teeth.

"I—" Valuai started, but a door to the far left of the room burst open, and Marruk, the eldest prince, rushed in. Three aides surrounded him. They each pleaded with him to stop.

"Mother!" Marruk yelled.

"Marruk, what are you doing?" Helena turned to her son, who stopped just a few feet short of her.

"He's dead!" Marruk screamed, and the room turned cold. "He's dead, and you hid it from us!"

"I—" Helena froze in her own shock. She knew exactly what the prince spoke of, and so did everyone in the room.

Maluai glanced at her sisters, and sensing things were about to get bad, she pushed Naluai behind her.

"Don't you dare lie to me!" Marruk screamed, his finger pointed at the shocked face of his mother. "My father lies cold and lifeless in his chambers, surrounded by fragrance to mask his decay, while you move around plotting to have things work in your favor. How could you? Do you have no shame? No loyalty? Did you love him so little that you would allow this to go on?"

"I did what I had to for our eumen. For Forge! Your father lost it," the queen shouted back. "Mining, ripping our home apart, and for what? To lose his own life as a consequence? We had to stay strong. All eyes are on us, and Wallai wanted freedom. I had to do what was right to keep up safe!"

"Don't lie to me!" Marruk demanded.

Cairaix ran back into the room, alerted by the screaming. "What is going on? Marruk, what's wrong?"

"Our mother is a murderer, and I will not stand here and let her go unpunished!"

Marruk's eyes blazed with fury, and his voice dripped with venom. Helena barely had time to react before he let out a blood-curdling scream and rushed toward her. Her son's hands wrapped around her throat before the queen could even react. Maluai was left dazed as everything happened in a blur.

The guards of Forge were too late to stop Marruk as he shifted into his true form and violently tore through his mother's neck with his beak. The Wallain guards pushed Maluai and her laenu back, but not before she saw the crimson splatters all around, and the metallic smell of blood filled her nostrils. Cairaix collapsed to the ground, tears streaming down her face, as Marruk reverted to his vanity form.

"Seize him!" Cairaix screamed and pointed at her brother.

As the guards approached him, Marruk turned to his sister, his expression twisted with anger. Unlike their mother, Cairaix proved to be a difficult target for the treacherous prince. Her brother ran toward her, only to have his jaw meet her foot. Cairaix leapt into the air and brought her right foot up, and she flipped backward. After impact, Marruk flew back into the waiting arms of the Forge guards, who immediately detained him.

New Days for all.

The new Queen of Forge was crowned with the Wallain royals, council members, and guards as witnesses. With the weight of her recent loss heavy on her heart, Cairaix stood tall as the Forge crown was gently placed on her head. Though the moment was sorrowful, the sun still shone brightly overhead. And while Maluai would have hoped it would happen in a more peaceful manner, she was happy the new Queen of Forge seemed to agree with her mother's vision for the future.

Fituen's unhappy appearance contrasted with the festive atmosphere around him. Maluai raised an eyebrow, observing his dissatisfaction. The princess had learned from experience that he was not a trustworthy person. She'd keep a close eye on him, waiting for any slip-ups.

When the ceremony ended, Maluai looked across the crowd, finding Wintia, who had been staring at her. But when their eyes met, she looked away, and before Maluai could decide if she wanted to speak, she'd disappeared.

"She won't speak to you again." Peliak, Jeraim's friend, approached the princess.

"I'm sorry?" Maluai turned to him.

"Wintia," he said. "I probably shouldn't tell you this, but Jeraim had a conversation with her before he left."

"He did?" she asked, shocked at the news.

"Yes, he told her to back off. Of course, he used different terms, but it got the point across."

"Oh."

"Have you heard anything?" Peliak asked, worried for his friend.

"No, but if I do, you will be the first to know," she promised. "I know we're all worried about him, especially with so much going on here while he is away."

"Thank you." He looked over his shoulder in the direction Wintia left. "I should go."

Maluai's mind wandered back to thoughts of Jeraim once Peliak had gone. She immediately withdrew herself from any festivities after that. The ceremony was finally over, and all the formalities were out of the way, so she could finally let go of her princess duties.

"I need a minute," she told Seru, who nodded. She wouldn't follow the princess, who was now free of the tight leash of her mother.

Maluai flew to their place. The peak that now overlooked two islands. The winds kicked up, and their warm caress came with memories of a euman she knew she'd never see again.

"Father," she spoke to the sky. "I'm not sure if you can hear me. But I hope you can. You've seen me through so much, even things I'm not entirely sure actually happened or were figments of my imagination. Through it all, you were there for me. I don't know what the future holds. I don't even know if wherever you are in your next life, or if you're able to sense the love that we have for you. Just know it is still here, and our love is strong. I and so many others will carry you in our hearts for centuries to come.

"This feels weird talking to the sky and hoping you hear me, but I just want to say I hope you're proud of me. I'm still not sure if I did exactly what you wanted, but I did what felt best for me. And there's something else. I never got to tell you about Jeraim. I never got to see your reaction to finding out your daughter gave her heart to a land griffin. I never get to hear your jokes about how he's not good enough for me.

"And I'll never know for sure if you agree with my choice, but I hope you would because he makes me happy. My heart feels so warm whenever I hear his voice, and I light up at the thought of him. It's the same way you expressed loving mother the way I thought I could never have because I'm different, and I spent my entire life hiding. I always questioned how that kind of love could ever find me. But it did.

"And no matter what happens in his challenge, whether he wins or loses, he has my heart, and he always will. I hope you would be happy for us. Things are good. They will get better, but we will always wish you were here with us for them. I love you now and forever."

With her last words, Maui heard the movement of wings, and inexplicably, her heart soared. She dropped her head back to look up at the sky and saw the wide graceful wings forming circles above her head. Her heart leapt, feeling like it would fly from her chest to meet him. He tightened his circles around her head, moving closer enough to brush her cheek with his wing before he landed in front of her.

"You're actually here," Maluai hesitated. "Does that mean?" she couldn't finish her question.

He said nothing, but he moved the color of his shirt to display a tattoo he now shared with her, one of intricate design, the symbol of their mother goddess.

"Thank the goddess." She jumped into his arms, wrapping her arms around his neck, and they kissed.

"I told you I would come back to you." He smiled.

"I would have waited one hundred years if it took that long." She couldn't stop her cheeks from lifting with her own smile.

"Now you don't have to, and we can live the life we want to live together." He touched her face. "Finally."

The cheers were so loud and sudden that they startled the couple. Soon, they could hear chants about the Iris and Lunai. Despite Jeraim's attempt at a covert entrance, the eumen of Forge were aware of his success.

"I think you're going to have to show up there before we can run away." She laughed. "Your people will want to celebrate their new champion."

"They're just gonna have to wait then, aren't they?" He leaned forward, kissing her. "I'm a champion now. I can do what I want."

Jeraim lifted her off the ground, his wings unfolding behind him as he carried her into the air. The celebration could wait.

Reviews help authors in so many ways. Sharing your thoughts could help this book land in the hands of a new reader who may enjoy it just as much as you did. So please take a moment to drop a review. I'll love you forever!

Thanks!

Leave your review.

T he Eldritch Trials is a collection of books in the same
world, but each book is written by a different talented
author!

If you enjoyed this story, check out the others in the collection.

https://mybook.to/D8BymgW

About the Author

Jessica Cage is an International Award Winning and USA Today Bestselling Author of speculative fiction and urban fantasy novels. Publishing since 2010, Jessica made a name for herself in Indie publishing through consistent efforts and organic growth of her platform. The author of 35 fiction novels and 18 short stories published in different anthologies, she continues to produce stories that give representation to marginalized communities in fantasy landscapes.

Jessica added a branch to her career to focus more on helping other authors reach their goals in 2021 with the start of her

Caged Writers Group where she offers guidance for new writers, and the launch of her first shared world book collection, Rise of the Elites which gave five authors direct access to Jessica's audience in a meaningful and lasting way.

Connect with Jessica on her website: www.jessicacage.com

Made in the USA
Columbia, SC
12 August 2023

21539848R00245